ACO

Queen of Poisons

ACONITE

Queen of Poisons

A Roaring '20s Mystery

№ 1 - Dr. Josephine Plantæ Paradoxes

L.M. JORDEN

SOLIS MUNDI

ISBN: 978-0-9838101-1-7 (Print)
ISBN: 978-0-9838101-2-4 (ebook)
Library of Congress Registration No. TXu2-285-878
Cover artwork by Alexi Jorden and design by L.M. Jorden
Cover photograph of Brooklyn Bridge courtesy of the New York Public Library Digital Archives

SOLIS MUNDI

Praise for Aconite, Queen of Poisons

"Aconite: Queen of Poisons by L.M. Jorden is an exciting and engaging story with a well-developed plot and characters..." - Readers' Favorite

"ACONITE is dynamite!... The characters leap off the page, the dialogue is witty satire." -ARC Review

"Pick your poison! ...This trailblazing lady doc has her work cut out for her, even before she takes on the medical establishment and becomes a murder suspect... an excellent romp with an entertaining cast of characters." - Amazon Review

This mystery featuring main character Dr. Josephine Reva is captivating enough, but knowing it is based on the real life of the author's grandmother, the first female doctor in [areas of] Brooklyn, NY, the story is even more delightful." - Amy Reade, author of A Traitor Among Us

"Dr. Josephine Reva, a Homeopath, is a fascinating spin on the doctor as sleuth. What fun!" - Anne Louise Bannon, author

"The novel is very well-written... a narrative voice that draws the reader into the story." - Richard Nochimson, author of Final Plans

"Vaudeville meets Prohibition. Give me a Booze Blank!"

"Commedia dell'arte! Roaring '20s lovers, doctors, cops, rumrunners.... Great ensemble scenes."

"I had no idea who the killer was!" - Marie R.

"Looking forward to the next book in the series!" - Amazon Review

For Nicolas, Alessandro and Tara,
with love to my brilliant stars

Dear Doctor, I have read your play,
Which is a good one in its way,
Purges the eyes, and moves the bowels,
And drenches handkerchiefs like towels
With tears that, in a flux of grief,
Afford hysterical relief
To shatter'd nerves and quicken'd pulses,
Which your catastrophe convulses...
-Lord Byron (George Gordon)

Also by L.M. JORDEN

The Dr. Josephine Plantae Paradoxes

Dr. Josephine Reva, Homeopath M.D. solves poison paradoxes in this riveting new series.

ACONITE Queen of Poisons - Roaring 20's Mystery
BELLADONNA Bitter Conduct - 1935 Mystery
CINCHONA Coney Island Bones - 1941 Mystery
DIGITALIS A Deadly Garden
GELSEMIUM Memoir of a First Woman Doctor
HELLEBORUS Death on the Hudson

See L.M. Jorden author's page:
www.lmjorden.com
https://www.amazon.com/author/l.m.jorden/
X or Twitter: lmjordenauthor
https://www.facebook.com/LMJorden/

Travelogue Novellas:
Istrian Odyssey: Food, Love and War in Croatia
The Bead Trader

ACONITE Queen of Poisons

BASED ON A TRUE STORY

In Roaring 20's New York, a feisty orphan rises from the slums to become a doctor. When no one will hire a female, Josephine Reva, M.D. hangs her shingle in Brooklyn as the area's first woman doctor. Her loyalty to the Hippocratic Oath will be tested under Prohibition, but Josephine has graver concerns. She's fighting for women's equality, and she isn't going to stop using her botanical poison cures.

Murder intrudes when a man is found dead from Aconite, a beautiful flower known as the "Queen of Poisons". The Chief Detective suspects Josephine, and the two begin a cat and mouse chase. Josephine must race to prove her innocence. She goes undercover as a flapper to spy, but complications arise when she falls for a debonair suspect.

Can Josephine unmask the murderer? Can she follow her heart and save her career, while keeping her dark secrets hidden?

The Law of Similars

Samah samam shamayti, Like cures like
—Sushruta Samhita and Ayurveda (1200-600 BC)

Through the like, disease is produced, and through the
application of the like, it is cured
—Hippocrates (460-377 BC)

Similia similibus curentur, Like cures like
—Samuel Hahnemann (1755-1843)

The author deliberately adopted a 1920's literary style: a liberal sprinkling of adverbs, dialogue tags, Jazz Age and Vaudeville slang, and old-fashioned verbosity. Some language from the 1920's is now considered offensive or insensitive, so please excuse the author's limited use for authenticity purposes.

Late Summer 1929

Prologue - Gravesend Bay

The Narrows is a funnel-like waterway where the Atlantic Ocean courses past the Bight, then spills from lower into upper New York Bay. The salt waters are pressed between Brooklyn and Staten Island before mixing with the Hudson and East River freshwater estuaries. The tides control the spigot.

Just to the south of The Narrows, lapping the shores of Brooklyn, lies Gravesend Bay.

Breakers washed against the docks, heaving them to and fro. The wood pylons pulled against restraining ropes, and hydrologic forces had splintered the wood into sharp-edged tinders.

Under a crescent moon, two shadows with flashlights searched in an old warehouse alongside the docks. They leaned forward, tugging out wooden crates filled with whiskey.

One used a crowbar, careful not to break any of the bottles.

"Take the Canadian, not the Scotch."

"Last time, it was the Irish."

"Hurry up! Hand me those empty milk bottles."

Clanking and the chugging of liquids pouring through a funnel.

"I added some medicinals. Tastes better than the Real McCoy. Let's bottle it when Prohibition ends."

"Why'd you change the ingredients? Speakeasies mix drinks with sugar anyway."

"That'll rot your teeth."

"Quit worrying and help me nail these crates back down tight."

As they hammered, the rat-a-tat-tat of machine gun fire sent stray bullets whizzing by their heads. They looked out to sea in alarm.

"This place'll be Grand Central Station soon."

"They're not gonna make it through The Narrows. Coast Guard's out tonight."

"Not our problem."

"They'll need a new drop off point."

"Could be anywhere from Bath Beach to Bay Ridge. We won't be so lucky to find the bootlegger's dock next time."

Gunfire echoed across the bay.

"That's close."

"Let's scram or we're gonna get rubbed out."

Moments later, an armored speedboat cut its roaring engine and coasted towards the dock.

Chapter 1 - An Invitation

Thursday morning...

A summer thunderstorm brewed in the city, with a headwind funneling between buildings and racing down the avenues, sending the 5¢ newspaper stacks flying and garbage cans tumbling. Soon the city was smothered in a dark cloud, as if a theater curtain had dropped. Rain pelted down on pedestrians, and these marching stick figures became frantically animated, ducking for cover. Dr. Josephine Reva, Homeopath M.D. peered out the streetcar window to watch the show. Human nature interested a scientist like her, and should anyone become injured—she tapped the large black medical kit on her lap—she was ready.

Josephine watched as people dashed across the avenue, nimbly leaping over puddles like acrobats. Some arched their arms above their heads in pirouettes, shielding themselves from the wet drops with their folded newspapers. The city was more crowded than she remembered; people sprouted like shoots between the cracks in the new asphalt. Old Tin Lizzies and the latest Model A's rattled by with wipers flailing, splashing mud at pedestrians and any open air Phaeton operators caught with their canvas down. Strangers hunkered together in narrow doorways, trying to keep dry. *Like couples in a struggle buggy,* she smiled.

As quickly as it began, the thunderstorm dissipated and rolled out to sea, leaving the promise of sporadic squalls. Josephine sighed in relief—no one had been injured.

Excitedly, she turned her attention to the invitation clutched in her hand. Engraved in elegant calligraphy on thick card stock —she'd been flabbergasted to receive it. *Why have the Manhattan big shots summoned me? I'm hardly noteworthy.*

A young medical school graduate, age 26 and the only female in her classes, Josephine found that no Manhattan hospitals would hire her. So she'd left for Bensonhurst, Brooklyn to become the area's first woman doctor.

She checked the invitation again to be sure her name was on it. *Why was I given the honor of speaking today before such renowned peers—male peers?*

No matter, the audience will be convinced by my speech. Josephine had been born with a fearless disposition, but what she planned to say was controversial.

Well, I'm still the only female doctor—I have nothing to lose.

A thunderclap exploded like a booming cannon. Josephine looked up in alarm. *Not a good omen,* she thought. But never one to let unscientific premonitions bother her, she brushed any feelings of foreboding aside.

She'd once loved stormy weather—it cleansed the city of dirt and grime. When she was a child, she'd run outside with the other orphans from a warren of tenements strung together with clothesline. They'd stomped in the puddles. Her home was the Convent of Santa Lucia in Little Italy. "Rain is nature's bath," the nuns teased, "and Lord knows you waifs need a good scrubbing!"

Mixed blessings. Josephine hesitated, weighing the invitation in her hand. The nuns always said that doubts did a person no good. *Fortes fortuna adiuvat, fortune favors the brave*—she recalled the Latin proverb the nuns murmured before they hit the streets to beg for alms. It had never failed them. In any case, she'd been given a once in a lifetime opportunity, so she'd best make it count. *What could possibly go wrong?*

She reached up to pull the trolley bell and began pushing her way to the exit, past the passengers packed in like sardines. At the next stop, she jumped down into the street's arena.

Steam hissed from the tracks as they cooled enough for her to tightrope walk across, just before the next cars barreled by.

The rain let up momentarily, as storms tend to do before they unleash more fury. She looked up at the sky—would today's event be more like the nuns' sun shower or a dousing from an open fire hydrant? She feared it would be the latter, but had no time to worry—motor cars were furiously tooting their rubber horns.

Josephine hastened out of the way. She pushed her hat pin in tighter to secure her fashionable cloche, bought for today's occasion, and pulled her traveling coat collar up against the wind. Shifting her heavy medical bag, she checked the address on the invitation and headed uptown.

There were still no pedestrian crosswalks, although reformers picketed City Hall to install them to save lives; therefore, Josephine was forced to jaywalk like everyone else. Motor car operators didn't stop or slow down for the masses of darting people. They even ignored the new traffic signalers topped with bronze statues of the winged god Mercury; indeed, the messenger god inspired them to careen down the avenues faster, as if at the Grand Prix.

Josephine spotted an opening and dashed into the fray, almost colliding with a Checker cab. The driver blared his horn and leaned out the window cursing and shaking his fist.

"Lady, get outta the road!'

"Go back to bed and take your medicine!" she yelled in response. *What doctor could resist a medical retort?*

The rain clouds above were now at the point of bursting. *The weather is "expecting" like most of my female patients,* she mused. Wet droplets soon fell on her face, and she feared she'd arrive drenched to the conference, like a drowned rat. That wouldn't do. She'd been sure to take her medical bag full of lifesaving instruments (a doctor must always be prepared), but she'd left a simple umbrella at home. Looking around, she spotted a forgotten one hanging off a pay phone booth, and made a beeline for it.

She examined her find: a little bent but not ripped.

"That's your share of the profits, courtesy of Gentleman Jimmy," a passerby called out with a laugh. "He knows how to keep the ladies dry." Josephine knew he was referencing the city's corrupt mayor, who was getting rich from his ritzy Central Park Casino club selling bootlegged liquor.

"At least he's not charging us for rainwater!" she bantered back. Prohibition jokes were all the rage.

That law has turned my medical practice upside down. I wrote fifty prescriptions for "medicinal" whiskey this week alone. Nonetheless, the extra money is helpful.

Opening the lopsided umbrella, she continued walking briskly uptown along Millionaire's Row. Fifth Avenue was a far cry from the tenements of her youth. An uptown building boom was going on. She dodged sky high construction cranes moving great blocks of marble onto twenty story megaliths. One day, she would live in one of these new luxury apartment towers, rising like mountain peaks. The billboards promised a view of Central Park and city lights. She imagined herself wrapped in satin and furs, sashaying through the brass polished doors that a white-gloved doorman held open for her.

Not bad for a girl from the slums!

The only office Josephine could afford was at the far shores of Brooklyn, so she'd moved there. That borough was booming, too, not upwards like Manhattan, but outwards across the flat plains of Long Island. While Manhattan's granite peaks rivaled Mt. Rushmore, Brooklyn consisted of low-slung houses made of muddy bricks. Unfortunately, her income reflected this disparity.

A loud taxi honk knocked Josephine out of her reverie. She'd dillydallied long enough, and surely the conference had started by now. Finding one of the newly built granite buildings with a classical colonnade, she eagerly climbed the steps and hurried inside.

Chapter 2 - The Law of Similars

The New York Society of Medical Professionals was buzzing with activity. Hanging her traveling coat and umbrella on a rack, Josephine looked for and found the Ladies Room. Standing next to impeccably dressed Fifth Avenue society matrons, she felt rather inadequate by comparison, checking her appearance before the large silvered mirror. *Being poor and unmarried never stopped me before,* she reminded herself. *I've just got to be bolder!*

All in all, a pleasing face—some said she was beautiful. *Well, I do have youth on my side.* Her mouth was a tad too determined. She wiped away raindrops from her thick round spectacles, or "cheaters" as they were called—they did help her look more learned. One eye was noticeably smaller, a subtle defect that helped her relate to her patients—no one was perfect, after all. Her irises were her most attractive feature—a striking celestial blue. Her mother had emerald green eyes, like the Bay of Naples, which she'd said she could see from her villa high in the hills. Her father's were dusty brown like the volcanic soil he came from. Josephine had inherited the rare genetic trait, but she couldn't ask her parents about it for her experiments. Both had died from the Spanish Flu.

Death no longer frightened Josephine. As a doctor, she'd seen it appear in many guises: factory accidents, drownings, explosions, ingestions of toxic products, cancers, fevers, hemorrhages, and sadly, stillbirths, to name a few. In her profession, it always lurked in the shadows, waiting to take her patients away in its icy embrace. Nor was she ignorant of the daily newspaper stories of rub-outs on the streets of New York and bootlegger shootouts along the waterfront. *How could someone be so full of sin that they would harm another mortally?* As a doctor, she was no longer innocent of its commonality.

A puff of powder to her nose and a touch of rose lipstick, Josephine continued making herself ready. Red lips would be too forward, brazen. *I've got to look educated and trustworthy, not like a flapper in a magazine.* Her black hair was bobbed to chin-length and unfashionably stick-straight. She glanced at the other ladies' permed hair in frothy waves and frowned.

Fortunately, her suit (bought for an extravagant $5.25) still hung primly—she'd over-starched and pressed it to a crisp to withstand the journey from Brooklyn. She kept tugging at the skirt. *Modern styles are cut too short for a respectable female physician. This doesn't even rest below my calves.* Next, she adjusted her slimming girdle, for there was no way to fit her curvaceous body into the boyishly skinny drop-waisted dresses without it. Lastly, she decided to leave her straw cloche hat on. With its pretty ribbon, it would more than make up for her simple attire.

As she left the Ladies Room, an usher weaved towards her, waving his hand. He picked her out of the crowd easily, for she carried her large black medical bag boldly embossed with her name in gold letters, like a badge. A graduation present from the nuns.

He shouted over the din that she would be speaking at three o'clock, just before the farewell reception. Good, she had plenty of time to mingle. If only she could meet an uptown doctor who needed a partner, a female partner. Or maybe she'd hear of a hospital planning to hire female doctors? *I'll be the first in line to apply!*

To move back to Manhattan and into one of those townhouses she'd passed along the avenue. Brass plaques engraved with Doctor Simmons, Allopath, Obstetrician, or Doctor Sloane, Homeopath, Specialist in Gynaecological Surgery. A door had opened and she'd briefly caught a glimpse of a marble black and white checked floor, a waiting room decorated with Persian carpets, high backed chairs, paintings on the walls, and even statues on pedestals. *A crowd of patients waiting—a doctor's dream!*

The audience of professionals and philanthropists began filling the hall, taking their seats with a clatter of chairs grating the wooden floors. Doctors shook hands and greeted each other sternly, straightening their wide lapels and removing their old-fashioned Homburg hats or fedoras. Their "appendages," as their wives were jokingly called, tagged alongside. Stylish taffeta dresses rustled as the women hugged and greeted each other, their large jewels and real pearl necklaces clacking loudly—a noise reminding Josephine of street kids shooting marbles.

The afternoon panel was entitled "The Future of Medicine," a timely subject in the decade after the deadly Spanish Flu pandemic and the start of Prohibition, which Josephine feared would continue indefinitely, with its resultant alcohol addiction.

Many panelists were adamant that medicine's future include Homeopathy, known for its diluted remedies which gently stimulated a person's own immune system to fight disease. The Homeopaths nodded to the statue of Hygieia in the hallway, goddess of prevention and hygiene.

Others were sure that Allopathy, with more toxic but faster-acting drugs, should predominate. The Allopaths with M.D. degrees nodded to the statue of Aesculapius, Hygieia's father, grasping his serpent-entwined staff, which they'd adopted as their symbol.

There were also the trained Naturopaths, Osteopaths, Chiropractors, Hydrotherapists, Phytotherapists. There were even numerous quacks who insisted on being included. The battle for the future of medicine had begun.

Josephine was a special case: she was a Homeopath with an M.D. degree, a rare combination. Only a few medical schools taught both philosophies of medicine and were accredited. She freely used both Homeopathy and Allopathy in her practice, and if she was forced to choose sides in the battle for the future of medicine, she did not know what she would decide. Her battle was of a different nature—it was to end the discrimination towards women doctors, which prevented her from working where she chose and where she would be most useful.

Josephine listened to the other speakers while waiting her turn. After a time, the usher approached and beckoned her to the dais. A ten minute break was called for the audience to stretch.

Josephine climbed the stairs to the dais, careful to pull her dress to cover her knees. She took out her speech and her expensive gold fountain pen, the one she'd been awarded at medical school graduation. One of only a few females in a college with hundreds of men, she was accustomed to speaking before a mostly male audience, most of whom did not agree that women should be doctors. She knew not to expect any courtesies—this would have to be a first-rate speech.

She cautiously reminded herself not to slip into her Boweryese accent—the nuns had made sure she practiced perfect elocution, especially when speaking to the upper classes. The Mother Superior had told her to keep her arms pinned to her sides, and not wave them about like the bakers on Mulberry Street.

Suddenly, Josephine was nervous. This was a prestigious panel on Manhattan's Upper East Side. She looked at the crowd. Elegantly dressed, they were fanning themselves with their programs. Most had no interest in Brooklyn, probably viewing it as some destitute area far away from their sumptuous townhouses, ritzy restaurants and clubs. Would they be interested in what she had to say?

What would they think of her, a first born American child of Italian immigrants? Since the 1924 Immigration Act with its strict quotas, Lady Liberty wasn't so welcoming. It was fortunate that Josephine's parents had arrived in the last century, and she was born in Manhattan as an American citizen. Birth meant everything.

Josephine's practice consisted almost entirely of newly arrived immigrants. She treated Italians, Germans, Africans, Chinese, Irish, Jewish, Russians and many others—a patient's origins made no difference to her. The babies she delivered would be American, too, like her. Much of the Lower East Side immigrant population was migrating out to her territory, and she welcomed them all.

Perhaps this speech isn't such a good idea. Josephine felt her larynx constricting. Her heart began racing. The usher announced that her lecture would begin in two minutes.

Now was not the time to falter, she reassured herself. *Fortes fortuna adiuvat!* If she could take control of her tachycardia, she'd get through this moment. Gathering her copious notes, she attempted to stack them with a confident knock on the lectern, but the sheets went flying.

"*Oh, applesauce!*" she cursed, then instantly clasped her hand over her mouth as her face reddened in embarrassment. The microphone was on and had sent her expletive flying across the hall. People looked up at her in shock. Her heart began pounding as fast as the El train, and sweat broke across her brow. She tried to apologize, but her voice exited as no more than a squeak.

Instead of panicking, her doctor training took over. She quickly put her finger to her wrist and counted the pulse beats to the second hand of the gold doctor's watch pinned to the front of her dress. Her diagnosis was accurate, but not helpful. Stage fright.

She bent behind the podium to pick up her notes.

The audience whispered. Undoubtedly, they chalked up her outburst to something "female." *That's a dreadful mistake,* she wanted to shout. *I'll convince you that women are just as capable as men.*

Finding her medical bag, Josephine searched inside for a leather case containing Homeopathic glass vials. With relief, she found the one labeled *Aconitum napellus*. The tiny white globules inside were extracted from the poisonous Aconite plant, diluted and then rolled in milk sugar. She placed one under her tongue.

Josephine looked fondly at the vial of *Aconitum napellus*. It was one of the first Homeopathic remedies she'd made with Professor Janus Heath in her school's laboratory. A devout Homeopath, he explained that Homeopathy was a series of paradoxes, based on The Law of Similars—*Similia similibus curentur*, or "like cures like". This doctrine held that a substance capable of inducing symptoms in a healthy person will relieve similar symptoms in a sick person. "We must imitate nature," he'd say. "When we chop an onion, for example, it causes watery eyes and sneezing. If we give the Homeopathic onion remedy, *Allium cepa*, it will cure these same symptoms Of a cold or allergy in a sick person."

The paradox was expected, explained the professor, because the goal was not to attack a disease with harmful drugs, but to gently stimulate a person's own "vital force" or immune system to heal illness from within.

Josephine remembered running to the laboratory, eager to begin the extractions and dilutions. Opening the door, she heard the familiar pounding of instruments and felt the hot steam rising from the giant steel distillers. Cloaked in swirls of billowing smoke, Professor Heath tended a mixture over a burner, stirring it briskly to and fro like a chef sauté-ing a sauce. Beakers next to him were filled with many kinds of natural wonders soaking in alcohol: colorful flower blossoms, plant roots, mosses, even frogs, snakes and tarantulas. There were boxes of mineral rocks, shells, and beakers of liquid quicksilver, precious silver and gold. She always remembered to use the tongs to handle the poisonous plants, snake venoms, and diseased tissues.

Josephine spent all her free time in the lab, grinding and "succussing," or vigorously shaking, the compounds to dynamize the ions. Chemistry had advanced to the point where ions were recognized to exist after molecules broke apart. Through succussion and dilution these ions were transferred to the surrounding water. Professor Heath said that chemistry proved that Homeopathic remedies held therapeutic value.

But in Josephine's last year of studies, the school's curriculum changed course from a mixture of Homeopathy and Allopathy to strictly Allopathy. It mandated the same chemistry labs and rigorous clinical practice as before, but the drugs used to treat patients were very different. No longer was she able to consult with the professor on which Homeopathic remedy would energetically (Allopaths thought inexplicably) stimulate a patient's immune system at the deepest level. She had to learn the entire Allopathic pharmacopeia. Its way of prescribing based on the most urgent (Homeopaths thought superficial) symptoms and disease categories was foreign to her.

But Josephine was smart and caught on quickly. Few girls undertook such difficult studies, but Josephine seemed to be called for it. The nuns, who were following her progress, said that she was like Esther, "born for such a time as this"—a girl entering a male-dominated profession.

Josephine checked her pulse again. The Aconite was beginning its work. Her heart began beating more regularly, and she breathed more evenly. She twitched her toes inside her shiny patent leather one-straps, another trick learned from the nuns to keep her body, and later her scalpel, steady.

For a last check on her appearance, she opened her compact mirror and dared to look in it. Her hair was now frazzled and the inky pencil line was smudged. *Not too bad,* she reasoned and smoothed her dress. Finally, she adjusted a single long strand of costume pearls, but they wouldn't sit right on her ample chest, no matter what she did.

Glancing around, Josephine noticed that some men on the dais were careful to catch her eye and nod. Were they Homeopaths or Allopaths? *It's not as if they wear a large H or A on their chests!* Josephine didn't want to offend anyone in either faction, so she politely nodded back.

The coming years would be decisive in the war between these two philosophies of medicine. Josephine, a graduate of New York City College of Homeopathic Medicine, was the event's final speaker. She realized she would have the last word.

Bravely, she stood back up to face the crowd.

Chapter 3 - A Lady Doctor

The hall quieted, as the head of the Society took the microphone and introduced Josephine. "Dr. Reva's perspective as a female doctor in the trenches will be most inspiring."

She thanked him and stepped forward to the podium to a smattering of applause.

In a smooth voice, she delved into a highly detailed list of facts and figures that she'd meticulously written down with the practiced strokes of her fountain pen. She looked up to see if the audience was astonished by her calculations.

But the men and women were squirming in their seats.

Josephine hadn't yet learned the first rule of public speaking in the Jazz Age: to entertain the audience with a witty, tap-beating monologue.

The usher rushed forward to put a footstool under her feet to lift her pint-sized frame, as if that would help.

"As I was saying, the mortality rates of immigrant women in childbirth are too high, due to unhygienic home births."

Josephine peered out at the audience and noticed the well-heeled ladies gossiping and smoothing their summer dresses and the gentlemen yawning.

Then the words of the Society's President echoed in her ears: "Dr. Reva's perspective as a female doctor in the trenches will be most inspiring." *Female? Trenches?*

"As you heard, I'm the first female M.D. in Bensonhurst, Borough Park and parts of Gravesend near Coney Island—in the trenches, so to speak."

Several audience members looked up. Most of them had been to Coney Island to visit Luna Park and promenade along the boardwalk.

"More female doctors like me are desperately needed in New York City. Why?"

The audience was now looking at her expectantly.

In the orphanage, Josephine had stood with Mother Cabrini as the nuns made an impassioned plea for funds to build more orphanages. Famous for miraculously building over sixty hospitals and institutions, Mother Cabrini spoke from the heart. Josephine put aside her notes.

"*Lemme*, uh, *Let me* tell you about my practice. Births make up over half my house calls. So, I usually work in the wee hours of the night—that's when most babies like to arrive."

There was a burst of laughter.

"After the trolley and buses stop running, I need a motor car to get to the home birth. Then, of course, I need a chauffeur because I can't leave my car on the street. I might return to find the white walls gone, or worse, it towed."

The audience laughed more heartily. They could relate. The injection of humor was working. But Josephine decided on another course.

"I climb to the mother's apartment—it's usually a 3rd or 4th

20

floor walkup—and set up my sterilized medical instruments. But what I find may shock you."

Josephine could hear some murmurs in the audience.

"It's dark, lit only by a gas lamp—I can't see my own hands in front of my face, let alone a baby coming. And there are germ bodies everywhere."

The audience murmured. Their homes were quite the opposite—bright and airy, scrubbed clean by domestic staff, full of fresh white bedding and with all the modern comforts of electricity and plumbing.

"Perhaps a midwife has been trying her best. But by the time they send for me, the doctor, it's usually too late."

The audience gasped. Josephine's tone became more impassioned.

"The mother is clinging to life by a thread and the baby is stuck inside the womb. The prognosis is dire—over half will die."

Several audience members' mouths hung open in shock.

"There's not much any doctor can do. So I take out my scalpel. Sometimes I can cheat death, but more often, I can not."

The faces in the audience turned grim.

"When I see a beautiful newborn turn cold and blue, my heart breaks. But what's worse to know is that my patient and her baby might have survived—if she'd chosen a hospital birth."

Josephine took a deep breath, and forged ahead. "And why didn't she? Well, I'll tell you. The mother was too embarrassed to submit to the intimate examinations of her private body parts by a man."

Josephine had spoken bluntly. Several gasps ensued from the

audience when they pictured exactly what she meant.

"But there's an alternative: the expectant mother is not embarrassed to come see me, another female—a Lady Doctor."

The women in the audience looked relieved, but the men seemed to be frowning. What could she do? It was time for another injection of humor.

"Many of my patients do become pregnant, well, repeatedly."

The audience tittered.

"When my patient disrobes in front of me, she has no fear for her modesty. Nor am I likely to cause jealous feelings in her husband."

Josephine could hear male voices guffawing, too.

"I can persuade the immigrant mother to deliver her baby in a hospital. It's hygienic and sterile. There's electricity and ether. I can deliver a baby safely with the assistance of my trained nurses. As you know from the facts and figures I gave at the beginning of my speech, the survival rates for both mother and baby are very high with a hospital birth."

A few members of the audience were now applauding.

Josephine still needed that inspiring finish to her speech, which the Society's President had promised.

"More women must be encouraged to enter the medical profession. We need more female M.D.'s, whether Homeopath or Allopath," she nodded to the gentlemen behind her, "to minister to the city's growing populations. Women doctors can work miracles. Thank you for your attention."

The audience rose to their feet in unison and applauded. They then funneled towards the rear of the hall to mingle and partake of the coffee, tea and pastries.

Josephine's face was flushed from the rigors of speaking. She felt the adrenaline coursing through her body and the thrill of having spoken up for a cause she believed in. A photographer came and snapped her picture, and the phosphorescent flash momentarily stunned her.

"We doctors enjoy hearing from a young Homeopath so rebellious." An elderly gentleman wearing a top coat and holding an ivory topped walking stick appeared next to her. "Your speech was full of plain-spoken vigor—a most unusual effect." He tipped his silken bowler, and walked on.

Josephine frowned. "Rebellious" was a peculiar word. She'd been called worse when she marched with the nuns demanding the right to vote. As for being plain-spoken, she could agree— she'd never been one to mince words. He'd labelled her a Homeopath, but she preferred to think of herself as a Medical Doctor, a woman of science. The few surviving Homeopathic medical colleges taught the latest in biology, chemistry, physiology, pathology and surgical procedures. Her school conferred M.D. diplomas, the same as fully Allopathic schools.

Although her speech was the last, Josephine had neatly avoided entering the fray between Homeopathy and Allopathy. Her message about including women doctors was divisive enough. It soon resonated like a piece of music playing—some would find it pleasant, others grating.

Two young ladies approached, wearing upturned ribboned hats and walking arm in arm, giggling.

"How did you do it?" one asked Josephine. "I mean, as a girl, get accepted to a male medical college?"

"More to the point," the other girl added, "why did you ever apply?"

Josephine knew that since the war had ended, more men were back home competing with women for limited places in the newly co-ed medical schools. The few remaining female medical colleges were forced to close due to Abraham Flexner's 1910 report mandating expensive research, equipment and laboratories, which these schools could not afford with their limited endowments. As a result, there were fewer female M.D.s in the 1920's when Josephine graduated than in the 1880's. Things had gotten worse for women doctors, not better.

"Well, I admit it was a long shot. But I loved reading medical journals, so I was prepared. The committee was convinced to take a chance on me. Well, I wouldn't stop talking until they said 'yes!'"

The other girl scrutinized Josephine. "Surely, you are a fine Lady Doctor," she said, twisting her hat ribbons. "But don't you agree that a woman's place is in the home with her husband, taking care of her own babies?"

"That's fine for some," Josephine bit her tongue. "But others like me prefer to work—some say we are *destined* to become doctors."

Josephine stared at the pretty girls as they walked off, smiling and twirling in a feminine manner among the crowd.

How different her life would be if she were married and had babies. She adored delivering babies, but raising them was a different matter. Babies grew bigger and needed constant supervision. How could she take care of a child while she worked such long hours? Would the child be left to wander the streets, like she and her siblings had been forced to do after their parents died? If she were married, she would also have to care for a husband. A husband would hardly let his wife work in such a difficult profession. While she was frightened of children, she was more frightened of a husband.

Yet Josephine realized that the social convention of marriage would be inevitable. *I'll put if off as long as possible.*

Several society ladies joined her at that moment, ebulliently talking. They offered their volunteer work and to donate funds for new city hospital maternity wards. "We must convince women to give birth in a hospital," one echoed Josephine. "Lady Doctors like yourself are capable of devoted service," said another. Suffrage, they all agreed, had given women the right to vote, but that had not led to more females working, especially in the male-dominated professions.

Soon, a stout man approached the group of ladies and introduced himself as Dr. Anthony Goldblum, a city Director of Preventative Health. A fellow graduate of Josephine's medical college, although many years earlier, he pumped her hand vigorously.

"I agree with you, Dr. Reva, on one point. Prevention is the key to good health."

"I must congratulate you, too, Dr. Goldblum, for your efforts to end the sale of spoiled and tainted milk."

"We must do our utmost to protect mothers and children," he proudly said, tipping his hat to the ladies. The ladies nodded pleasantly in return, then left to rejoin their husbands. Dr. Goldblum turned to Josephine, continuing in a hushed tone. "On matters of public health, no matter my recommendations, my reports are rarely enacted. Conservatives won't regulate businesses, while Progressives find it expedient to do so. They are locking horns."

He motioned towards the far end of the dais where New York Senator Royal S. Copeland and Governor Franklin D. Roosevelt were surrounded by other important politicians. "With my next report, they'll listen to me."

He looked determined.

"I would've done much more during the last Spanish Flu pandemic to halt mass infection," he continued in an angrier voice. Josephine remembered that Senator Copeland, a Homeopath, had become New York City's Commissioner of Health. While leading the city through the Spanish Flu influenza pandemic, he was greatly admired for his calmness and practicality amid the chaos. He mandated sanitary protections and quarantines to fight infections, and his policies met with success in curbing the death toll. The good press had catapulted him into the Senate.

"I lobbied for much stricter measures," Dr. Goldblum continued. "I wanted to outlaw spitting and close all places where the public gathered, including theaters and restaurants. I wanted to mandate mask-wearing immediately—that's the best protection from germs floating in the air. Of course, no one listened to me, and the disease spread miserably."

Public health was certainly contentious. "However, schools were kept open," Josephine countered. "Immigrant children needed a safe place and to be kept off the streets."

The Spanish Flu had swept through her family's Little Italy tenement when Josephine was fourteen years old. When her parents fell ill, she became responsible for their care and that of her four younger siblings, who were also sick. Consulting with the neighborhood pharmacist, she administered Homeopathic *Gelsemium*, and concocted herbal teas to keep them hydrated while they battled fever and pneumonia. Josephine's siblings survived, and Josephine had only gotten mildly ill. But her parents, who hadn't been of sound constitution to begin with, succumbed in one terrible night.

Her sadness was interrupted by a loud scratchy voice, playing like the needle at the end of a record.

"The most effective cure for influenza," Philomen Quinn ordained, "are forsythia buds plucked in the early fall. I make a purified extract and advise one ampule every three hours. The demand is so great that I must produce a steady supply for the season."

Josephine turned to find the tonic salesman who set up his stand on her street corner selling his unregulated bottles. He must be doing well, Josephine noted, for he had a pot-belly under his new suit and his mustache was neatly trimmed by the barber. "Forsythia and herbs are fine, but it's your other ingredients, Mr. Quinn, that are questionable. The morphine, whiskey and addictive substances you add to the natural healing qualities of the plants —"

"Now, Dr. Reva," Dr. Goldblum interrupted. "My man Quinn here was a very good pharmacology student. I admit he's young, but he's learned plenty. Morphine and cocaine are no longer permitted. I'm sure he's following our new protocols against addiction."

"Alcohol is a necessary ingredient to extract the potency of the herb," Quinn protested. "I strictly follow all guidelines. My main concern, of course, is the health and well-being of my customers."

"Customers?" Josephine harrumphed, "they're not customers. They're my patients!"

"Now, now Dr. Reva, do calm yourself. There's no need to get emotional," said Dr. Goldblum. "You must begin to think about modern medicine fabrication and synthesis. Alcohol extraction is perfectly legal, medicinally speaking, under the Volstead Act. We require stringent testing. I understand you're a female, working in a man's world, but you ought to let us men take care of the practicalities."

"Indeed," said Quinn, indignantly. "We know what's best for the future of medicine."

Josephine started to protest and her face flushed a bright pink. Nonetheless, she was on a mission.

"Dr. Goldblum, perhaps you know of a hospital willing to hire female physicians?"

"Certainly not." He turned back towards Quinn. The two stood closer, both stout men in their herringbone suits with belted backs. Even though they had been condescending towards her, she couldn't help being amused by their appearance. They reminded her of crowing roosters, like the one a patient once tried to give her in lieu of payment.

Quinn put his arm around Goldblum's shoulder, speaking under his breath. Josephine could just hear bits and pieces of their conversation: "regulations... production... three-fold." Goldblum nodded vigorously in reply. Josephine watched the two men walk off, their heads bobbing together.

"That was a truly inspiring speech, Josephine." Dr. Israel Kleiner approached and graciously shook her hand. A former dean and professor at Dr. Copeland's Homeopathic college, he was a kindly man wearing wire-rimmed glasses. Dr. Kleiner was mild-mannered and soft-spoken, rather dovish, Josephine thought, but she admired his modesty. He'd earned a PhD in chemistry at Yale University, and had once been a researcher with the Rockefeller Institute, surrounded by other brilliant minds. But his work on diabetes didn't gel with the institute's need for bacteriology research, and he was forced out. *Their loss was our gain,* thought Josephine.

"Thank you, Dr. Kleiner. I hope to inspire more girls to join me in this difficult profession. Maybe a few society daughters, those who can afford it, will take up the study of medicine."

Dr. Kleiner nodded thoughtfully. Another scientist pulled him away to discuss biomedical research.

Three of Josephine's former classmates, Abraham, Vicenzo and Jameson had been tagging along behind their former Dean. They liked to call themselves the "Yorkvillains," a play on the name of the Yorkville area where the medical school was located.

Josephine remembered they had been trouble-makers who rarely studied but somehow managed to earn passing marks.

"I'd say you really hit it out of the ballpark, Joe," Abe said, "clear to the moon." Josephine didn't know if that was a compliment, but she decided it probably wasn't. In the last year of medical school, the boys had masculinized her name to "Joe," which in their minds was a form of acceptance. She hadn't minded but for their constant teasing—they never let her forget that she was the only girl in their classes.

"You're now a crusading Lady Doctor," said Vic.

"Or *Doctress*," joked Abe. Doctress was the name for a female healer who used mysticism and herbs.

"I'm a scientist," Josephine retorted. "I earned my M.D., the same as you."

"Maybe what you needed was a M.A.N," Jamie snickered. "If you remember from anatomy, we certainly are not the same."

The Yorkvillains laughed.

Josephine turned red. At least, these Yorkvillains hadn't heckled her while she spoke to the Society. Flustered and remembering that she had to be ladylike if she was going to get a partnership, she decided to ignore them.

She turned back towards Dr. Kleiner, who was still standing quietly a few paces away.

"I enjoyed your speech, Doctor," Josephine began. "I didn't realize you were the first to show conclusive results that pancreatic insulin was responsible for hypoglycemia."

"Yes, back in 1913, my research found the cause of diabetes. I had started working towards its cure."

"To hear your work was pushed aside was alarming."

"Well, there were many worthy research subjects," he began judiciously. "As you heard today, I still needed to show how the pancreas extract lowered glucose through metabolism—and for that I needed the methods being used in German labs. I made several trips there, but the war interfered. By July of 1914, my wife and I barely escaped to Paris and back to America."

"That must have been harrowing. But I can't understand why the leaders failed to support you in continuing your research, war or no war."

"Our soldiers needed antisera for bacterial infections. My research on diabetes was sacrificed for the greater cause."

"But the world would have had insulin years sooner, saving many children from a horrible and painful death."

"True. I had shown promising results. Years later, in 1922, my research did help the Canadian team. They extracted animal pancreatic insulin, just as I had suggested. The drug was injected into a child, curing him." He looked proud.

"But they got all the glory. They won the Nobel Prize. You were thrown out before making that breakthrough. Weren't you angry? I'd have been mad as—"

"Only when I heard they patented insulin. I wished that it be available to all who needed it for free."

"I'm sure the Institute regrets their decision."

"One's efforts are not always appreciated."

At that moment, the usher who helped Josephine at the dais brought over the footstool and laid it at her feet.

"You may put this back in the office," he said, and walked off.

Dr. Kleiner pointed downward. "I see you, Josephine, also know the price of being ahead of your time."

Josephine shrugged. "He probably thinks I'm the cook, too."

She asked Dr. Kleiner if he knew of any partnerships, but he said regrettably that he did not. Picking up the stool, she said good day and headed further inside the large building.

She found the office, but the receptionist motioned her onward to the library. Josephine continued down the serpentine hallways, marveling at the polished stone walls and thick oak doors leading to various rooms. Having access to New York's wondrous museums and societies never failed to amaze her, far from the humbler places she was used to.

The library was tucked away in a cozy salon lined with bookshelves stretching from floor to ceiling, and stacked with leather and cloth-bound medical books from ages ago. Burnished oak moulding, marquetry cabinets and inlaid floors decorated the room. Josephine envied the solid oak tables topped with bright electric reading lamps covered by green glass globes, and felt an urge to climb the tall library steps to reach the uppermost books. Putting the footstool back in its place, she thought back on the many nights she'd used a footstool to climb out the window of the orphanage to escape to the New York Public Library to read medical journals by electric light. Looking around this room filled with books on science, she imagined herself sinking into one of the armchairs and never leaving.

Out of the corner of her eye, she spotted Professor Janus Heath. She couldn't wait to speak with him and find out where he'd gone. But he was talking to a man she saw only from the rear and the two seemed to be in a heated discussion. So as not to disturb them, she walked over to the archivist and asked to see some of the rare collections.

"Perhaps a book by Dr. Sigmund Freud?" he asked. "We have a signed edition of his work, *On the Interpretation of Dreams*."

"No, thank you. I've already read that."

The archivist looked at Josephine then consulted his notes. "An 1880's female doctor donated her private collection. We've a lovely copy of a Roman work by Apicius, *De re coquinaria*. It's a hand-scripted vellum, in Latin, of course. The illustrations are particularly good."

Josephine understood the title, for she'd been schooled in Latin by the orphanage nuns to assist at High Mass. *On the Subject of Cooking*. She frowned for an instant, for she could barely boil an egg. She then realized that such an ancient cookbook would be full of knowledge of herbs, and medicinal botany was a subject that intrigued her. "Yes, that'll do nicely."

She cradled the ancient tome, which was in remarkably good condition. Choosing a large comfortable looking armchair to the rear of the two men talking, she begin leafing through the translucent pages. She scanned a few recipes for unusual herbs and found *Silphium*, a large stalk-like plant with a pungent and flavorful sap, whose disappearance during Roman times was a mystery. She knew that its common name was Laser, it originated in Cyrene, eastern Libya, and Theophrastus wrote that it only grew wild and couldn't be cultivated. Josephine remembered that Laser was considered magical and a powerful aphrodisiac. Ironically, it was also used as contraception, so it probably went extinct from over-picking. Alexander the Great carried it in his satchel and Julius Caesar stockpiled it—Laser was worth its weight in gold. Emperors minted its image on coins. Only the wealthiest could afford Laser, and the rest had to be content with common garlic.

Tavola Mediterranea, a healthy Mediterranean diet, interested Josephine, for her mother espoused Neapolitan recipes. One day, she'd travel there, to eat freshly caught fish cooked with white wine, spices and olive oil. The gift of gastronomy hadn't been inherited—the most Josephine could manage was heated soup or a bowl of spaghetti. Turning more pages, she found one particularly strange recipe when she was interrupted by shouting.

"You have to face the inevitable," the man with his back to Josephine leaned towards Professor Heath. He got up abruptly, throwing back his chair, and stalked out of the library. Josephine caught a glimpse of his angry profile. It was Dr. Goldblum, the man she'd just met. *That's odd*, Josephine thought.

Professor Heath was left staring bleakly, eyes downcast. He shook his head slowly, and sank lower into his chair. Josephine watched him as he picked up several pieces of paper from the table in front of him and put them in his breast pocket. He looked so forlorn that Josephine decided to go over to him.

"How have you been, Professor?" she asked. Professor Heath rose to shake her hand. He still had eyes like a hawk, but she noticed that his face was lined. Tall and gaunt, he must have been nearly sixty, and his hair and beard had feathered in gray. His chest puffed out and his middle was considerably larger than she remembered.

"Oh, Josephine, what a pleasure. Do sit down, please." They sat in the armchairs. "I remember how we used to make remedies together. I've moved to Brooklyn, too. You must come visit my new laboratory. It's bigger and better."

"Sure, that'd be wonderful, Professor," said Josephine.

"And you may call me Janus because now we're colleagues—today you've given a fine speech." He looked at Josephine who frowned. "Your first? I thought so. Don't worry, it gets easier."

"I'm glad I didn't make a fool of myself.'"

"You spoke from the heart. Much more interesting stuff than the others."

"Mothers and babies, that always gets people's attention. But the part about Lady Doctors—I'm not so sure if that didn't fall upon deaf ears. I was hoping to find a partnership here in Manhattan."

"Ah, but more women in medicine is a future we can be sure of. *Tempora mutantur, nos et mutamur in illis.*"

Josephine smiled, remembering that quoting Latin in medical school was a necessary pastime, if students didn't want to lose points by failing to name body parts on exams. She loosely translated his expression. "Times are changing—we, too, are changed with them."

"Yes, that's so, isn't it? But you're only a fledgling, just out of the college and internship nest, and only one year into your practice. You need to let the rest of society catch up to the idea of female doctors." He seemed to be encouraging her, so she relaxed a little.

Janus poked at the ancient book in her hands. "What's that you have there? It looks very old."

"It's a cookbook from ancient Rome. Did you know there's a recipe for flamingos, of all things?"

"Apicius was a glutton," he retorted with some hostility. "He ate anything, no matter how exotic, and served it up for dinner. Apparently, so did most Romans."

"We're no longer living in the Roman ages, thank goodness."

"Oh, aren't we?" Janus answered cryptically. "It's the Roaring

20's. Gluttony wherever one looks nowadays."

With that, he got up, looking almost as angry as Dr. Goldblum had been. Josephine was startled, but he gave her his calling card, then left the library.

Josephine went to return the recipe book. She hadn't meant to cause any offense, but it seemed that by her very presence, she did exactly that. What had Dr. Goldblum said about her—a woman working in a man's world.

She leaned back in her chair and wrapped her arms around her tired body, cradling herself. She'd worked all night delivering a baby, and another patient was due—a toll call from her Brooklyn hospital might come at any moment.

Josephine decided it was time to leave and make her way home to Brooklyn. If the streetcars and buses were running behind, she might miss her patient's birth. But first, she must make the rounds and be sure to greet anyone important who could help her find a partnership or help more girls become doctors. If they were Progressive, as Dr. Goldblum seemed to suggest, so much the better.

Still on the dais was Franklin Delano Roosevelt, the newly elected Governor of New York. She pushed her way through the throng around him.

"Oh, Dr. Reva," he turned his wheelchair towards her, "a most delightful young lady. I thank you immensely for livening up our conference."

"Your welcome, Governor. Congratulations on your election," Josephine said, taking his outstretched hand. She noticed it was cold and his grip was weak. "I hope you can help more women find places in medical schools."

"Yes, I agree with your point, and I'm sure Eleanor would, too. Our immigrant communities need more female doctors."

"I'm sure you'll do your utmost."

"Lady Doctors are most capable," he agreed, smiling pleasantly at Josephine. "I'm thinking of adding one to my staff."

Josephine looked awkwardly down, for she had read that the Governor was flirtatious. The Governor laughed heartily. Josephine told him she agreed with his policies and reforms thus far.

"I hope we have the pleasure of meeting again, Governor."

"I believe we will," replied Mr. Roosevelt.

A group of well wishers closed in on the Governor, and he was wheeled away, presumably to a waiting motor car. Josephine was glad that the Governor was in good humor. She would have liked to have taken his case Homeopathically, because she sensed, from her simple interaction, that he seemed to suffer from a general weakness. Could there be something else, not polio? she wondered. A degenerative disease? Nonetheless, his mind was as quick as a fox, she mused. The famous Mr. Roosevelt had listened to her speech. She felt very good, indeed.

Despite that New York was considered a launching pad for the Presidency, the previous Governor Al Smith, another Democrat, had been defeated, she'd read in the newspaper, by "three P's: Prohibition, Prejudice and Prosperity." The American people weren't ready to elect a Catholic, citing the ridiculous fear that the Pope would then be in charge. Josephine sighed. She'd been dismayed by Mr. Smith's loss. Not only had he helped dressmakers like her mother with workshop reforms, but he was also a "wet" candidate, meaning he wanted to end Prohibition. *It's time this ridiculous law was repealed.* Josephine knew from practicing medicine that when you forbid people from doing something, often enough, habit will overtake them. But Smith's candidacy did show that the Democrats could unite wealthy and poor, and this could be very useful. *I suspect Mr. Roosevelt will go farther.*

Josephine spotted Senator Copeland waving at her, and headed over. He was a sensible Midwesterner and Homeopathic medical doctor who moved to New York to further his political ambitions. Josephine remembered his lectures at her medical college, discussing Homeopathy with fervor, with his piercing but sorrowful eyes under bushy eyebrows and strong jowls. She thought he was in temperament something like a bulldog—tenacious until the job was done. She remembered that arguing with him was futile, because he remained eloquent and immoveable in his debate. If only Josephine could do the same, but her character was quite the opposite. She was fiery and quick to engage in battle.

Senator Copeland was standing next to a rather corpulent woman in an indigo polka dot silk dress wearing a stylish hat pierced by a large ostrich feather.

"Dr. Reva, this is Mrs. Henrietta Porter-Graves, one of the supporters of the Society."

Josephine said a polite hello. Mrs. Porter-Graves took her hand and held it warmly.

"I'm so pleased to meet you, my dear. Your story is inspirational. The Senator tells me you were an orphan, raised by Mother Cabrini. I must hear more. I'm wondering if you'd be inclined to come and speak to our ladies' group? So many of us have daughters, and some of them are simply not cut out for marriage. It would be a good idea to find them employment where they could do some good for others."

Josephine managed to suppress a laugh. "Well, being a medical doctor is certainly no walk in the park, that I can say." She looked at Senator Copeland who seemed to be pleased by the conversation. "It's rigorous training, and very hard work. But I'm sure that some of your girls might find a calling in it, as I have."

"Indeed," Senator Copeland said. "Josephine would be just the person to inspire other young ladies to enter the field of medicine. Her training was in Homeopathy, and women are ideally suited with their questioning natures and patience to take cases and prescribe our remedies." Then he looked sternly at Josephine. "I'm sure Josephine is a devoted Homeopath."

"Um, I certainly learned it well, but I haven't altogether decided."

"You may want to give that more thought," the Senator said, adjusting the red flower in his lapel. "The remedies are like this carnation, a perfect symmetry of petals. It will be my legacy to see the Homeopathic Pharmacopeia recognized as the wondrous gift of medicine that it is. This knowledge will continue, even if the winds are blowing it asunder."

"The remaining Homeopathic medical colleges train students in both philosophies of medicine: Homeopathy and Allopathy," Josephine explained to Mrs. Porter-Graves. "Senator Copeland's school and mine offer the most advanced scientific instruments and laboratories." She didn't elaborate that in her final year, the dean of her school was overseeing a full transition to Allopathy.

"New York Homeopathic Medical College was originally founded with faculty trained at Columbia University, and our affiliation with Flower Hospital offers excellent student clinics," Senator Copeland added. "There are labs in bacteriology, chemistry, biology, physiology, histology, dermatology, and ophthalmology, my specialty."

You get everything you would get in an Allopathic school and besides this, you get Homeopathy."

"That's very interesting," said Mrs. Porter-Graves. "I, for one, prefer Homeopathy. Those little pills dissolved in water help my rheumatism. I find enormous relief, and with so little after effect. Of course, wintering in Palm Beach also helps." Mrs. Porter-Graves let out a substantial laugh, and her large pearl necklace bounced on her chest. Senator Copeland laughed, too, throwing back his head.

Josephine could only stare, for she had never seen real deep sea oyster pearls that large. Mrs. Porter-Graves continued, "One must escape New York's cold winters. And I sail the *Ile de France* over to Cap d'Antibes in the damp springtime. Oh, I know—my daughter can become a physician on board the ship."

"A shipboard romance, I can see the headline now," joked Senator Copeland. "But seriously, your daughter would be most welcome at our colleges. We've been accepting female students, like Josephine, who show exceptional promise. All girls must, of course, pass university preparatory science classes. She must be capable of long and laborious study of the sciences."

"If I could do it, then I'm sure your daughter can, too, if she applies herself entirely."

"Josephine was a scholarship student," interrupted Dr. Kleiner, who had been listening. He already knew Mrs. Porter-Graves and needed no introduction. "She was one of the most highly ranked students, receiving a First on the New York State Regents in Physiology. It would be most generous of you, Mrs. Porter-Graves, to help support another female who displays such promise while your daughter attends and launches her career. They could both follow in the footsteps of the great American women doctors, Elizabeth Blackwell and

Mary Putnam Jacobi. Dr. Jacobi, as you well know, was the first female Fellow at The New York Academy of Medicine."

"I believe the city is ready for more of us Lady Doctors," said Josephine, aware that that wasn't true yet. Not one doctor at the conference had asked her to join his practice. But she remembered what Janus Heath had said: times are changing. But how much more time was needed? Brooklynites in her neighborhood were already used to the sight of her in a white lab coat carrying her medical bag through the streets. Cab drivers no longer bothered honking at her. But there was the front-page murder trial of a female practitioner in Brooklyn Heights, Mary Dixon Jones. She was arrested after a patient died, even though her surgical skills were said to be among the best. That was about thirty years ago, but other Lady Doctors faced revocation of their licenses. A woman doctor could never let her guard down.

"I'll come speak to your Ladies' Group. Please let me know when and I shall be there." Josephine handed Mrs. Porter-Graves her calling card, and saying her goodbyes, headed for the door.

"More female doctors, ha!" Abe made a guffawing sound. "I'll say, you never give up, Joe." The Yorkvillains were blocking Josephine's exit. "That was all fine during the war, when you ladies were needed, but men are far more suited to the profession."

"How much of a success has it been for you?" Vic stepped forward. "I don't see your office anywhere near ours uptown."

"We're on Park, and you're—where was it? Oh, yes, Brooklyn," added Jamie sarcastically.

"Fashionable, ain't it?" mocked Abe. "All youz livin' in Bwooklyn, wit' de best 'ospitals like Doctors, fine restaurants and speakeasies, Broadway thee-ay-ters..."

"...and the ritziest Jazz clubs like The Oasis." Jamie added. The others laughed.

"You boys never grow up." Josephine crossed her arms. "Your teasing is still child's play."

"Ha! Remember we locked you in the morgue for the night," Abe continued. "Pennied you inside, jamming the door with copper tops."

"And remember that time on rounds," Vic snickered, "when we sent you to examine a typhoid patient." They laughed some more, oblivious to the danger they had put her in.

"Doctor Josephine Reva!" An usher shouted over the crowd carrying a silver tray with a card on it. "Doctor Josephine Reva! You have an urgent telephone call!"

Josephine made a face at the men and raised her hand. She picked up the card, then went to the telephone booths, hearing guffaws echoing in her ears. She wasn't going to let those Yorkvillains ruin her triumphant day.

Chapter 4 - A Citizen Tip

Later that night...

B rooklyn Nine Six Two," the rookie officer on duty answered the telephone's clanking noise, yawning and half asleep. Nearly 2:00 a.m., he thought, and no major crimes to report. When was he going to see some action?

"Please standby and I'll put the call through." The operator connected the two parties.

"May I please speak with Detective John O'Malley?"

The female caller's voice had a touch of flirtatiousness, and the young officer perked up. "Yup, he's here, d'ya wanna speak to him *personally*?" He pushed the telephone candlestick stand forward so the other officers could listen.

"Yes, officer, and jeepers, you don't sound half bad yourself! But my call is urgent, if you would be so kind."

The rookie smiled, remembering the daringly modern women he encountered in the Jazz halls. This one sounded classy, so he shouted towards the Detective's Room.

Chief Detective First Grade John O'Malley, a grey-haired lanky man of thirty-nine, woke up from his snooze, unwound himself from his chair and stomped over.

"Dames calling you at work, O'Malley?" the rookie snickered. "She sounds like the cat's meow!"

"That's *Detective* O'Malley to you." The detective scowled, for he discouraged any kind of familiarity with his rookies. Perching on the desk, he grabbed the telephone stand and placed the bulbous receiver against his ear. His steel-blue eyes squinted and his forehead creased. Pulling at his neatly trimmed military-style mustache, he patiently listened.

"Uh huh, a what? A Lady Doctor, you don't say. May have known the victim. You saw them both arguing where?" O'Malley was jotting down some notes. "She knows plants and what? Poisons! Uh, I see. Suspicious, I agree." He listened some more, frowning.

"That's very observant, Miss, and the Brooklyn Police Department appreciates your call," he said with a final grimace, disconnecting the line. How he hated to be polite, but the Commissioner's orders specifically aimed to encourage citizens to report on crime.

Most of these citizens are cranks, O'Malley thought, and there's no use being polite when it only encourages them. This caller sounded like she was wasting his time.

But after scratching his pencil some more on his official notepad, he looked up, perplexed.

"Should I round up the boys?" the rookie grinned hopefully. "Another speakeasy raid?"

"Nope, you've gotten your wish tonight. A body down by the water at The Narrows. To top it off, it seems we've been given some instructions by the murderer."

"She was on the phone? Did you get her name?"

"Haven't you learned anything about these calls yet? She was just a local gossip, a patsy." O'Malley was annoyed. He was in no mood to teach rookies how to evaluate these confounded citizen tips. He much preferred strong-arming his army of paid street informants.

Besides, something about this call told him he wasn't making it home anytime soon.

"Get me a coffee—black," he growled at the rookie. Then he called over his sergeant and handed him a sheet torn off his notepad. "Top Priority, send for the Coroner's unit."

As the sergeant's eyes grew wide, O'Malley checked his notepad again. "And send a car to this address to collect a Lady Doctor, whatever that means—name's Josephine Reva. Treat her with respect until I figure out what use she'll be to me."

He'd certainly heard an earful about her.

Chapter 5- Births and Jazz

Meanwhile...

"Push!" Josephine repeated, encouraging her patient. "Almost there, Rachel, one more push!" This delivery, Josephine's second of the night, was proving long and difficult, even more so than the twins she had just finished delivering. The baby was stuck facing the wrong way and wouldn't fit under the pelvic bones. Josephine prepared to use forceps, which the nurses had ready in the autoclave, but she decided to wait.

"Rachel, can you raise up? That's it, thank you, I just need a few inches more for the baby." Josephine manipulated the tiny shoulders a quarter turn to squeeze through, as the head crowned.

Suddenly, the baby slipped in a mass of gushing fluids into her hands. The nurse wiped Josephine's brow.

"Congratulations, it's a girl!" Josephine announced, smiling in awe at the innocence and beauty before her.

Rachel held up her arms for the newborn. "Oh! Let me see her!"

"Here she is, healthy and well."

"I'm going to call her Bina, that means wisdom in Hebrew. In honor of you, Dr. Reva." The baby let out a hearty cry.

A male voice interrupted, "Nurses, step aside. I'll finish here."

Josephine looked up, startled. "I'm not a nurse. I'm Dr. Josephine Reva, and this is my patient."

"I, uh, didn't realize," he said with a hint of disbelief, still looking over Josephine's shoulder. "Hmmm, this patient isn't unconscious on ether and morphine. Dr. Reva, why didn't you sedate and operate?"

Josephine took a deep breath, then answered in medical terms. "The baby was only occiput posterior. Mother's conscious state allowed her to move freely, which prevented labor from arresting. Now, if you don't mind..."

"Birth is a dangerous pathology. It requires sedation and interventions. Letting nature take its course, even for a moment, puts both mother and child at risk."

Josephine bit her tongue, for the doctor was correct, according to the textbook. She, too, had learned in obstetrics to treat birth like an illness, but her experience taught her otherwise. "Look at this healthy baby, and then tell me that Mother Nature didn't know what she was doing."

The nurse recorded the time of birth at 2:00 a.m. "She's pink and perfect!" Josephine quickly allowed a moment for the mother to grasp the little one's hand and stroke her head.

"God be praised, we're both alive. It's the first time I'm awake and can hold my baby," Rachel said. Josephine smiled, but was thinking that it hadn't been that easy—there was a moment when she was ready to use her scalpel. Birth was still dangerous, even in a hospital.

She swiftly cut the umbilical cord then scooped the baby to the neonatal exam table, where she aspirated the baby's nose and placed her stethoscope on the baby's chest. She was relieved to find a strong heartbeat. The nurses then swaddled the tiny baby. They would administer the silver nitrate eye drops for possible eye infection.

Josephine ordered the nurses to increase the mother's intravenous drip and cover the mother's modesty. She began to close the episiotomy.

"Good work, Dr. Reva," the doctor returned to observe. "Very even stitches."

"Uh, huh," Josephine muttered. While sewing wounds, she usually bit on a piece of thread to help her concentrate. She had seen her mother do this and the habit stuck with her and comforted her. She quickly finished, then sat back with relief.

"Although your methods are radical, the outcome was productive," the doctor declared. He seemed to be complimenting her while also berating her. "I look forward to our next meeting."

"Radical" and "rebellious"—she'd been called enough names in a day. She looked at him sharply and spat out the thread. "Surely not in my delivery room!"

This doctor, like the others, would soon learn it was best to leave her to her job—her patient survivability rate was very high. Josephine didn't agree with the current research telling doctors to sedate the mother until unconscious and operate by forcibly opening the cervix and then extracting the fetus with forceps. Yanking a baby out of a woman's body—the thought made Josephine cringe! She was a woman, after all, and had the experience of female anatomy. She encouraged her mothers to stay relaxed and move about to let the cervix open gradually as it was designed to do. "Imagine tossing a pebble into a pond and watching the concentric ripples expanding, or a rose bud opening its petals," she would say.

She turned to the doctor, determined to change his thinking.

"If the mother is sedated to the point of unconsciousness, she can't experience the heavenly moment of holding her newborn and hearing its first cry."

He looked at her with a mixture of disbelief and disdain. "We doctors must think foremost of patient safety and hospital expediency."

"Well, what of the newborn? Isn't she a patient of ours as well? A baby seeks its mother's fresh milk. How can a baby nurse if the mother is knocked out cold?"

"We're not on a farm, Dr. Reva," the doctor retorted and walked out.

By now her blood was boiling. It wasn't often that another got the last word. She quickly washed her hands, then followed him into the hall and the nurses could hear the loud argument which ensued.

When she returned, one of the nurses consoled her. "He had no right to talk to you like that."

"Well, it's not surprising. Most doctors think of pregnancy and birth as a disease."

"Most doctors are men, and they don't trust us to have minds as well as bodies," she nodded at Josephine. "You didn't do anything wrong. Look at all the beautiful babies you delivered tonight." She pointed to the string of bassinets being wheeled from warm baths to the nursery.

Josephine heaved her shoulders and removed her soiled white medical gown and head cap from over her short hair. Washing her hands thoroughly, she carefully cleaned her spattered spectacles, and she sat down to make notes in her patient files. After another check on her mothers and babies in the ward, she'd update their charts and wait for the arrival of the next shift.

None of her other patients had due dates for a week, so she cleared off her shared desk, then went to see the babies curled up in their bassinets. How peaceful and innocent they looked. Even when they cried, they were adorable. It was amazing that such painful labor could result in such gifts of joy.

Josephine headed to Recovery. It was a relief to see the mothers wide awake and happily talking to each other or resting, with no sign of any fevers. The nurses were pleased, too, for Josephine had not cut anyone open and their work would, therefore, be less.

"I'm resolved to never go through this myself," she whispered to a nurse, once out of earshot of the new mothers. The nurse replied that Josephine was still young, then knowingly smiled. It wasn't the pain of labour or the peril involved that dissuaded Josephine. It was the effect a child would have on her ability to work. And her work was something she would never give up.

Josephine gathered her files and said goodnight to her staff.

Dominick, Josephine's chauffeur, was patiently waiting outside next to the sleek silver Packard Club Car Sedan. A muscular Italian with dark curly hair and flashing black eyes, he'd had no trouble persuading Josephine to make such an extravagant purchase. "It's faster and more reliable—I'll get you to the hospital quicker." Then he'd given her his Rudy Valentino look. Dominick usually got his way.

Dominick was by now well-accustomed to these midnight runs. He'd been brushing the red plush seats, buffing the dash's burl wood inlays, and shining the chrome drum-style headlamps. He'd even cleaned the spokes of the white walls and the various pipes and vents that streamed out of the powerful engine. Satisfied that the Packard was gleaming, he stood leaning with one long leg against the front curved fender and the other perched up on the running board, reading the midnight edition of the *Brooklyn Daily Eagle*.

"How'd it go, Doc?" he jumped forward as Josephine approached, taking her heavy medical bag and opening the car door for her.

"Smoothly, thank goodness," she answered. "But a new doctor thought I was a delivery nurse."

"I can believe it," Dominick laughed. "That poor man! I'm sure you read him the Riot Act."

"I certainly did." She settled into the back seat, and Dominick took the wheel. He drove out the hospital grounds and the large vehicle soared over the rutted streets.

"Mind if I turn on the radio?" he asked. "The Cotton Club is broadcasting tonight."

"Sure."

Dominick rustled the knobs and found the station. Music piped into the car.

"It's Duke Ellington. Wild *Jazz*. Some call it *Jungle Music*. That's crazy, huh?"

"What's that?" The upbeat tones were unsettling her, but she found herself tapping her foot.

"Great rhythm. Just listen to that saxophone—it's smokin' hot!"

"I'll say it is." The music was starting to wind its way into her body, and although exhausted, she felt suddenly enlivened.

"That banging piano, it's the bee's knees, ain't it? You just wanna get up and dance!" Dominick was tapping the steering wheel in rhythm.

"That's too much excitement for me."

"You've gotta hear *West End Blues*," Dominick continued. "Louis Armstrong's trumpet—it's not like any ole horn. Not like an elephant, either. There's nothing like it. They say it's all the rage in Harlem. I've got the recording, if you want to hear it sometime?" He looked up in his rear view mirror and Josephine caught a flash of his lively dark eyes as they passed under a street lamp.

"We'll see," was all she said. In the cocoon of her back seat, she let the music and swaying motion of the car rock her as they drove at what seemed like breakneck speed. Electric street lamps bathed the car in a syncopated beat. She fell back against the red buttoned cushioned seats.

But she couldn't let herself relax for long and turned on the motor car's reading lamp. Dominick had wired it especially for her. "Say, where did you put my medical journals, Dominick? I've got a lot of reading to catch up on."

"They're where they always are, Doc. In the pocket hanging off the seat in front of you."

"Thank you." Josephine fished around. She tried to bury her nose in a journal, but found that the motor car pulsed over the potholes to the same rhythm as the music. She started drumming her fingers on the journal pages.

"How many babies tonight?" Dominick interrupted her thoughts. "I've got a bet with the boys. Did you crack one hundred yet?" Dominick kept a tally, for racehorses, baseball and other things.

"Let's see, three more, twins tonight! My grand total, including clinic and internship, is one hundred and one. And the hospital is expanding the maternity wing."

"That's great, Doc, congrats! Those immigrants make babies like gumdrop candies. Plenty more coming—you'll be rich!"

"It's never been about the money," Josephine responded tacitly. She could watch Dominick's eyes in the rear view mirror.

They drove through the sleepy streets towards Bensonhurst, the lively jazz music keeping them awake for the ride. Josephine was ready to collapse into bed. If she was lucky, she'd get a few hours of sleep before opening her office.

The Packard's headlamps lit up the brick facade of home as Dominick swung into the driveway. "What's that?" Josephine said. She'd seen a glimmer of something shiny at her front door.

Dominick parked, then got out of the car and bounded up the front steps to the office. "Well, well, it's a vase of flowers!"

Josephine got out and walked up the stairs. "Flowers, for me?" she exclaimed with mock delight. No one had ever sent her flowers. The pretty colorful stalks were arranged in a large bouquet covered in cellophane.

"They're not roses," Dominick said with relief. His heart skipped a beat. He'd never seen the doctor step out with any man, and hadn't thought she was interested in romance. Now he appeared to be wondering. "There's no card."

"Well, who on earth sent me flowers?"

"You must have a secret admirer."

"Don't be silly, Dominick."

Dominick's expression changed to puzzlement. Josephine had no lover, so why would anyone send her a vase of flowers? It seemed she had attracted a man's attention. They both remained quiet for some time.

"Such an extravagance," Josephine said at last. "I'd best get these lovely flowers inside, and get some rest."

Josephine looked sideways at Dominick. He'd never come up the stairs to escort her to her door, and she hoped he didn't expect to be let inside.

"Uh, I'll go put the Packard to bed," he said, "and you need your sleep, Doc." He gave her a final look as she turned the key.

Chapter 6 - The Narrows

Friday...

J osephine tossed and turned in light brain-wave slumber, the kind where memories and regrets torment. She was having one of her nightmares again. Yesterday's events in the maternity ward and her earlier encounter with those darn Yorkvillains had festered in her mind, like an untreated wound. If only she'd learn to hold her tongue when necessary—a woman shouldn't be so contentious. In her dream, her empty mouth moved but her throat found no voice.

Medical College 1922. Josephine was a whiff of a girl, who did she think she was? "You'd better get back to the kitchen where you belong!" a boy shouted as she walked the hall to her classroom, her unfashionably long skirt brushing the floor and her oversized hand-me-down shoes clicking noisily. She yelled back, "I belong right here!" The college boys turned to gape, shaking their heads. "Tiny Joe," they scorned. "That ragamuffin! She should be seen but not heard!"

Josephine awoke with a start. *"A minore ad magna!"* she remembered shouting back, delivering one last zinger. *From tiny to mighty.* How she'd relished confounding those boys, using her fluent Latin like a weapon. The nuns had given her a classical education at the orphanage, and knowing the ancient but dead language had proven useful for the study of medicine. "I could name every body part and associated diseases, all in Latin," she proudly recounted, "but those boys couldn't even spell 'hematemesis', nor even 'humerus.'"

The nuns at the orphanage had warned, rightly so, that Josephine was too precocious. "Why don't you learn a ladylike profession like dressmaking?" they suggested. But Josephine stubbornly refused—"I will become a doctor!" The nuns had laughed and patted her head, saying it was improbable for a girl. "A doctor, no, but you'd make a fine nurse." Only Mother Cabrini's intense gaze had given her the answer she needed.

Josephine sat up abruptly as she did every morning, earnestly checking to see that her Medical Doctor diploma was still proudly hanging over her desk. *Victoria!* She still had to pinch herself that it hadn't all been a dream.

After graduation, Josephine planned to join Mother Cabrini's order as a missionary doctor in China. True, she'd have been a nun, but the thought of working in the exotic wilds of barbaric lands had been stimulation enough. But New York's immigrant population was doubling, the tenements overflowed and immigrants were flocking to the outer boroughs—Brooklyn, it was agreed by the nuns, needed her services more.

The porcelain mantel clock chimed 5:30 a.m. Josephine could hear the cart vendors and shop owners unfolding their awnings as they called to each other. Brooklyn was becoming a thriving metropolis. Her office would soon be a whirlwind of patients. With an odd mixture of excitement and dread, she anticipated some life-or-death emergencies

Arising quickly from her feather-stuffed mattress on her iron rail bed and finding her slippers, she scuffed to the kitchen and found matches to light the gas lamps. Electric bulbs were costly, so she saved those for the newly-wired examination and waiting rooms down the hall. Her office was set in an alcove in the hallway, just a few paces from her small bedroom. Walking by, she saw the vase of flowers on her desk. *Such a beautiful bouquet!* She could see an artist's palette of bright purples, reds and pinks through the filmy cellophane. *They'd look nice in my patient waiting room. I'll arrange them after I get ready. I wonder which one of the men from the medical conference sent these to me?*

She went to her armoire and pulled out one of the plain gingham house dresses, a simple checked rectangle without any form. She slipped it over her head, feeling its scratchiness against her skin. The dress had little style but fit neatly under her lab coat.

Seating herself at the oak mirrored vanity table, Josephine rubbed sleep from her eyes and put on her huge round spectacles. Taking her hairbrush, she stopped for a moment to analyze her dream—wasn't that what Dr. Freud recommended? Did a dream represent some of her hidden emotions? Sexual, he'd said, and she turned to look at the vase of flowers. The only time she'd ever been kissed as a child was when little Spikey Brown grabbed her in the school yard. She'd sent him reeling with a well-placed kick. No boy had ever tried to kiss her again, until her fiancé, and that hadn't ended well either.

She gazed at her reflection—with her classic heart-shaped face and striking blue eyes, a man just might find her attractive. But having passed her 26th birthday, that bloom of youth was fading, and she was soon to be considered an old maid. Her prospects for marriage were dimming like the gas flame flickering before her. No matter, she said, remembering that she'd need a husband who'd let her keep working. Would she ever find such a suitor?

Perhaps if she wore some make-up and changed her eye glass frames? She'd seen the new cat's eye style, and it looked vampish. Dare she risk it? "Courting" had long gone out of fashion, so it was high time she started to "date," that peculiar custom of doing nothing that led to marriage. But the boys at medical school had only laughed when she suggested going to Fingerly's on the Avenue for a pastry. Nor was she any good at fluttering her eyelashes flirtatiously—her regard was one of keen intelligence and her demeanor serious, as befitted her studious nature. Besides, she was a career girl and didn't want any children—how would she ever attract a mate?

At the moving pictures, Clara Bow flirted with her gorgeous leading man, the two tumbling together on the rides at Coney Island. She was shocked when the starlet's skirt blew too high in a gust of wind, revealing her bloomers. Josephine was certainly no "It" girl. Perhaps a girl had to plot to seduce a man like Clara did in "Mantrap"?

She brushed her dark hair into its plain bob. With some flair, she tried pinning a silver clip to hold a curl on each side, like Clara Bow, and that did something to accentuate her high cheekbones. Then she added a dab of rose-colored rouge and lipstick. "Well, this will do nicely!" she said aloud. But it was unlikely that any handsome bachelor would stroll into her office that day, unless he were sick. Besides, it was unethical to date a patient. She pulled out the hair clips.

Outside her window, the neighborhood awoke with a bristling cacophony of snorting horses, squeaky pushcarts and squawking motor car horns. Josephine could hear the vendors readying their shops and the barkers' cries touting their latest tonics and "cure-alls."

The clock chimed 6:00 a.m., but the telephone hadn't rung yet. She'd have time for a quick cup of tea and breakfast. She went to the front door. There it was—her delivery! Warm bagels with her favorite topping of creamed cheese were tenderly wrapped and pushed through her mail slot every morning by Samuel Bloch, the delicatessen owner. Ever since Josephine delivered his baby boy, he always repaid her in kind.

While she ate, Josephine thought about ways to grow her practice. Predictably, it was the women who came first to see the new "Lady Doctor." It was true, as she'd said in her speech, they were embarrassed by "intimate examinations," and most of her cases involved pregnancies or other "female" problems.

The women soon brought their children along, and recently, started forcing their husbands to come. These men came grudgingly. Well, Josephine reasoned, one couldn't expect the men to come voluntarily. But lately, they, too, called her "Doc" and admitted that "her touch is the same as any man's."

Now her daily ledger was almost full. Office visits and prescriptions paid $2, and house calls $3—Josephine had amassed quite a bank account. Many couldn't pay such high rates, but Josephine never turned anyone away—there was a large stack of IOU's in her drawer that she knew she'd never call in.

Opening her practice out in Brooklyn had been a compromise. She'd already made enough money for a downpayment on her two-family building and put away a little savings. Frugality was ingrained since her childhood of deprivation; coins she received were conserved in a jar for the silver and copper would be worth more in the event of another war.

Every so often, there were those hair-raising ambulance rides, which paid the exorbitant sum of $5. Josephine loved these the most, but not for the money. Thankfully, the wealthier hospitals had purchased motorized ambulances, and Josephine could sit inside, rain or snow. A few years' ago, there'd been only horse and cart ambulances in her territory—Josephine had insisted on riding up front with the driver who held the reins and cracked the whip. They'd sped through the crowded streets as folks stopped to stare at her, their jaws dropping to see a female in the doctor's seat.

The sound of the front door bell shattered her reverie. More insistently, several knocks followed by a voice shouting: "Doctor, it's URGENT!"

Josephine grabbed her overcoat, hat and medical bag and rushed out the door.

* * *

A sleek black Town Car stood conspicuously in the street, engine racing. A man in a blue double-breasted uniform opened a rear door. He wore a badge, but Josephine didn't treat any police officers yet. Then she remembered her training at The Tombs, a cold, damp miserable prison in lower Manhattan.

"Am I being called to an execution?" she asked with dread.

"No, a murder," the driver said brusquely.

"A murder? I'm not a coroner."

"Chief Detective's orders."

Taking stock of Josephine's diminutive stature wrapped in a shiny fabric, fashionable cloche hat with its big ribbon bow, and genuine leather medical kit embossed with her name, he became more respectful.

"Er sorry, Ma'am, if you please." He held the door for her.

"It's Miss," Josephine corrected him as she stepped into the limo.

She noticed the change in the officer's demeanor. A dressy exterior conveyed respectability. *"It's like sewing fancy buttons on an old coat,"* her mother, Grace, had laughed as she tailored. This was one of the few memories Josephine had left of her mother. She sighed, twisting in her seat to examine her new surroundings.

This is the Ritz! she thought, examining the puffed, soft calfskin leather seats, vanity mirrors and wood trim. She pushed on a panel and a bar full of crystal bottles and snifters popped out. "Tsk, tsk," she sighed. Wasn't whiskey illegal, even for the police? She wondered what important conversations needing libations were held in this private compartment.

The motor car sped off on 18th Avenue, as the dawn broke over the flat sandy dunes of Long Island. But the car didn't head towards the Brooklyn Bridge leading to Manhattan. It turned south towards The Narrows, where the sea was sandwiched between Staten Island and Brooklyn before spilling into the harbor of the great metropolis of New York.

The Town Car slowed over a rutted road leading along the waterfront. The site was at the ruins of the Narrows Fort, where Brooklyn militia fired upon passing British man-o'-war convoy ships as they sailed to blockade Manhattan during the American Revolution. It still offered a commanding view of the lower New York Harbor.

Seagulls feasting at the water's edge were disturbed by the car's rumbling and flew up in a great fuss of squawks. The area was now a deserted construction site. Steam rollers and diggers sat idle, and dirt was pushed into piles. Crumbling docks roped over thick wooden piles led out to the channel. Josephine could see the Statue of Liberty and knew the faint outline of Wall Street buildings in the distance was just around the bend.

Josephine adjusted her spectacles. There was a dead body on the ground, its face covered by a white sheet.

"Surely, there's no use for me here," she harrumphed. "I treat patients who are still breathing!"

"Please step outside, Miss Reva," the driver had opened the partition and spoke to her directly. Unwillingly, Josephine stepped out into the foggy mist, and the Town Car sped off.

Policemen had cordoned off the area from the gawkers. The officers expected that a lady would be nauseated and proffered Josephine their white handkerchiefs.

She brushed by them. "I'm a medical doctor, I've seen my share of dead bodies." Indeed, she'd been hardened by treating horrific road accidents, heart attacks, diabetes and, sadly, childbirth deaths, But she'd never seen a murdered corpse.

A police officer removed the white sheet. The victim's face was a distortion in agony, the throes of death etched in a weird grimace. His eyes were wide open, with eyeballs popping out of their sockets in shock. His mouth hung hideously agape as if gasping for air. His neck was swollen like a grapefruit filled with oozing bodily fluid.

"He's been outside overnight, so he don't look too fresh." An officer wearing three stripes on his armband spoke to her.

Josephine flinched. She recognized the victim. It was Dr. Goldblum from the conference.

"No need for an I.D. His wallet was found on him," the sergeant continued. "But we found some weeds in his mouth."

"Weeds?" Josephine could only repeat. She was distracted from mentioning that she knew the victim, albeit slightly, and thought it best to keep this to herself for the moment. "I know nothing about murder nor weeds."

"Well, maybe it's some kind of plant or something. We heard through the grapevine that you're the one to call about this stuff. Not like the, er, the other doctors." He reached out to take her medical bag. She snatched it back.

"You mean the male doctors? Or maybe you're referring to Homeopaths who deal with botanicals, extracts from trees, elements like phosphorus and sulfur, compounds of calcium carbonate, silver nitrate..." she trailed off, and the sergeant looked rather sorry he'd said anything at all.

Josephine approached the body. Dr. Goldblum was bloated almost to the shape of a small-sized whale. The humidity was rising in misty ringlets from the water, and Josephine wondered how much longer the body could remain in the open air. She removed her overcoat in the heat, keeping her lab coat on and opened her medical bag. She looked over Dr. Goldblum's body, and saw a bruising to the back of the skull and smattered blood. She also noticed that his clothing was rumpled, but his pockets weren't turned out. She wondered if this was a mob rub out. *Best leave that to the police.* She noted the skin's blue grayish tinge, a deathly pallor, and bent closer to the victim's gaping mouth and sniffed. She didn't smell cyanide or bitter almonds, or any remnants of chemicals.

"We found this," the sergeant showed her a tray. "It was in his mouth."

Josephine was looking at a clot of purple colored matter. She retrieved a pair of long-handled tweezers from her medical bag. After picking at the dry, clotted mass, she was surprised to find large petals. "It's not a weed at all. It's a flowering plant," Josephine said. That inkling of knowledge seemed to impress the policemen, and they stood straighter.

She looked more closely, picking out a vividly purple blossom in a strange shape.

"*Aconitum napellus!*" she suddenly exclaimed as if greeting an old friend. "Aconite—the first Homeopathic we learned in medical school. It's a wonderful, beneficial plant." She remembered how the remedy had helped her recover from stage fright at the conference.

"Except it killed this poor bugger. Must've choked on it."

"Aconite is also called Monkshood—look here, the petals form in the curved shape of a monk's hood. It's as if they're hiding something, or like a monk praying. That's how it's easy to recognize." The sergeant leaned forward but Josephine stopped him. "Be careful! Don't touch it! It's highly toxic."

The sergeant pulled back and nodded, as if confirming his suspicion. "So it was poison."

"He killed himself with Aconite?" she wondered aloud.

"We think he was murdered. See that blood on the side of his head—someone clubbed him before poisoning him."

"That doesn't make any sense. Why not finish him off with the club, or even a gun?"

"Good question, and that's what we were hoping you could answer."

Josephine felt that familiar but uncomfortable flush she'd known from medical school, of being surrounded by males. Was she supposed to come up with a clever response? Or show some knowledge of criminal behavior?

"Aconite is also known as Wolfsbane." Her brain began with the basic textbook information. She thought harder. "Shepherds in Italy used the toxin to trap and kill wolves who hunted their flock. To me, that sounds like a mob warning."

The policemen nodded approvingly. Josephine was enjoying what she thought was her first police recitation.

"But Aconite is normally used as a Homeopathic cure, not a poison," she continued, feeling the need to defend her beloved botanicals. *Aconitum napellus* was one of the most dispensed remedies in the repertory.

"What exactly do you mean?" Another man stepped forward. Josephine noticed he was tall, thin but healthy in body. He appeared to be well-dressed, wearing wire-rimmed glasses, a dapper Panama hat and Chesterfield worsted coat. Josephine couldn't help noticing his attractive but lined older face and blue-grey eyes like mist. He introduced himself formally as Chief Detective First Grade John O'Malley.

Josephine instinctively drew back. She had learned something about New York City cops from her childhood on the streets. The surest way for a cop to rise to the rank of Detective was to be on a gangster's payroll or smooth the way with family money. Which sort of detective was this O'Malley? She noticed the bulge of a gun holster hidden under his loose coat. A necessity—Brooklyn was a lawless place. How many criminals had he killed? But he looked cunning— the kind who laid the trap and then let others do the shooting for him. She had best tread carefully.

Josephine took the tweezers again and pinched a bit of purple dust from the flowers. "This whole flower is deadly, as deadly as that gun you're carrying." She couldn't resist letting him know that she was as observant as he was. "But if you took a small amount, like this, and diluted it, it would be beneficial. A Homeopathic pharmacist could easily turn this into a remedy."

"Please go on," Detective O'Malley said.

"This particular species, *Aconitum napellus*, is the most deadly of all. Any part of the plant can begin to kill on contact—Aconite is known as the Queen of Poisons. When ingested, like this poor man, it would have been hopeless. There is no effective anti-toxin."

The detective was staring intently at her. She paused, then continued. "Death by Aconite is difficult and painful. The initial symptoms are gastrointestinal. Then there's a feeling of numbness in the mouth and face, and headache. Then motor paralysis begins. He would have felt weak, unable to move and had great difficulty breathing. Finally, cardiovascular symptoms appear—hypotension, sinus bradycardia, and ventricular arrhythmia. That's paralysis of the heart and respiratory center."

The officers looked grim.

Josephine then added what she felt they should consider. "The post-mortem signs are only those of asphyxia—a lack of oxygen. Most coroners fail to discover Aconite at all."

Josephine wasn't done yet with her recitation.

"On the opposite hand, when carefully diluted into a Homeopathic remedy, *Aconitum napellus* has a beneficial effect. It cures headaches, fevers, anxiety, even stage fright. You see, its medicinal proving is related to the deadly symptoms it causes. *Similia similibus curentur* or "like cures like,"" she explained. "That's the premise of Homeopathy—the Law of Similars."

The Chief Detective had been listening patiently. "In this case, we have a murderer who didn't try to hide the cause of death. So would any pharmacist have this Aconite plant on hand?"

"Goodness, no!" she said. "There aren't many Homeopathic pharmacies left. Nor many Homeopaths, for that matter. The AMA and others are seeing to that."

"The AMA?"

"The American Medical Association," she explained. "It's a large organization of Allopaths—that's doctors who promote orthodox medicine. Only Homeopaths with M.D.'s are allowed as members."

"Then this Aconite is illegal?" interjected the sergeant.

"No, not at all. Homeopathic drugs are considered medicines. The physician's Homeopathic Pharmacopeia, in fact, lists all the cures." Josephine smiled, remembering that it was New York Senator Royal S. Copeland who avowed at the conference that Homeopathic remedies would be included in any new drug regulations.

Detective O'Malley interrupted. "So these Homeopathic drugs, like Aconite, are no longer used by most doctors?"

"Yes. There's a battle going on in medicine. Making Homeopathic remedies takes time and has to be done with great care. First, you take the poisonous plant *Aconitum napellus*, for example, then extract the toxic phytochemical Aconitine. Then you must dilute it many times over in water with vigorous shaking—what Homeopaths call "succussion." Only an infinitesimal amount of the poison molecule remains—it becomes perfectly safe, but still holds its therapeutic value. But with Allopathic drugs, chemists modify the compounds. These drugs remain toxic, although highly effective at treating symptoms."

Josephine then became excited. "There's so many new discoveries. I just read an abstract in the British Journal of Experimental Pathology. Dr. Alexander Fleming, he's a professor of bacteriology in London, he found a penicillin mold growing on a melon—imagine that! Penicillin drug could be a panacea—although it does seem unlikely." She looked up.

"You see, with all the new discoveries, those with an M.D. degree, like myself, are converting from Homeopathy to Allopathy."

This shift had happened right in the midst of Josephine's medical training. Josephine thought about the two systems of medicine she had studied, each with its own distinctive philosophy. Modern Allopaths sought to treat symptoms with powerful, but toxic, drugs. Homeopaths, on the other hand, disapproved of suppressing symptoms, claiming this only served to mask the underlying illness. But Allopathic drugs did bring immediate relief of symptomatic pain, Josephine reasoned. It was clear from the conference that many of her colleagues remained devout Homeopaths—but she kept this to herself.

Josephine looked again at the purple Aconite flower, deadly yet so beneficial.

"Taking a case Homeopathically means interviewing the patient extensively to discover the underlying cause of illness—what are their fears, their movements, whether they like sweet or salty foods, and how they sleep at night." She looked pointedly at Detective O'Malley. "It's rather like being a detective, searching for any clues that might help break the case."

Detective O'Malley wasn't sharing her enthusiasm. He was studying her as if she were under a microscope. "Is that so? Please go on."

"Homeopathy believes that an illness can be cured by the right remedy, diluted to such an extent that it produces very slight but similar symptoms in a healthy person. Many medical treatments derive from Homeopathy, like vaccination. It, too, uses the Law of Similars; injecting small amounts of cowpox causes similar effects to smallpox, leading to disease resistance. If, for example, a patient was suffering from severe nausea, he was given a remedy which in a healthy person would provoke mild nausea. But the dosage is extremely important, and we had to be extra careful not to poison our patients!" She gave a nervous laugh.

Detective O'Malley looked at her sharply. But surely, he didn't suspect her?

"Medical schools don't even teach pharmacology anymore," she lamented. It'd been one of her favorite classes.

"I see," said Detective O'Malley, as he pointed a finger at her, "but you studied it. Poison is a woman's weapon."

Then he continued in rapid fire. "You clearly know how to concoct a deadly dose of Aconite. And you have a motor car at your disposal, my deputy saw it in your box. You and the deceased knew each other. To top it off, you were seen arguing with him at a medical conference."

"I don't understand," she stammered defensively, and her voice pitched awkwardly higher. While at the orphanage, she had learned it was better to deflect a direct question that she wasn't prepared for. "You want my help, but then accuse me of murder?" She twitched her toes, trying to remain steady on her feet.

"Where were you yesterday between 5 pm and 2 am?"

The detective looked at her with a steeliness that told Josephine she'd best cooperate. "I own a motor car, yes, but I don't drive. I don't even have an operator's license," she said indignantly. "And last night, after midnight I was at the hospital delivering babies. Before that I was home asleep. No, before you ask, no one can verify that part. But my chauffeur lives downstairs. Perhaps you can talk with him?"

O'Malley took down the name and phone number of Dominick.

"Why were you arguing with the victim?"

"I wasn't arguing with him at all. I was arguing with that Quinn fellow, the tonic salesman. But I did see someone else arguing with Dr. Goldblum—Janus Heath—but I can't really call it an argument, they just disagreed."

"What did they disagree about?"

"That's just it, I don't know. All Dr. Goldblum said was 'you have to face the inevitable.' I don't have any idea what he meant."

"Had you ever met Dr. Goldblum before the conference."

"No. I only spoke to him for a few minutes. He seemed pleasant enough." He certainly hadn't been pleasant, more like condescending and a chauvinist, but it was not a good time to bring that up.

Detective O'Malley raised an eyebrow. But now he sounded more annoyed than accusatory. "Did you meet him again, after the conference?"

"No, of course not."

"Did you notice anything strange about him at the conference?"

"No," she answered. "If anything, I'd say his preventative measures for public health were admirable. We agreed that the sale of spoiled milk was dangerous for mothers and children. He was doing good work for the city. He said he was working on a new report, something that would make his superiors listen up."

Josephine was suddenly curious. Why had someone murdered him?

O'Malley jotted down the information. "You'll leave a statement with my rookie. We'll question all possible suspects, and get to the bottom of this."

To Josephine, the detective seemed to be swinging from good to bad, like a dizzying pendulum. Was that designed to catch her off guard? Had he noticed her nervousness, and would he see that as a sign of weakness, or worse, of guilt?

"Miss, er, Doctor Reva, please give us a list of Homeopaths and Homeopathic compounding pharmacies that you use." He didn't appear to be making a request, more like an order. "And any doctors besides yourself who'd have an Aconite plant."

Josephine suddenly felt her throat tighten again. The nerve of this detective—*now he wants me to be an informant!* In her old Little Italy neighborhood, informing to the cops was a death knell.

"I'm afraid I can't help you, Detective. I haven't kept in touch with any of my classmates, and like me, they graduated as Medical Doctors." She didn't mention that they could still be Homeopaths or Allopaths.

The detective continued to stare until his gaze felt like a hammer blow. Was he considering taking her to the station house and questioning her under a harsh light? She felt a cold sweat running down her back. How could she allay his suspicion of her?

There must be something here that can help me identify the real Aconite killer. Josephine looked at the body again. She then reached for the tray of Aconite. The flowers were still vividly purple.

"Aconite," she hesitated as if she recognized something important, but couldn't figure out exactly what that was, "doesn't grow wild in this kind of barren landscape, sandy loam at the water." Once again, she put on her scientific voice. "It grows mainly in the cold mountain climates or along riverbanks in Europe. But this Aconite is fresh."

"Interesting," the detective interrupted. But he didn't seem interested at all, certainly not in a botany lesson nor another of Josephine's recitations. He was intensely staring at her. "Would you kindly then check your own supplies?"

Josephine withered. "I don't have any plants, because as I've told you, I graduated with an M.D., that's Allopathic medicine. Most of us have converted. Do I need to spell it out again?" He looked affronted by her outburst, but she was determined to assert her innocence, even if that meant denying her love of Homeopathic remedies.

"You can't seriously believe that I killed this man." She stared directly back into Detective O'Malley's cold eyes. The two faced each other defiantly, until Josephine turned away.

She looked again at the body laying on the ground.

The victim wore a tailored expensive suit and vest made of imported herringbone tweed in bright grey-green. Yes, that was just like the suit he wore at the conference. He did have expensive taste. A thick gold watch chain was peeking out of his pocket, and he wore a large gold ring.

"The victim liked to dress well. You can tell by his clothes and all that gold," she pointed at the body. "But it obviously wasn't a robbery because the murderer left the goods behind. There's signs of a struggle, which could be from either a fight or from the victim as he struggled with the toxin. Then the blow to the head, delivered at close range. I'd say he came here to meet his killer and probably knew him." She gave a satisfied nod to Detective O'Malley, who seemed to be looking at her queerly.

Josephine inspected the detective's stern face. He must not sleep much, she mused, and she was sure the ever-expanding tentacles of the New York City criminal network kept him busy. Prohibition hadn't been kind to cops. They now had to chase bootleggers and mobsters who made millions of dollars and who could afford more powerful guns, faster motor cars, huge ships and even seaplanes to make their drops and run from the cops. She couldn't help feeling sorry for him and reverted back to the caring physician.

"If you don't mind my saying so, you should eat more fruits and vegetables."

"Excuse me?" he exclaimed.

"You could use a few more vitamines, A, C, D, and the B complexes in particular are very invigorating. There's been a lot of new research."

The sergeant tittered, then coughed to conceal his amusement.

"Let me give you my card, Miss, um, Doctor Reva, and would you call me if you think of anything that's *useful.*" Detective O'Malley's grey eyes pierced her own.

She had a disquieting feeling that he knew more about her than he was letting on. But she had noticed details about him, too, like how he wore a gold Claddagh wedding band and kept touching it fondly, caressing it. But she didn't dare ask him about his personal life or habits, as a Homeopath would.

"Yes, of course," she said, relieved that the questioning was over. "Please take me back to my office. My patients must be waiting."

As the patrol car drove off, Josephine took a last look at the waterway. "What are they building here?" she asked the officer at the wheel.

"Doncha' read the papers?" he responded. "The Narrows is like a chokehold between the lower and upper bays, see. It leads to the major warehouses of New York. Hundreds of ships pass by here each day, right by these docks. They're gonna build a bridge across The Narrows, the Liberty Bridge, to connect Brooklyn and Staten Island."

"Oh, I see. More trucks, buses, ships and motor cars."

"Yeah, dat's progress. It'll be the fastest - the Circumferential Parkway. It's gonna stretch from the Brooklyn Bridge to Jamaica Bay, maybe even farther to the tip of Montauk." he said proudly.

"Golly!" said Josephine, feeling a touch of queasiness from riding in a car as far as she had today. She instinctively thought of all the accidents waiting to happen. But she'd best keep talking and see if she could glean any more information from the driver.

"So that man's death has something to do with that?"

"Not likely," said the officer. "But The Narrows is notorious for rum-running gangs. They try to make it through the channel when the Coast Guard ain't looking."

He turned his attention back to the road and closed the partition.

Josephine's mind was restless. Was Dr. Goldblum a rumrunner? That seemed unlikely. She thought back to the conference. Well, of course, he must have made the rounds to talk to as many people as possible, the same as she did. She'd heard his speech. He obviously was bitter towards other doctors and politicians who weren't following his reports on prevention. Then oddly, he walked off arm in arm with that creep Quinn, but argued with nice Professor Heath. But surely, many people were arguing about medicine that day. Was Dr. Goldblum an Allopath or a Homeopath? Only a Homeopath would have *Aconitum napellus* flowers.

She had so many questions. Whom was he meeting? Why did he come to this deserted area? Such a large gold ring he wore, but she hadn't had the nerve to inspect his fingers frozen with rigor mortis. Why had he been hit on the head and also poisoned with Aconite? And how dare that impertinent Detective O'Malley suspect her!

* * *

The officers watched Josephine get in the car. "Wowee, what a nice chassis!" said the sergeant.

"I'll say! She had the prettiest blue peepers I've ever seen," the rookie added. The men gawked at the petite figure.

"Should we tail her?" the sergeant asked O'Malley, pleased with expectation. "Are we looking for a what d'ya call it, a Homeopath?"

"No and yes" answered Detective O'Malley impatiently, "Get me a list of all Homeopathic doctors and pharmacies in Brooklyn. We need to trace the source of that Aconite plant. And find me a copy of any report the dead man was working on for that conference." O'Malley didn't say anything more as he watched Josephine leave. Then he turned and gazed at the waterfront.

Bringing Dr. Reva to the scene of the crime hadn't worked as planned. She hadn't looked at the dead man with any sign of emotion, but with more of a clinical nature. She strangely liked to dress for outings in her white lab coat, and didn't seem to care as much as most dames about her appearance. He noticed that when she got nervous she talked a lot, and he'd certainly given her enough rope to hang herself. Poisoners were usually women, he knew from experience, because the crime didn't require any strength. Women could put poison in a man's drink. "Sweet is revenge—especially to women"—that's what Byron meant. These creatures usually broke down under questioning and confessed, such was their emotional nature. But this young miss seemed to be made of steel.

Under questioning, she became defensive, which was not, in his experience, the behavior of a murderess who committed a crime of passion. Besides, she was probably too small and weak to deliver any knock-out blow to the victim's head, unless he had already been on the ground. One thing was certain, she kept proclaiming she was an Allopath, but she had shown a lot of love for Homeopathy. Why was she lying?

O'Malley rubbed his temples. What a problem this murder was causing him. A quick arrest would be just the ticket he needed. Another year until rising to Second Grade Detective, maybe even Third Grade, if he solved this crime, and then he could retire to his Hudson Valley country estate, earning a comfortable pension. He imagined his garden there, the one his beautiful young dead wife had tended so carefully. All those flowers in bloom, just as pretty as she was. And they smelled so nice! Just like Evelyn. How he longed to hold her and smell her perfume. Just once more. The flowers kept blooming, but Evelyn didn't.

Soon he could retire and spend more time in her garden. He'd be glad to leave Prohibition investigations behind, with the sidestepping of corrupt officials and shootouts with gangsters and bootleggers. This wasn't looking like a bootlegger case. They didn't kill people with purple flowers. And the complications—he'd have to read up on medicine to boot! He rubbed his temples some more.

He thought about that telephone call - the murderer was cunning, using a gossipy caller to point the finger at an unmarried, lonely female doctor who studied poisons. She was indeed the perfect foil. That Dr. Reva is certainly feisty, he thought, and with enough smarts to carry out this bizarre crime. No one would miss her if she went to prison. She had no alibi for the entire night, she knew the victim and she certainly had the knowledge, means and opportunity. But what about motive? He kept coming back to that, and rubbed his temples again.

A lover's quarrel? Could Dr. Reva be part of some lover's triangle? Love or money leads to murder, but Dr. Reva didn't seem like she cared much about either.

The rookie was right, she certainly had beautiful blue eyes, like forget-me-nots. Their color made him think of his late wife's eyes, so like flowers, too. How he missed Evelyn, her softness, the way they had danced…. All he had left of her were memories, some photographs and her beautiful garden. Soon he would be there. One more case. And this wasn't the typical mob rub-out—he was hardly likely to get shot. Evelyn would have been less worried about his investigations. But would she have minded him chasing a female suspect?

Dr. Reva probably hadn't committed the crime, he had to admit his sixth sense told him so, but she'd certainly been acting suspiciously. She knew the victim. She argued with him. She was an outsider, a female in a man's profession. He'd have to keep her on his suspect list. But if she didn't do it, then who?

She did possess that one important thing—access. And she would be the perfect person to bother this circle of Homeopaths, like a flea bothers a dog. He was willing to bet that this little Lady Doctor would be the key to unlocking this case. He must force her to be that key, twisting in the lock.

Turning back to the crowd of gawkers, he motioned to the irksome reporter lurking behind the ropes to come forward. It was time to set his plan in motion.

Chapter 7 - Bensonhurst

Saturday...

Josephine awoke with a start. Still bothered by the sight of the corpse the day before, she sat up quickly. *The nerve of that detective, dragging me all the way out to The Narrows, away from my patients. Why was he so insistent that I must know more than I could possibly know about Dr. Goldblum's murder!* Did she? She thought a moment. "That's preposterous!" Stifling a yawn, she arose from bed.

Walking by her alcove office, she noticed the vase of flowers still in its cellophane wrap. *I'd better change the water or the flowers are going to die.* Josephine untied the bouquet and lifted it. The bright lilies, peonies, carnations, and baby's breath flowers illuminated her drab office with their cheerful colors. *So pretty!* She separated the stalks and found buried inside, a dark purple array.

She looked closer. The stalk held several cascading flowers in the shape of something peculiar. A helmet? *No, it's a monk's hood. Aconite!* She'd never seen a live Aconite plant before, only powdered flowers in Janus' lab and the dead petals pulled from Dr. Goldblum's mouth. Here was a living plant. She was fascinated.

Gingerly pulling away the other flowers, Josephine left the Aconite stalk standing alone in the vase. *It's so beautiful! Who would send me Aconite? Whoever sent it would surely hope that I'd recognize these blossoms and wouldn't poison myself.*

She took the other flowers, so ordinary in comparison, and searched for a canister to display them in, for she'd never bought a vase. She found an old jar in the dust bin, filled it with water and cut the stalks in half to fit. She then put this arrangement on one of the side tables by the magazines in the waiting room. *These flowers do brighten things up*, she thought, pulling back the curtains.

Returning to her desk, she carefully carried the glass vase with its lone Aconite stalk into her bedroom, placing it in the center of her mirrored dressing table. Sitting down, she brushed her hair beside the Aconite's multi-tiered reflection, which radiated from all vantage points in the trifold mirror. She felt a shiver run down her spine. *The murderer must have sent me this. Did he want me to touch it?*

Aconite is wolfsbane, as she'd told the detective. *Perhaps it's a warning from the shepherd who doesn't want his flock disturbed? Does he think I'm a wolf?*

What applesauce! Ridiculous! It's probably those Yorkvillains trying to rile me, as usual. Josephine had no time for pranks. Besides, what could she possibly have to do with Dr. Goldblum's murder? She moved the vase away to a side table.

It was time to start her day with some brisk morning stretches. Being a General Practitioner, or G.P., required physical agility and strength. At any given moment, she might need to wrench a dislocated shoulder back into its socket, climb stairs up and down to visit sick patients, rush to the hospital to complete a forceps delivery to save both mother and child, or tie a tourniquet tightly to stop arterial bleeding. Reach up, twist and touch toes, again.

Even with street marches for women's equality, most people still refused to believe that a female doctor had the stamina required of the job. She would prove them wrong.

While her body limbered up, her mind wandered to her favorite reading materials, medical journals, and articles about the famous Dr. Sigmund Freud. *A female doctor poking and prodding undressed strangers—he'd probably have fits!*

But she couldn't get the picture of that dead body at The Narrows out of her mind, all bloated and distorted. It reminded her of medical school. *Autopsy class, her male classmates formed a wall and turned their backs to her, preventing her from examining the male cadaver. "It's not fitting for a girl to see a man's bits," they'd said. She tried standing on tiptoes, but couldn't see past their broad shoulders. She raced outside, tears in her eyes, expecting to fail the class. A street vendor took pity on her, and with a sly wink, handed her one of his apple crates. She'd marched right back to the autopsy and stood upon the crate for a full view of the cadaver, towering over the boys.*

Josephine smiled at the memory. A victory! But those boys never let up. *I had to carry that crate around and stand on it for the rest of the school year.*

Wrapping up her exercises, Josephine went into the washroom and turned the spigot, which groaned and complained. "Applesauce!" she muttered when only a few drops sputtered out, "so much for modern plumbing." Fortunately, she'd filled the porcelain basin earlier while preparing the bouquet of flowers, and leaned over to wash her hands and face.

The shock of the cold water invigorated her, plunging her into the present. *Detective O'Malley must believe that I'm involved in Dr. Goldblum's murder. Why else had he brought me to the scene of the crime?* She decided there and then that she would pay a quick visit to Professor Janus Heath's Homeopathic pharmacy. *Why was he arguing with Goldblum? Did he keep fresh Aconitum napellus flowers in his laboratory? Had he sent me the Aconite bouquet?* She would ring Professor Heath straight away.

Josephine grabbed a towel and then opened her armoire, glancing briefly to the left where the lovely frocks with pleated skirts and low necklines hung. She wouldn't dare to wear any of these beautiful but risqué dresses. Her patients had sewn them to her measurements, even if it was hard to make out her form under her lab coat, but they were dressmakers and had a practiced eye. These dresses were offered as partial payment for the good doctor's treatments, but with an ulterior motive. There were so many parties, the patients hinted, and the "giggle water" could be found in speakeasies. If Josephine would only come out with them, they implored. "You need to find a husband," they said, "before it's too late." *Perhaps they are right.*

The much larger collection of plain house dresses in gingham and broadcloth hung to the right, with respectable neck ties and vested fronts. She pulled out one of these, her usual choice, but then she changed her mind. It was Saturday after all, a slower day of the week when people were hung over or busy planning the next evening's fanfare. Her choice in streetwear was rather limited to afternoon tea style or flouncy, so she decided on the former, choosing a demure olive green chiffon with a modern dropped waistline. It had a long bibbed V-neck in pale ivory with a large fabric flower in repoussé at the shoulder and a few smaller matching ivory flowers on the pleated skirt. Her patients really did beautiful needlework. She touched the petals in the design, feeling a sad nostalgia for her mother, who had tediously worked the embroidery needle. On her vanity table, she searched for and found a pair of cultured pearl earrings—they'd been her mother's, brought with her from Italy. *Wear these,* Grace had said, *and always remember that you are a lady. I doubt we'll ever be rich again, like my family, but maybe one day, a wealthy gentleman will ask for your hand in marriage.* Josephine had promised her mother then that she'd have a career and earn her own wealth.

Josephine slowly donned her white lab coat, then pulled on white stockings and shoes. *A capite ad calcem*—head to toe in doctor's white. Not the same white her mother had hoped for. *If she could see me now, I wonder if she'd be proud of me?*

Most G.P.'s worked from home, so Josephine had never bothered to decorate, nor was it necessary with all her patients coming and going. The rooms were spartan. She had a housekeeper come weekly to scrub and scrub again the floors and walls with borax powders.

The living room was converted into the Waiting Room, with rows of hard-backed chairs neatly lined up. Posters courtesy of the AMA hung on the walls extolling the virtues of cleanliness. "Wash your hands with soap!" "Beware of bacteria!" "Eat three servings of protein, dairy, fruits and vegetables per day!" "Empty the bowels!" they cried out, with wholesome illustrations of mothers and children. A few magazines rested on the side tables, along with a silk potted banana plant a patient had brought in to brighten up the place. *How happy they'll be to see these fresh flowers! If they're not allergic!* Checked curtains on the windows, which another patient had added, gave both privacy and a homey feel.

The master bedroom was converted into the Patient Examination Room, and all her medical equipment rested therein. Most of this room was taken up by the large examination table with stirrups, and there was a large overhead light swinging on a mechanical arm, an extravagance for sure, but it brightened the room considerably. In the large marquetry wall hutch she kept her prized bin-aural stethoscope. With it, she could listen to a patient's heartbeat in stereo. There were jars of various cleansing tools, cotton swabs, iodine, rubbing alcohol, sterile gauze rolls, tongue depressors, and numerous trays with different sized scalpels, tweezers and cauterizing tools. In drawers could be found gloves and aprons, and sterile cloths. In the smaller drawers were sterile threads and many different sized needles, pulling tweezers and scissors. Porcelain coated basins in different sizes were nested on the countertops. The shelves of the hutch were packed with labelled bottles and jars containing various medicaments and Allopathic colored pills.

Josephine surveyed both rooms, and slid her finger along counters, window panes and chairs, satisfied that all had been dusted to her satisfaction.

Once again, she found Sam's hot bagel at the front door and sat down to eat at the tiny kitchen table, sipping her morning tea. She had mixed the leaves herself, after a visit to the Indian market: chamomile, lemon balm, and linden for calming; peppermint, spearmint, and lemongrass for taste and a touch of licorice for sweetness; and after the tea wallah extolled the benefits of turmeric she added a pinch this as well. Her muscles and joints could use all the help they could get.

The warmth of the late summer day flowed in through her open kitchen window. The need for fresh air flow had been a main staple of her former Homeopathic training; the dead disease-borne air needed to be filtered out and new air circulated in. It was such a beautiful day. There were no emergencies, so she could sneak out for a quick constitutional to the corner and back before any patients showed up. She put on her light coat and sensible walking shoes, then a cloche hat and headed out the door to the street below.

Josephine's modest home was one of the many identical brick row houses squared with iron gates that defined Bensonhurst. There was a postage stamp-sized front and back yard and the lower level, in a modern improvement, had a short drive enclosed in wood for the new-fangled automobile. Patients had to climb the concrete staircase to reach her office front door on the second level, but they didn't seem to mind, and for those that couldn't she always made house calls.

It was tight quarters, but an improvement from the two room tenement her entire family had squeezed into on Baxter Street, in Little Italy where she'd been born. It was also larger than the entire ward where she'd been raised in the orphanage.

Small as her home was, she had everything she needed. With the apartment for Dominick below and parking for the Packard, she felt that she had made a sound investment—she even collected rent from the tenants on the top floor. She'd soon pay off the house, and values were constantly rising in Brooklyn.

Despite the weed-ridden front garden (she really must do something about that), her home was beautiful in its modest way. But she couldn't forget her dream of living in an Upper East Side stone-facade townhouse, like the ones she passed on her way to the medical conference. How that would have impressed her siblings! But that future seemed to be running away from her, like the galloping horses at Belmont.

There'd been little choice but to start her own practice in Brooklyn after no Manhattan hospital would hire her. Even Columbus Hospital, founded by her mentor, Mother Cabrini, wouldn't hire female doctors. That mistrust of women was ironic, thought Josephine, considering that the Mother herself had been an icon. When she'd found this rowhouse for sale, the nuns agreed that Brooklyn should be her mission.

Moving so far away had brought its share of travails. *Those Yorkvillains were right, it ain't Park Avenue!* Josephine sighed as she walked down the block. At the turn of the century, hundreds of thousands of immigrants had moved to the borough, first in areas closest to Manhattan like Brooklyn Heights, then further out to Carroll Gardens and Park Slope. By the late 1920's, the population had spread even further afield; now the scraggly pine sweeps of Josephine's neighborhood were being bulldozed for more housing and grid streets.

Because the sprawl stretched for miles to the southernmost elbow of Long Island at Gravesend, it was impossible for Josephine to call upon many of her patients by foot.

First, she had tried to manage by buses and taxis. But that had proven slow and even dangerous; there were no traffic lanes in the streets, nor even stop signs at intersections—streetcars, buses, motorcars, vendors, some horses and pedestrians criss-crossed together at any moment, most going the wrong way. Out of such randomness arose chaos, Josephine knew from experience—she was often called to the scene of horrific crashes to treat the bloodied and gravely injured. She had thought about learning to drive herself, but gave up that idea after arriving at the scene of one particularly gruesome hit and run where a man died, mangled beyond recognition.

The most practical solution for making house calls was to purchase a motor car and hire an experienced driver. *Abundans cautela non nocet*, she thought, one can never be too careful. The expense weighed on her pocket, but there was a benefit: having a man around provided safety from the criminal element. She certainly wasn't afraid to venture out in the middle of the night to deliver babies, but once, in a seedy area, she'd been jumped on. Dominick had appeared out of nowhere and punched out the group of thugs trying to glom her medical bag. "Doc, when punks hold you up at gunpoint, you'd better let go," he warned. "Never," she replied. He'd looked at her pint-sized frame and said, "Then you're gonna need some protection."

At her insistence, Dominick lived in the small apartment adjoining the garage, rent free. Living in close quarters with such a handsome bodybuilder had caused the gossip mill to churn. But Josephine hadn't hired him for his brawn nor his movie star looks. She needed him to keep the motor car running. Dominick was also a first-rate mechanic.

Soon the neighbors became used to her "arrangement," and waved to her motor car with Dominick behind the wheel.

She worked day and night to build up her practice, but there was another risk. Josephine had to defend her territory, admonishing her patients not to buy useless and dangerous tonics from "medicine men," and educated them on "science-based medicine." Perhaps she was too stern—there had been several complaints that her bedside manner was not "lady-like." Sometimes, it seemed like she couldn't please anyone. Her best recourse was to be "tiny but mighty," and let the chips fall where they may. She held her head a little higher and continued on her walk.

Josephine reached the avenue and was just about to turn back when she spotted Philomen Quinn setting up his stand at the far corner, raising a large banner that read "Famous Dr. Quinn's Indigestion Bitters." *He's no Doctor, and he's certainly not famous.* Wearing ridiculous looking Edwardian coat tails, a checked vest and a top hat, "Doctor" Quinn began loudly touting his wares.

"Hair loss creams! Baby sleep aids! Anti-infection gels! Rheumatism and ligament oils!" he shouted out in a sing-song. "Specially made for King George and Queen Mary of England at Buckingham Palace!"

Josephine crossed the street, not knowing what to expect. Just last month, she'd been furious to find mercury in his ingredients for baby's teething gel.

"Good day, Mr. Quinn," said Josephine, choosing her words carefully. "Nice to see you again after the conference. Mind if I take a look at your tonics today?"

"Not at all, Dr. Reva, you won't find anything amiss," Quinn replied with some acidity.

She picked up the Baby Sleep Magic Potion with the cute label of a baby asleep on a crescent moon. "Hmm, no alcohol or morphine in the ingredients, I hope?" she asked, noting the ingredients list did not specify opiates. Most of these "medicines" were made in a lab somewhere, under questionable purity and with few inspections. "We don't want to turn babies into future addicts, do we?"

"Not a trace of morphine," said Quinn. "That would be illegal under the Harrison Narcotics Act of 1925."

Josephine nodded, but wondered if he simply hadn't found his supplier that week. Enforcement of the Harrison Act was weak—the police were too busy keeping up with illegal bootlegging and organized crime. She untwisted the cap of the Baby Sleep Magic, and put it gingerly to her nose.

She gagged. "That's chloroform! And I smell valerian root." There was no mistaking the slightly putrid smell of valerian, but it was herbal and safe in limited amounts, and considered quite soothing. The chloroform, however, was overwhelming and odious, and could kill a baby.

"My Baby Sleep Magic Potion works like a charm," Quinn announced to the crowd, picking up a bottle and waving it in the air. "Puts babies gently to sleep! Only fifty cents!"

"Fifty cents, Doctor," he said to Josephine, pretending to make a sale. "You opened it, now you're gonna have to purchase it," he muttered under his breath.

Josephine replied in outrage. "I'm not paying you for chloroform!"

But there was a stooge in the crowd who shouted, "Baby Sleep Magic worked for my little one, and it was perfectly safe!" Others in the crowd nodded in agreement. Someone jostled her brusquely and Josephine felt unwelcome. Realizing the futility of arguing, she decided to put the Baby Magic in her medical bag and pay him anyway, announcing to the crowd that she would test it. Who knew what was truly inside this or any of Quinn's bottles? But she didn't have time to survey all of his many products. Calling the authorities hadn't worked, although she had tried that many times. They came and took away his stand, but he always popped back up out of his hole on a new street corner, like the weasel he was.

"Tonics, elixirs, gels for fast relief! All work miraculously, folks! Hey Doctor, don't go! You look like you need my Ligament Rubbing Oil. Soothes those tired and aching bones."

The crowd laughed.

"Not on your life!" said Josephine, furious that he'd gotten the better of her. Well, at least he seemed to have stopped adding morphine, opium and cocaine, and that was an improvement. But ethers? That and the rest of his questionable ingredients were legal as long as they weren't opiates and were plainly labeled. The lack of regulation bothered her, and she could well understand why Dr. Goldblum had been frustrated. It was *caveat emptor*, or buyer beware. All she could do was warn her patients to stay away. Quinn the medicine man had every right to do his own form of prescribing.

Josephine walked briskly back home with much annoyance. She arrived back to her office, washed her hands, and set about preparing her examination room tools for the busy day ahead. Sure enough, her tidying was soon disturbed by a loud commotion of animated voices in the waiting room. Dominick, hearing her return, must have turned the street sign to read, "The Doctor Is IN." He was always eager for a house call to get out the new motor car.

But so many voices! What was he offering—free consultations?

Thank goodness the door to the waiting room was still locked. Where was Dominick anyway? Perhaps he took the morning off to do some errands. She wouldn't need him for a while anyway. She passed her ordered desk and patient files, neatly stacked. But something caught her eye that was out of place. Pushed under the door was a local newspaper. Picking it up, she saw her picture from the conference, and read the headline in bold type:

"Lady Doctor Questioned in Health Director's Murder!"

"Homeopathic-trained physician Dr. Josephine Reva, an attractive young miss barely taller than her medical bag, was escorted by police yesterday to the scene of City Health Director Anthony Goldblum's grisly murder. Dr. Goldblum, who led the Bureau of Preventable Diseases, recently formed a panel to investigate allegations of wrongdoings by doctors and others practicing irregular medicine. These allegations are said to arise from the Carnegie-funded 1910 Flexner Report, which closed down most women's and Homeopathic medical colleges. Dr. Reva, 26, possesses a Medical Doctor diploma from one of the few Homeopathic medical colleges still in operation, the New York City College of Homeopathic Medicine, the same school Dr. Goldman attended. She completed clinical practice, then an internship at Metropolitan Hospital on Welfare Island. She is currently the only female physician in the populated areas of Borough Park, Bensonhurst, and parts of Gravesend. She is reported to have been raised and mentored by an iconic woman, Mother Frances Cabrini, the founder of Columbus Hospital. A medical miracle reportedly took place there, which was recently avowed by the Vatican: a baby blinded at birth was completely cured by prayers.

It is not clear how intimately Dr. Reva knew the murdered official. When asked if the young miss was a suspect, Chief Detective John O'Malley replied, "No comment." He said that the cause of the victim's death was undetermined pending further toxicology reports."

Josephine gasped. *That big shot detective is trying to implicate me!* She reached for the telephone and started to click the receiver. But then she relented, hooking the handle back on its post. *Detective O'Malley isn't going to stop harassing me unless I prove my innocence. I'll have to do a bit of sleuthing of my own. If that clod O'Malley can do it, it can't be that hard.*

There was much commotion in the next room. So many patients today, she thought ruefully.

For the first time, she hesitated before opening the door.

Chapter 8- Brooklyn Precinct 962

Meanwhile...

Detective O'Malley leaned back in his comfortable oak armchair. How he loved this new invention—a spring coil hidden under the seat let him swivel in any direction and push back with his weight to a delightfully supine position, almost like reclining in bed. Nothing like a little nap, he said to himself. He was relaxing with his feet up on his desk and his arms crossed behind his head, ready to take a snooze, when his rookie opened the door yelling.

"That chauffeur is here." Why did that rookie always yell? Couldn't he knock and talk in a pleasant voice? Youth!

"Don't just stand there, send him in."

The rookie nodded and left to fetch Dominick. He returned with the chauffeur in tow.

O'Malley ordered his sergeant, who was peering in, and the rookie to leave. "Don't disturb us." He beckoned for Dominick to take a chair.

"Why am I here?" Dominick asked nervously. "I ain't done nuttin'."

"Yeah, that's a change of pace—here's your record," O'Malley answered curtly, throwing a file across the desk to land in front of Dominick.

"That was a long time ago, kid's stuff."

"Relax, you've got a good job now, and no one need be the wiser. In return, I've got a little job for you to do." O'Malley leaned back further in his chair, furling and unfurling his clasped fingers.

"You'll be my eyes and ears, reporting to me on that Lady Doctor, Dr. Josephine Reva," said O'Malley.

"But she's my boss," Dominick protested. "I won't tell you nuttin'. I ain't no stool pigeon."

"You will be," said O'Malley, "or I'll have you arrested."

"For what?" Dominick called his bluff. But his brow was starting to sweat.

"For whatever I want," replied O'Malley, who then threw an envelope in front of the chauffeur. "Like gambling? I hear you have some large debts. And those gangsters aren't going to forgive you. That envelope is for you, and there'll be more where that came from. You'll be working for me on the side, in whatever capacity I see fit."

Dominick took the envelope and his fingers pulled apart the five dollar bills stuffed inside. "That's a lot of dough," he said. He groaned, realizing he was now, whether he liked it or not, one of the detective's street informants.

"Go on, get outta here and to work," O'Malley waved his hand. Dominick left the room, and the detective picked up the file. He glanced through the rest of it, finding a document of interest. It was an old military discharge paper honoring Dominick for valor.

Chapter 9 - Patients and Remedies

*We should imitate nature, which sometimes cures a chronic afflic-
tion*
with another supervening disease...
—Samuel Hahnemann (1755-1843)

J osephine's Waiting Room was chock full of locals from the
neighborhood. Had they come for medical ailments or to
relish gossiping about that newspaper article?

Josephine resolved to make sure that the day's examinations
were about her patients' complaints, and not about her role in
the murder investigation.

"I'll see whoever was here first or who's in a state of emergency," she declared in her professional voice.

"Doc Joe!" A stout woman holding a baby cried out.
Josephine ran over to her. Maria had been one of her very first
patients and Josephine felt a fondness for her and her family.
Maria had had terrible birth pains and Josephine had to coax the
baby, who was breech, out feet first. That was a night when she
wished Maria had opted for a hospital birth. Since then,
Josephine had delivered Maria's second child, a son, much more
easily at United Zion Israel Hospital.

"What's wrong, Maria?" Josephine reached for the pulse of the large ebullient woman, and started to count while looking at the gold watch pinned to her lab coat.

"With me, nut-tin'! But you, whadda dey do to you?'

Did they take you to the Big House?" someone from the crowd shouted.

"How can anyone tink you killed tat man?'

"They have a witness who saw me arguing with him before he was murdered, although I was actually arguing with that tonic salesman."

"*Dio buono*, my God!" sobbed Maria, sinking into a chair.

"Please try not to get upset, Maria," Josephine patted Maria on the shoulder. "You'll elevate your blood pressure." She took her stethoscope and checked Maria's heart rate.

"Maria's worried about you, Doc, we all are—*porca vacca!*" exclaimed Antonio, Maria's husband. Josephine was grateful for their concern, but she couldn't help being amused by the country slang of a cursed pig and cow. Even though the couple had done well for themselves since opening the newspaper, candy, book and ticket kiosk at the streetcar stop, she knew that they had been born peasant farmers outside of Naples.

Josephine's mother, Grace, came from the same region, but was born into an aristocratic land-owning family. Unfortunately, a sibling's romantic scandal caused Grace to be packed off to America. The harsh New York City sweatshop conditions led to her demise - she fell terminally ill with Tuberculosis and the pandemic influenza was too much for her. A tragic end, sadly mimicking Puccini's Mimi in his opera *La Bohème*—Josephine had tears in her eyes, imagining her mother while listening to a recording of Nellie Melba and Enrico Caruso's duet. Josephine and her younger siblings had been left as street urchins until the nuns found them. Josephine wasn't embittered; but she did rue the hand of fate and often thought how different her life would have been if she had been raised in the bosom of her mother's wealthy family in Naples, probably married by now and living an elegant life as an aristocratic lady. But then would she have pursued medicine? Probably not.

Her mother had taught her Italian and Neapolitan, and that made it easier for her to learn other Romance languages. Although first generation American, she still felt akin to her immigrant patients. She loved the "melting pot" of New York. Many held her up as an example of how far one could rise in America, in a single generation.

"We came as soon as we saw that awful article!" Sophie leaned over. She was young and pretty, about 25 years old and a second-generation New York-born woman of English and Welsh descent with a small oval face, gentle green eyes and light reddish hair coiffed in a wavy bob. She and her husband, Andrew, an immigrant Scotsman, had been trying for several years to have a baby with no success. Sophie wore a black and white striped dress with white collar and a smart hat pierced by a perfectly matched eagle feather. Josephine glanced around the crowded waiting room, and saw that most of her patients likewise were wearing their Sunday best.

"Don't you worry none, Doc," said Andrew, taking off his fedora hat. He was young, sturdy and tall, with slicked back blond hair and light blue eyes. He and Sophie owned the green grocers on the avenue. "It's just muckrakers looking for a story. Obviously, you wouldn't harm a flea!"

"For goodness sake, no!" said Sophie. "Who would think such a thing! You'd treat a flea if it came in this office. But of course it wouldn't—there are no fleas. I mean, it's very clean."

"Yes, every'ting is spic 'n span clean!" Maria cried some more. "*I miei bambini,* my babies— it was no picnic! You stayed wit' me te whole night!"

"Maybe we'd a better give 'er some whiskey," Antonio said, looking around for a glass.

"Yes, that's a fine idea, indeed! A draught to tide you over, Doc," added Michael Finnegan, a black-haired well-dressed Cork dandy who owned a pub. He had a profitable business serving alcohol before Prohibition closed him down. Now he served coffee, root beer and soda.

"Not for Doc Joe," said Antonio, "I mean my Maria. She'sa hysterical."

"Alright everyone, let's be calm," said Josephine. "Maria needs to relax."

She spoke again to Maria. "Let me give you something. You have finished nursing, haven't you, Maria? I have to think of this little one," and she took Maria's baby Gianni in her arms, cradling him and cooing. She then asked Sophie to hold the baby and mind Chiara, Maria's first-born toddler daughter, so she could continue working.

All eyes were on Josephine as she took out her keys. She went into the hallway and behind her desk, where she unlocked the liquor cabinet. Her patients peered around the doorway as she took out a big bottle of Scotch Whiskey, an imported brand allowed to doctors. She poured out a dram. Then she carefully replaced the liquor, locked the door and put the key in her pocket. She also went to her desk, unlocked the top drawer and took out her official Prohibition Prescription Blanks, issued by the United States Treasury under the National Prohibition Act, and put that in her pocket, too.

Josephine returned to her patient and handed her the glass. Maria drank the drops of golden liquid at once.

Michael licked his lips wistfully. "Yes, sirree, that's the Real McCoy!" He let out a low whistle. "I haven't cast my eyes on that much whiskey since they closed my bar."

"You know, Doc, a drink would do you good, too. I mean you can hardly expect to remain calm when those gumshoes think you murdered a Health Director!" Andrew said.

"Uh, I hate to be the bearer of bad news, but my cousin's on the force." Michael reluctantly added. "They're planning an arrest. Doc could be sent up the river for good!"

"Oh, no!" Maria fell backwards again, as several men caught her.

"Quickly! Help me get her into the examination room," shouted Josephine.

Antonio hauled the plump Maria down the hall and helped her lumber up onto the exam table. She was flush and sweating from the strain. Josephine pressed a cool cloth to her forehead, and Antonio tenderly smoothed her dark brown ringlets between his fingers.

"Your blood pressure is too high and your pulse is jumping again," Josephine said as she unwrapped the blood pressure band from Maria's arm and pulled off her stethoscope. "And the extra pregnancy weight needs to come off, Maria, it's no good for your circulation. I'm preparing a special diet for you, just like in Italy: olive oil, beans and vegetables, fresh fish, lean meats. No more candy. You must be sure to follow it this time."

"*Grazie*, uh, tank you, Doc Joe," Maria said.

"And how about you, Sophie, have you eaten yet?" Josephine turned to the young woman. "Let's test your glucose levels."

"I fasted all morning, like you asked. Besides, I've been too worried about you to eat anything," Sophie looked about to faint, too.

"I don't know wadda we do wit'out you, Doc Joe!" said Maria, starting to feel the effects of the whiskey. "We'll bring you plenty of food! As soon as I can get up, I'mma gonna cook sometin' nice for you!" She fell back down on the table.

Michael and Antonio said they would do it and walked over to the kitchen and opened the icebox.

"*Madonna mia!*" Antonio exclaimed, "Holy Mother of God, it's empty! Whatcha doing, starvin' yourself?"

"That's one way to disappear from the law," cackled Mike. Antonio gave him a sideways look. "I'm trying, you know, to make the Doc laugh," the former barman said sheepishly.

"Don't worry, I have plenty of canned goods," Josephine called over her shoulder. She could find nothing amusing about running from the law, but it was just like the men to joke. "Please find some juice for Sophie's test and water for Maria's whiskey." She wanted to keep the men busy while she continued working.

"And here, run to the druggist for this prescription." She tore off the top sheet of her Prohibition Rx pad and handed it to Antonio. "Hurry up, now!"

Antonio ran out with a worried look on his face, obviously concerned for his wife. Andrew and Michael began lighting up some Roosters, but Josephine pointed to the AMA posters on the walls that forbade smoking. They complained under their breath and went outside.

Josephine looked again at her Rx pad. *That's odd, the certification numbers don't match—there appears to be one missing. Did I forget to mark one? Or did the Prohibition authority misprint this pad?*

The telephone rang, interrupting her thoughts. Sophie ran to answer it. "Yes, this is Ambassador 2-0037. Yes, Dr. Josephine Reva's office. Oh, dear! Poor boy, bring him right over."

"Doc Joe," Sophie shouted over the din of the noisy office and babies crying, "you've got an emergency coming! Oh, someone rang named Professor Janus Heath. He wants to meet you this afternoon - here's the address."

"Ok, thanks," Josephine had no time to think about Professor Heath. She turned back to her patients. "Now that you're resting, Maria, let me examine your adorable baby," said Josephine. "He is uncomfortable."

Maria handed over her crying baby wrapped in swaddling. After listening to little Gianni's heart and prodding his tummy, Josephine determined that he was having a bout of colic.

"It will pass," she said. "Give him some gripe water for the gas, rub his tummy and apply warm heat. If that doesn't alleviate his pain, try pushing his knees to his chest gently like this," and she showed Maria what to do. Josephine thought about *Chamomila*, a Homeopathic remedy for colic, but brushed the thought aside.

"He's teething, too," Josephine said, feeling the little baby teeth emerging under the gums. "But be careful you don't buy Calomel from that quack on the corner, or at the pharmacy. Mercurous chloride is a poison that causes horrible things, even death. Instead, let Gianni chew on a cool wet cloth. The cold will make his gums numb, and he'll soon be better once his teeth cut in." How she wished there was more enforcement of toxic ingredients in medicines. The Pure Food and Drug Act of 1906 now forced manufacturers to label their toxic ingredients. It was still up to doctors like her to warn their patients.

Next she confirmed that Sophie had fasted since waking, and conducted an oral glucose tolerance test. Sophie drank a sweetened juice. In a few hours, she would test the blood and urine for diabetes. In the meantime, she attended to the other patients waiting.

Raging and shrieking, Josephine's emergency patient was brought in. The anguished mother was holding onto her adolescent child. "He was feeding the machines, and his finger got caught. It's smashed awful."

The boy was in severe pain. Josephine could see that his finger was severely gashed and dislocated.

"I'm here to help you," she said, trying to calm him. "Keep steady. Lemme examine your finger closely."

But the boy flailed about and howled. Noticing the rags the child was dressed in, Josephine was upset. It just wasn't right, she thought, a child his age should be in school, not working with dangerous machinery.

"Let's calm him down, so I can clean and stitch the wound."

There had been a child with fright that Josephine attended to at Flower Homeopathic Hospital during her clinical rotations. She remembered he had been quickly soothed. *That's it, Aconite! Indeed, it's the perfect remedy for this case of fright, too. But I've got no more in my kit.*

Suddenly, she remembered her medicine cabinet— had she kept any of her old vials? She stood on her tiptoes and reached up to the top shelf and felt around. Yes, there it was— the box! Her fingers touched the warm oak as she inched the box forward, hearing the clink of the glass bottles inside. She pulled the box down and onto the counter, her fingertips rubbing the letters of her name embossed on the lid. Each glass bottle was carefully labelled and contained a number of small white tablets.

The boy cried again shrilly, and Josephine decided to take out the first bottle. She had always kept them in alphabetical order. *Aconitum napellus.* She pulled off the cork stopper, tapped out one tablet on a plate and offered it to the boy. "This medicine is sweet, it's made with milk sugar. Put it under your tongue and let it dissolve." The boy dutifully obeyed, grabbing for what he thought was a candy.

After only a few minutes, the boy stopped howling, "You're a real soldier," Josephine told him. "Do you ever watch your mamma sew?" He nodded. "Well, I'm going to do a little sewing to close this cut on your finger. It's going to look just like your mamma's stitches." Josephine scrubbed her hands thoroughly, then prepared a local anesthetic, cleansed and stitched the wound. "There, these stitches are small and neat, just like my own mother's," she told the boy, remembering her mother's tiny petit point that decorated the expensive linen tea set tablecloths and napkins she had brought with her from Italy. Such fine workmanship!

"Now you're going to be alright. And you'll even have a story to tell all your friends!' Josephine said as she bandaged the boy's finger. Turning to the boy's mother, she advised that the boy would probably regain movement with time in the damaged finger. "Please come back in a week to remove the stitches, and remember to keep the area clean with this ointment." Josephine refused the dollars offered. "Please promise that you'll find a safer job for your son," she said, "or next time it could be far worse. He might lose a finger, or, God forbid, his hand." She didn't want to frighten the mother, but she wanted to warn her of the danger.

Josephine looked at the open box of remedies. *Well, I might as well continue.* She took out two more bottles.

She gave Maria's baby a tablet of Homeopathic *Chamomila.* "Give him another every three hours until he feels better. We prescribed *Chamomila* for colic at Flower Hospital clinic, with great success. If he's still got gas pains, you can then give a tablet of this, *Carbo vegetalis.* It's very effective. Do your best to place the tablets under his tongue as I just did, and let them dissolve in his mouth." She neatly folded two little paper envelopes for the remedies and handed them to Maria.

It was time for Sophie's glucose tolerance test. Josephine determined that her patient was not yet diabetic, but had a little sugar in the urine and showed signs of weight loss.

"We need to do a blood test regularly, Sophie," she warned. "if you want to have a child soon. I'll monitor your estrogen level with the new test available, and then we'll have a better idea on a course of treatment." She thought briefly about reaching back into the old wooden box to find a remedy to help Andy and Sophie conceive, but then shook her head. *I'm an Allopath now. I shouldn't have given out the other remedies. But the Aconitum napellus did work.* Josephine let her hands linger over the bottles as she closed the box.

She looked at her watch pinned on her lab coat and realized it was time to head over to meet Professor Heath at Green-Wood Cemetery. *What an unusual place to meet! I suppose Janus wants to enjoy the warm air and the park-like grounds. I wouldn't mind a walk there among the graves— it's the only greenery we have in Borough Park.*

She announced that office hours were closed for the day until 6 p.m.

Going down the back stairs, she called for Dominick to get the Packard ready. As she put on her hat, Josephine felt more determined than ever. *I'm going to get to the bottom of this. Janus Heath and Dr. Goldblum were arguing—but why? Did Janus send me the Aconite flowers? Could Janus be Goldblum's killer?*

Chapter 10 - Rum Row

P atients filed into the street, but Andy and Mike stayed on the front balcony overlooking the driveway. They lit up more Rooster cigarettes and exhaled in relief. They watched as the garage doors folded opened. A distinctive roar was heard as the engine kicked over, and Dominick backed out the elegant silver motor car in a cloud of smoke, leaving it running to warm the engine. He went back inside to close up.

"Ain't she a beauty!" sad Andrew. "I'll say she is!" instantly replied Michael.

They both laughed in guffaws, thinking of the Marx Brother's "Cocoanuts" vaudeville show.

Samuel Katz, the rotund delicatessen owner, rounded the corner carrying a bag full of steaming bagels. "This joint is hoppin'!" Sam collected the latest Jazz discs and played them on his Old Vic, the syncopated music blaring from the bell horn. "I never saw Doc's place so lively!" He turned towards the exiting patients, handing out bagels. "Here, everyone, my latest batch! Free samples!" Patients murmured in appreciation.

Gabriel, a neighborhood bookie, appeared behind Sam to help. He was about eighteen years old, short and skinny with a shock of dark hair and bags under his eyes from working the fights at night. "I was gonna see a man about a dog, but Sam found me." The others laughed, knowing full well that Sam was 'the man,' and 'the dog' was whiskey. Sam's deli turned into a jumpin' speakeasy every Saturday night. With Orthodox Jewish people moving into Borough Park, many were appalled that Sam was running a Blind Pig on the Sabbath, hence the need to speak in code when out on the street. But Sam's Deli and weekend Gambling Parlor Gin Joint was making too much money for Sam to mind what other people thought.

"Whoo-ee, look at that spit 'n polish!" said Gabriel, walking over to the motor car. "Doc Joe must have a house call."

"You should see the latest roadster model. It's got a disappearing top that folds down right into the trunk. The front wind-screen stays up, so the driver doesn't get any bugs in his eyes," said Andy.

"How considerate of the common man!" smirked Gabe. "Hey, where's Dominick?"

"Probably off to some professional chauffeuring school!" joked Sam.

"Pull a lever, turn the wheel, open the door!" Mike gesticulated each move, and the men laughed. "How hard can it be? I bet this baby drives itself!"

"Naaw, he's one helluva mechanic," said Gabe. "And a soldier—he told me he built ambulances in the war."

Mike and Andy walked down the steps to greet Sam and Gabe, and grabbed some of the hot bagels. As they ate, the men walked around the front of the motor car's long hood.

"Yes, sirree!" whistled Mike. "This model's the Deluxe, with a juiced up 8-cylinder engine!"

"Salesman must have talked her into it," Andy said.

"Suicide doors, and look, jump seats! Wow, eight people can fit in here! This mustta cost a pretty penny!" Gabe peered through the window. "There's even a silver tissue box for the ladies! And it's wired with a reading lamp, and there's even glass bottles on a tray!"

"Holy Be-Jesus!" Mike let out another whistle. "A traveling bar, what d'ya know!" He tried the door. It was locked.

"Doctors get special permission to carry booze," explained Sam. "My Rabbi, too. Every now and then we get sizzled over a bottle of imported Bordeaux—he saves it for bris!"

"My priest saves Irish Whiskey for Baptisms and Last Rites. You're zozzled coming and going!" Mike joked.

"So Doc Joe gets the Real McCoy," said Andy, thoughtfully.

"Yeah, only doctors and religious folks are allowed. It's a confounded shame Doc Joe doesn't drink!" said Mike.

"But she sure does prescribe it," Sam said. "I get a prescription every now and then."

"You mean a Booze Blank?" exclaimed Gabe.

"How's that?" asked Andy.

"A Booze Blank—that's a whiskey prescription. It's perfectly legal. You get one from a doc for colds and sneezing." Sam explained, and he sneezed repeatedly for effect. "See, it's a chronic condition!"

Antonio returned from the chemist carrying a paper bag.

"Here, Andy, you can share dis pint wit' us. I gotta plenty o' wine at home," said Antonio, opening the paper bag to reveal a bottle of Canadian Scotch. Neighbors knew he stocked bottles of grape juice in his basement and let them sit a little too long. Once a week, a truck came and hauled off the fermented "juice."

"Hey, Antonio, Doc Joe must have given you a Booze Blank," Gabe said, while the others were delightedly examining the legal whiskey bottle.

Once the excitement of the liquor purchase had passed, they turned their attention back to the motor car, running their hands gingerly over the rounded bumpers, head lamps and mirrors, then stepping on the running boards and prodding the white wall tires.

"How much does this baby cost?" asked Andy.

"I dunno, maybe two or three grand!" answered Mike.

"Wish I 'ad one, for my kids," Antonio said.

"Shouldda stopped having babies, and you'da saved up for it!" Gabe teased.

"Doc Joe ain't got no husband, no kids. She can afford it." Mike added. "She probably could have bought a Dusenberg!"

"Naw, that's ten grand," said Gabe.

"This baby was expensive enough, like $2500," Sam said.

"Wowee!" exclaimed Mike. "I should've gone into medicine!"

"They'z making money now because everyone wants a Booze Blank. Some docs are duplicating them and getting a kickback," said Sam. "Of course, our Doc Joe ain't doin' that."

"Poor fella'," Andy said, gesturing towards the door off the driveway where Dominick lived in the basement. "He's always at the beck and call of the Doc."

"Are you kidding, Andy?" Michael rebutted, "I wouldn't mind driving a nice posh model like this around!"

"But he's gotta drive rain or snow, day or night!" said Andy, "Those babies ain't born when it's convenient!"

"Dominick's got a sweet deal."

"There's better ways to make some real money," said Gabe.

Michael and Andy stopped arguing. "Whadd'ya mean?" they asked.

Gabe looked closely at the motor car. "You know, there's lots of places to stash bottles in here." Gabe pointed to the large passenger compartment and the cargo boot. "A moonless night and a drive to the docks. I bet this V-8 could outrun the flatties!"

"Four or five grand, easy peasy!" Mike slapped his hands together.

"Five grand is peanuts," said Gabe. "You ever see those twinkling lights far out at sea. They'z the Mother Ships, anchored out on Rum Row. That's what they call the route between here and St. Pierre and Miquelon—French islands off Nova Scotia"

"So what?" said Mike.

"In France, there ain't no Prohibition," Gabe continued. "It's legal to buy and sell liquor there. Them islands are one giant liquor warehouse." The other men turned to look at Gabe with interested expressions, so he continued.

"Mother Ships load up legally with the really good stuff— imported Irish and Scottish whiskey, French wine, cognac and champagne. Then they sail down here to Gravesend, Brooklyn, just before The Narrows. They anchor in international waters at night. Everybody's in on it—anybody who's got a boat goes back and forth - fishing boat, trawler, even a sailboat, you name it. The mob's bought a whole flotilla of armored speedboats, to outrun and shoot at the Coast Guard. They can haul thousands of bottles at once. Those Mother Ships make nearly one million dollars each trip alone, and they do it every single night!"

"That's some serious dough," Sam said, letting out a long whistle.

The men went silent, thinking of so much money and how they could get in on it. "Except you need a boat. Or at least a truck or a car to get to the dock and back," Gabe completed their thoughts and the five stared at the Packard.

Andy shook his head. "No way. Doc's in enough trouble as it is."

"Lads, we've got to put our minds together. Doc's in a pickle, and those coppers don't care who they arrest," Mike said.

"She's clearly being framed," Andy agreed.

"Right, let's see that newspaper again," said Mike. "Maybe there's something that'll help us find the real killer."

"It says the dead guy was found down at The Narrows," Gabe said. "That's where the bootleggers come in. Do you think it was the bootleggers?"

"Might be," Mike agreed.

Josephine came outside and walked down the steps towards her waiting car. The men tipped their hats and started to disperse.

"Let's get back to work, Gabe." said Sam. "See youz later tonight at my place?" he winked.

"You bet!" the others replied.

Through the curtains, Dominick watched them leave.

* * *

Sophie and Maria came downstairs holding on to Maria's toddler and baby. They rejoined their husbands heading back to their respective shops. At the corner they said their "see ya laters", the men winking and the women excitedly discussing what they would wear that evening to Sam's.

Sophie was not feeling all that chipper, and Maria noticed.

"What's te matter, Sophie?" she asked.

"It's just that Doc Joe said I need more tests." Sophie looked distraught while cradling Gianni in her arms. "You know, to have any children."

"Dontcha worry, Doc Joe will figure itta out. Sometimes, when you least expect it...."

"That may have worked for you, Maria, but it's not working for me. I don't know if I'll ever have a child. You're so lucky, you have two."

"Oh, Sophie, dere's always a way, if God is willin'. And ya have to follow Doc Joe's orders, 'cause we wancha to be healthy so your baby's healthy and you both survive te birth."

Maria took Gianni, hugged Sophie and went into her apartment.

Sophie held tightly to Andy's hand. "I don't want to go back to our apartment and find it so empty. It's makes me sad that we still don't have any little children running about, like Maria and Antonio have."

"Listen to me, Sophie," Andy looked into her eyes. "I love you more than ever before. And whatever God above has planned for us, that's fine by me. We'll keep trying—I can't say that I don't like the trying part!"

She smiled as they kissed and he went into their grocery store. She turned towards her doorway, but out of the corner of her eye she spotted Quinn surrounded by a small crowd. With determination she walked over and pushed her way to the front.

"Dr. Quinn," she said in a low voice, almost whispering. "Might you have anything for infertility?"

"Who's problem?" whispered Quinn back to her. "Yours or his?"

She appreciated his being discreet. "Uh, I don't know for sure, but I think it's mine."

"Well, then I have just the tonic you need. Mother's Special Cordial. This will open the, uh, female parts to be receptive."

"What's in it?"

"My special extracts of red raspberry leaf, nettle, alfalfa, dandelion root and a touch, or two, of whiskey, to relax you so the tonic can take effect and make its way into the body."

"Anything dangerous?"

"Nope, these herbs have worked for centuries. The only thing is that you'll have to take a bottle a week. Until you get pregnant, that is, which will be soon. And what a joy that will be!"

She paid him two dollars, took the bottles and went upstairs to her apartment happily, almost skipping.

Chapter 11 - Green-Lawn Cemetery

Dominick looked in his rear view mirror and pulled the sedan slowly out of the driveway. He got out to open the passenger door for Josephine to climb inside. He drove around the corner past Maria and Antonio's newsstand and he tooted the horn. Josephine waved as they passed Sophie and Andy loading up their grocery truck.

"Best to let 'em think there's nothing's wrong, Doc," said Dominick, "but I'm worried about you. That Detective O'Malley is ruthless, I hear. I think he planted that story in the paper."

"I have a plan," Josephine said. "I'm going to do some sleuthing of my own. I'm going to ask Janus Heath exactly why he and the deceased had words at the conference."'

"You saw 'em together?" Dominick asked with a wary look. "And they were arguing? Doncha think you'd better let the police investigate?"

"It was only for a moment that I saw them together. Dr. Goldblum was angry, but Janus had seemed, well, meek. He's harmless. He couldn't kill anyone. Besides, I didn't think it was important. In any case, I told Detective O'Malley about it, sort of."

Dominick looked in the rear mirror at Josephine with a worried expression.

They passed the bagel shop, waving at Sam and Gabe, who were loading up their delivery jalopy. Then they came to Quinn's stand of tonics with a large crowd in front.

"I see that quack is still selling his snake oil," muttered Josephine as they passed. "'Doctor Quinn's Rheumatism Tonic'—that's a new banner!"

"There's your competition," Dominick agreed.

Quinn was briskly selling his wares and deviously tipped his hat as Josephine passed, looking her directly in the eye.

"'Doctor,'" Josephine exclaimed, "he's not a doctor! I can't believe he attracts so many foolish—what does he call them? Oh yes, 'customers.'"

Dominick continued splashing the Packard through potholes as wide as foxholes along the crumbling streets. He made slow progress, due to the wandering children, wayward vehicles going the wrong way and jaywalking pedestrians rushing into the streets at lunchtime. He hopped the car slowly over the crisscrossed streetcar tracks, like a boat entering a wake zone. Checking his rear view mirror, he decided to take a circuitous route on 15th Avenue passing Temple Beth El, then turned up New Utrecht Avenue, towards United Israel Zion Hospital and the dispensary.

"Are you taking me on a grand tour of Borough Park, Dominick?" Josephine asked.

"I thought you'd enjoy seeing the hospital in daylight for a change. How the neighborhood is growing! They're building everywhere. Look at that new synagogue!" Dominick whistled.

"More and more Jewish immigrants—you'll be happy about that."

"Whatever helps get more hospital beds. Besides, if Jews expand the hospital, then they are welcome here—their charities have taken the reins, thank goodness," said Josephine.

"There aren't many hospitals that will treat 'em."

"Such segregation and prejudice! It's getting worse. There's Jewish blocks, Italian blocks, German blocks in our own neighborhood."

"You don't have to worry none, Doc. All people will come to you—they all get sick at one point or another. Everybody needs a doctor."

"Of course, I treat everyone—we're all homo sapiens." Josephine was very against Social Darwinism's belief that humanity should be classified in ways similar to animals, with "survival of the fittest" as its core, and saw this as the basis of Fascism growing in Italy. She'd read about it in the Italian newspapers Maria had given her. "A human body is like any other— we're all made of blood, bone, tissue and organs. That I can treat. Prejudice, unfortunately, I can't.

"Speaking of it," she continued, "alarming news is coming out of Italy. The *Corriere* said that Mussolini has seized more power." She paused to open her window, fanning herself. "Even after D'Annunzio, the madman poet, failed to annex Fiume just over the Croatian border, you'd think the Fascists would give this crazy idea up. They want to be a great empire again, like the Romans or the Germans in the last war."

"That's just like 'em," Dominick added. "But even worse, the Germans are now going after the Jews. It's gonna get ugly over there. I'm glad I left Sicily, and thankful to be right here in Brooklyn. Nothing ever happens here, just the way I like it."

"But it's bad here, too. Coloreds are barred from clubs and schools, and there's a Jewish quota," she said with disgust. "At least my college ignored it," she added proudly.

"Yes, you've mentioned that your school had more Jewish, Italian, and even some female students," Dominick smiled at her in the rear view mirror, knowing that she wasn't done expounding yet.

"Did you also know that our sister college, New York Homeopathic Medical College, was one of the first to graduate Colored doctors? After the Civil War, in 1870, Susan McKinney-Steward graduated as New York State's first Colored woman doctor. Guess what? Her grave is at Green-Wood Cemetery. Let's find it today. I want to pay my respects."

"As you like, Doc. It's a nice gesture."

"Slavery ended, what, sixty years ago, but everywhere we've got segregation." She wanted to denounce it, but she was just a female doctor, trying to break through her own barriers. She wanted to tell this to Dominick, but she couldn't find the words

"History repeats itself," Dominick said, as if reading her mind. "It wasn't that long ago that we Italians and Irish were called Blacks. Well, probably many still think like that—there's no end to it."

Josephine turned to look back at the Jewish hospital's growing footprint. She'd heard that the hospital would be fundraising - how she wished she could be involved. Would they welcome her? She was a lone female doctor, an Italian-American and a Catholic—no, it was quite impossible. No matter, she hardly had time for such things. "I hear they're having a gala to raise money," she said to Dominick, pointing to the hospital. "I'd like to see the purchase of some new medical equipment. I read about new machines for measuring electrical currents in the heart and brain."

"Wow! You know, there's new electric automatic traffic signals, too. I'd like to see one on every street corner." Dominick sighed. "They've got a few signal towers in Manhattan, but a man still needs to climb up to operate those."

"Indeed, we both need new inventions." Josephine was still thinking about the hospital. She remembered again when Mother Cabrini was planning a new hospital wing. This woman had built so many hospitals and institutions—Josephine had been amazed listening to Mother Cabrini and the doctors discussing their plans. She had even dared to imagine herself one day using her medical expertise in such a philanthropic way. Perhaps when she returned to Manhattan? But that was looking more and more like a long shot, with her being a suspect in a murder investigation. She'd have to remain in Brooklyn for now, and while her life seemed modest, she was beginning to find it fulfilling. No, she decided, she wouldn't be helping to build new hospitals, at least not anytime soon.

After a few more quick turns, and a few more checks in his rear view mirror, Dominick bobbed the car over the next set of streetcar tracks and wove his way towards the cemetery. He followed the black metal fence to the corner of 5th Avenue, just before reaching South Slope, and turned right to arrive at the cemetery's main gate.

Josephine didn't find it odd to meet at a graveyard. For many Brooklynites, cemeteries were a spot of green in a city being taken over by concrete. She certainly wasn't superstitious and was too practical to believe in any ghosts. But it'd been only a few days since she'd seen Professor Janus Heath at the conference, and although he had seemed upset, he still was the kind old Professor she remembered from medical school. But why had Dr. Goldblum gotten so angry at him? Did they have another falling out later, and could Janus be Goldblum's killer? The thought seemed preposterous. But she had been reading Freudian psychology, and learned that those who seemed meek and mild-mannered may well turn out to be psychotic.

Suddenly, she felt that what she was planning to do was dangerous. She shouldn't be getting mixed up in a murder investigation! Then of course, there was that Detective O'Malley—it was as if by accusing her, he was throwing her into the investigation. Besides she was curious and puzzled—why would a murderer use Aconite as the coup de grace to kill a city health director? Was the Aconite plant sent to her as a warning? She was suddenly glad that big, strong Dominick was with her. It was unlikely that Janus would try anything with alarm clock Dominick around.

The Packard maneuvered through the solemn gothic-styled stone gates of the cemetery. Dominick took the first left and headed up Battle Hill. He pressed the gas pedal and the car surged forward, easily climbing to the highest hilltop in Brooklyn. As they drove upwards, Josephine was amazed by the commanding views of downtown Brooklyn. She could see beyond to the blue waters of New York Harbor, even as far as Lower Manhattan's financial district with its skyscrapers in the distance.

Dominick stopped the motor car, and turned to Josephine. "Did ya know, Doc Joe, that the most important Revolutionary War battle took place right here on this hill?"

"No. And I didn't know you read up on old war history, Dominick. What happened?" She was half-listening, thinking about how she would question Janus. She tried to remember what O'Malley had done when he questioned her—he'd listened a lot and prodded her to talk more.

"Well, the Battle of Brooklyn is really the story of three generals: George Washington, of course, for the Americans, then William Howe and Admiral Richard Howe, for the British." Dominick continued, intent on regaling Josephine with his military knowledge. "Of course, there were other minor generals commanding different flanks. Washington only had a few thousand men, so he was vastly outnumbered. He was gonna have to find a way to outwit the Brits, and he had to protect the two most important places, Lower Manhattan and Brooklyn Heights, from invasion. This very hill was important because they could see everything from here."

"That's interesting, Dominick. Please go on."

"As you probably know, Brooklyn Heights was within cannon striking distance of Manhattan."

"No, I didn't know that," mused Josephine. "There aren't that many cannons firing upon New York these days."

"Ha, very funny! Howe had 20,000 men to Washington's 3,000 or so. It was August, 1776 and the first major battle of the war. In those days, they'd announce it. Like you'd read it in the newspaper.

"General Howe landed at Gravesend, just south of your house, Doc. Admiral Howe was waiting there at The Narrows with a fleet of battleships to blockade the harbor. The Americans were expecting a confrontation here on this hill. But the British decided to sneak around to the side, which Washington had left undefended."

"Why would General Howe do that?" Josephine asked. "It must have meant marching far out of the way. I'd think that would be tiring." Josephine nodded for him to continue, while looking for Janus. She was glad that Dominick was distracting her.

"Not really," answered Dominick,"when I was in the army we had to march twenty miles every day and this was only a few miles or so. The Brits had good reconnaissance because General Clinton knew the terrain. So, the British snuck up, surrounded the Americans from all sides and eventually took this hill. Then they marched straight to Brooklyn Heights and got ready to take Manhattan."

"So the Americans didn't see any of this coming?" asked Josephine. She was trying to recall if Janus was still making remedies or if he'd been driven out of business, like most of the Homeopathic pharmacists.

"Nope. The Americans could only flee across the Gowanus Canal and many drowned. That should have been the end of them all, but it wasn't. That's what makes this story interesting."

"Why? What happened?" She was keeping an eye out for Janus, and glad that Dominick was distracting her from worrying. Did Janus pose a threat? He'd always been so kind to her.

"General Howe was the winner, but he got cocky. That's when he made his biggest mistake—he could've crushed Washington's army trapped between his forces and Admiral Howe, who was gonna sail through The Narrows. But General Howe did what he thought was the honorable thing—he offered Washington a surrender.:

"Did he take it?"

"Nope. He sent two lesser Generals to General Howe's boat to pretend to negotiate a surrender. The winds that night changed to southerly, and that prevented Admiral Howe's fleet from entering the harbor—remember they only had sails and oars back then, no motors. Then a thick fog set in, so the British went to sleep, thinking that the Americans would sit tight until morning. But Washington and his men got busy. They grabbed every boat they could find and escaped during the night under cover of fog, right under the Brits' noses!

"The next morning, the winds changed back and the fog lifted, the British warships came blazing in through The Narrows, but the American army was long gone!"

"So they did a disappearing act!"

"*Davvero!* True! In the end, the British won the battle anyway and occupied Manhattan and Long Island, but the Americans survived. It was lucky, they could've been slaughtered like sheep."

"Wow! Those three generals—they each made a lot of bumbling mistakes!"

Josephine saw Janus' car and started to open the door. She must remember to ask him if he had any blooming Aconite plants. "Well, I'm about to become a detective—wish me luck." Dominick turned off the engine. "Listen, Doc, be careful. I'll be watching and waiting alongside if you need me."

"Josephine!" Janus' voice called out. "I'm up here at the Altar of Liberty, by the statue of Minerva."

Josephine climbed among the graves to the crest of the hill. She hugged Janus' tall gaunt frame. He wore a gentleman's striped suit with starched color, a tightly high-buttoned vest, and an old-fashioned Bowler on his head. His eyes still twinkled mischievously, like a chemist's fire burning. "It's been a long time!" he laughed. "Since only a few days' ago! To what do I owe this honor to be double-blessed?"

"Oh! It's I who am honored! What a scenic place to meet—such beautiful views."

"It's the highest point in all of Brooklyn."

They gazed out over the grey cemetery markers to the lower New York Harbor. Janus reminded Josephine of a hawk, perched high and ready to swoop with his scientist's eye perusing the ground as if all the objects were his prey to gather for another experiment.

Janus pointed to the Statue of Liberty in the distance, and the southern tip of Manhattan, then turned to point at the bronze statue behind them. "This statue of Minerva, she's lovely isn't she? She's facing Lady Liberty across the bay with arm raised. It's as if they're waving hello to each other."

"Minerva, the Roman Goddess of Medicine!" exclaimed Josephine. "It's fitting that we meet here."

"She's also the Goddess of Wisdom and War. Smart and fearless, like you, Josephine. You were one of the few women to undertake such rigorous training—and one of my best students." He looked at her proudly.

"I guess Minerva was my inspiration then," she laughed. "But, Janus, I wanted to talk about Dr. Goldblum's death."

"Indeed." Janus looked at the view pensively. "Let's talk about that in a moment. Did you know that many of New York's most illustrious are buried here at Green-Wood? And there are many stories to tell—the dead do speak."

Josephine was wondering what he meant, when he pointed to a distant monument in a peaked gothic style.

"There's the Brown family plot, and a monument to the wreck of one of their ships, the S.S. Arctic. Unfortunately, the crew's dereliction of duty resulted in the drowning of the passengers. The crew saved themselves first, letting the women and children drown. A tragedy—an utter failure of honor."

"That's a terrible story!"

Janus looked down the hill from where they stood and pointed to a patch of green far below. "I wish to be buried there, in my family plot, in this beautiful rural place. Far away from the crowded and corrupt city, where they're digging up cemeteries to build more apartments. This earth here won't ever be disturbed. It would be comforting for me to rest here when my time comes, knowing that I'll not be turned out of my eternal bed by the bulldozers of progress."

"Janus, what do you mean?"

"Progress knows no boundaries, that is all."

There was silence, and Josephine fidgeted. She didn't know how to get around to the subject of the murder politely, so she just blurted it out. "Janus, I saw you argue with Dr. Goldblum. Did you kill him?"

Janus looked startled, but he pointed to an ornate mausoleum below. "Look at that. The Billingfords built it. The family got very rich after patenting a stylish fountain pen. Everyone needs a fountain pen." He reached in his pocket, but only pulled out a gold fountain pen.

Josephine looked at him questioningly. His face flashed heatedly and his eyes flared. "Some say there was a fellow who designed a better fountain pen, but he didn't patent it."

Josephine took a step back, for she had never seen Janus angry. He was now as angry as Goldblum had been.

"My family has been making Homeopathic remedies for over a century," Janus continued, his hawkish beak turning sharper. "But Homeopathic medicines are by their very nature not easy to patent."

"Is that what you and Dr. Goldblum were arguing about at the conference?" Josephine asked. "You'd better explain. I understand little about business."

"I'm sorry." He was flustered but quickly regained his composure. "Our family laboratories were inspired by Minerva, the goddess of medicine you see here. To make medicines to heal the poor and sick is my family's great honor." He looked at the horizon. "Oh, there's still plenty of money in it, and my family became very wealthy as we expanded our laboratories. We use only natural ingredients: minerals, plants, etc... It's their naturalness that makes them healing and pure. But, alas, these things can't be patented."

Janus sat down on the steps of a nearby mausoleum, to collect himself before he continued. He motioned for Josephine to take a seat beside him. "It's a question of honor. This is what I tried to tell that Goldblum fellow. He never was a bright bulb, one of my most un-noteworthy students."

She sat down cautiously. But he smiled paternally at Josephine.

"You were one of the brightest. You could grasp the electromagnetic power of the Homeopathic compound when diluted beyond the Avogadro Number." Josephine nodded.

His tone became pensive once more. "My divulgence is not meant to endanger you, Josephine. I was glad you called. I needed to confess to someone who would understand my motives. Better than the police, I'm afraid." He looked guiltily at his former student. "I confess I knew full well what I was doing."

"Janus," Josephine said slowly. It still seemed unlikely that he could harm a fly, but many seemingly nice people were capable of murder. "Tell me what exactly happened." She looked nervously over her shoulder to make sure Dominick hadn't walked off to explore any Revolutionary graves. He was leaning against the mausoleum with his arms crossed, protectively watching Josephine.

"Dr. Goldblum called after the conference to meet me. He apologized for getting angry with me at the conference, and he said he had something to show me—his report. I suppose he came as a gentleman would, to warn me about it...." Janus trailed off anxiously. "I suggested we meet here, it was such a lovely day.

But I couldn't believe what he was threatening—that all I had worked for—everything would be lost.

"You, see, he was going to put an end to my Homeopathic pharmacy, the nail in the coffin, so to speak.

"Goldblum decided that the provings we Homeopaths rely upon were not adequate. This, of course, was just a silly excuse. His true aim was to start patenting and selling new drugs, Allopathic ones. He said that if I converted and joined him, we'd be rich."

Josephine was beginning to see a connection. "So Dr. Goldblum wanted to put you and Homeopathic pharmacies out of business?"

"Yes, I was shocked," Janus said. stamping his foot. "But Goldblum talked about making money! How gauche! As if that's all that matters in life!"

Josephine didn't want to interrupt Janus' confession. He seemed to be getting fired up again. Dominick looked ready to jump into action. She remembered the words Detective O'Malley used. "Please go on, Janus."

"He wanted me to set up a new laboratory. But Allopathic drugs are made from high concentrations of substances at toxic levels. This indeed requires them to have extensive safety controls to protect the patient. But Homeopathic drugs are diluted to extremely low levels of toxicity—that's why they are safer to begin with.

"You see, Goldblum's report was about to change everything!"

Josephine had come to find a blooming Aconite plant, but now she was finding that Goldblum's report was the real danger.

So that's why Dr. Goldblum was murdered! But how had Janus done it?

"My life's work was going to be destroyed!" Janus was red with rage. "Distilling the purest and finest ingredients, preparing that wonderful Mother Tincture. It's Minerva's teachings that I needed to protect..."

"What happened next?"

"We argued some more. But it was impossible for Goldblum to consider the presence of the potentized active compound in my remedies complying with any article of his report. In practice, this would have excluded from patentability all of my Homeopathic medicaments, even those I created in twelfth times dilutions!"

"Janus, how did you kill Dr. Goldblum?" Josephine interrupted.

"We had a long discussion, right here before this statue of Minerva. Finally, Goldblum assured me his report would state that Homeopathic remedies could still be sold. But that was disingenuous, he was merely trying to soften the blow. My remedies would soon only be available in pharmacies without any prescription. Such a dangerous thought! Patients shouldn't be allowed to medicate themselves with my remedies! You see, Goldblum warned that my remedies, which I create so carefully, would soon be picked up willy-nilly by any common layperson, like gumdrops at the drugstore counter! A person wouldn't even need to be under the care of a Homeopathic physician. Our business is already suffering—that would be the death knell!

"And then he had the nerve to suggest that there was still money to be made. I told him that his whole idea was scandalous!"

"Then, you gave him an Aconite flower from your laboratory?" prodded Josephine.

"No!" Janus looked surprised. "We argued. I kept trying to reason with him, at first," Janus looked down, shaking his head. "We disagreed on the fundamentals of the Homeopathic provings. We've already published our findings. Goldblum said that wouldn't matter any longer."

"So when you both couldn't come to any mutually agreeable position, you got angry?" Josephine cautiously prodded him further.

"Yes I got angry! Of course I did! And I regret what I did next." Janus rose up and brought his fist across the air. "We were like schoolboys again. We fought, and I being the more agile man, had the advantage. He was a coward and ran behind the gravestones. I gave chase. He tried to round the monuments, seeking cover behind that large one over there, but I snuck up upon him and butted him. He fell, striking his head on a tombstone."

Janus pointed to a nearby grave that had a blood smear across the top.

"Goldblum was stunned, but he wasn't dead. I assure you that. He said his head was pounding. He even asked me for a tablet of Aconite. The irony!"

"I expressed immediately my regret for the row. He was unwell, but he insisted he could make his way home. I don't know what then happened, I can't understand it myself."

"Aconite is a remedy I make often. There wasn't any attenuated poison from the flower or root in the dose I gave him, I swear! But something must have gone wrong, the poison molecule must have taken hold and he died."

Janus sank to his knees against the base of the Minerva sculpture. "I am responsible, I killed Goldblum."

"Janus—did you give him a tablet or fresh Aconite flowers?"

"A tablet of course," he looked up at Josephine. "The plant itself is highly toxic and would have caused almost instantaneous respiratory and cardiac arrest, leading to a sure death."

"Where were you that evening?"

"I was working with my former students in my lab, making remedies."

"Janus, you didn't kill Goldblum!" Josephine exclaimed with relief.

"I didn't?"

"No! You struck him, and yes, you gave him a tablet of *Aconitum napellus* for his injury. But that didn't kill him. Goldblum was killed at The Narrows—I was there and I saw that Goldblum had fresh vividly purple Aconite flowers in his mouth!"

"But that's impossible," Janus declared.

"Did you send me an Aconite bouquet?"

He looked bewildered. "No, of course not. I'm not the romantic type."

Josephine was relieved, for she would never have believed that Janus could kill anyone. But if Janus didn't kill Goldblum, then who did?

"Janus, this means that the murderer is still out there," she said with alarm. "Have you told me everything?"

"Of course," said Janus. He stared at the statue of Minerva with a worried expression.

Josephine watched him. Who else knew enough about Aconite to prepare a deadly dose and would also have a motive to want Goldblum dead? A Homeopath, perhaps the same one who had sent her Aconite flowers after the conference. True, she was outspoken, 'rebellious'—but who would want to frame her and end her career?

Chapter 12 - Booze Blanks

E vening office hours resumed. Josephine was back home, at
work, where she felt more calm, but the events at the cemetery had unsettled her. *Someone, a Homeopath, is trying to frame
me for murder.* She thought back to the conference and all the
doctors and professionals there. Who were Homeopaths and
who were Allopaths?

Josephine's notoriety had brought a steady stream of new
patients, and her office waiting room was again full. Using her
newly purchased flexible bin-aural stethoscope, with two tubes
to listen with both ears in stereo, she could diagnose patients
more easily. For example, she easily determined that a patient's
raspy cough was severe bronchitis. She prepared a prescription
for cough syrup with morphine and an expectorant syrup of
ipecac to loosen the phlegm and advised warm compresses to be
applied to the thorax and chest. "If you get a fever, call me immediately."

Another patient had a low-grade temperature, a sore throat
and swollen glands. 'Possible Tonsillitis' she noted in his patient
file. She had been very good at cutting the tonsils with her
scalpel, but nowadays this was done in a hospital by otolaryn-

gologists. "Let's have you gargle and apply warm mustard compresses to the throat. I'll give you a prescription for a vodka gargle with mint, eucalyptus and thyme. It's much safer and better than what you can find from those quacks at the corner selling their tonics. If the infection doesn't go away in three days, or if you get a fever, call me immediately. I may have to refer you for a tonsillectomy."

Sophie, seeing how busy the office was, had appointed herself as office secretary, finding patient files and answering the telephone. "Doc Joe, Professor Janus Heath rang again and wants you to meet him tomorrow at his laboratory. One thirty in the afternoon. He said he has something important he needs to show you." Josephine thought about that for a moment— Janus had confessed to fighting with Goldblum, not killing him, but he seemed suspiciously nervous at the cemetery, like there was more that he wasn't willing to say. He'd certainly incriminated himself by harming Goldblum, so she felt sure he was holding something back. "Please ring him and tell him I'll see him tomorrow."

"Next patient," she called. Sophie handed her a file, and she noted that having a secretary was helping her see more patients quicker.

Andy entered, holding his head. "I feel terrible, Doc. I'm spending a lot of time in my cellar where it's cold 'n damp."

"Well, you can't get a cold from a cellar unless there are germs down there. Has anyone been in that cellar with a cold?"

"Maybe," said Andy sheepishly, not wanting to reveal that bootleggers go in and out of his cellar. They came just two days ago to haul out a new batch of whiskey from his still. Josephine already suspected that most of the men were brewing their own and selling as much as they could at a profit. She had overheard at the grocers that they were earning $15 a case!

Josephine took out her Prohibition Rx pad and wrote him a prescription for *Fructus spiritus*, or whiskey, to be taken with meals. "Do stay out of that cellar!"

She looked at the prescription pad and saw that the next number skipped ahead by one. That's odd, she thought, there must have been a misprint at the US Treasury.

"Thank you, Doc Joe," he said, ecstatic that he was going to get his own bottle of imported Scotch, and legally, too. Back in the Waiting Room, he whispered to his friends, "I got me a Booze Blank!"

Mike was next. He complained of a cold and sneezed several times in a row into his handkerchief. "That repetitive sneezing is indicative of an allergy, not a cold," Josephine said, placing a thermometer in his mouth. "Maybe it's a reaction to something here, like the antiseptic."

"No, Doc, I'm sure it's a terrible cold, and whiskey would really warm me up," he managed to sputter out while keeping the thermometer under his tongue. As soon as it was removed, he forced a loud sneeze again. "I feel bleary and weak."

"Well, you don't have a temperature, your lungs sound clear and your heart is fine," Josephine said, after listening to his chest. "But you do look a little piqued. Your blood vessels are dilated on your nose, hmmm, have you been drinking much?"

"Well, I really need whiskey so I can sleep at night. My head is all congested."

"I'll write you a Prohibition prescription for three days. You'll be glad to get some of the real whiskey to put you to sleep! But please don't drink that illegal moonshine, it's tainted with poisonous alcohol - it can kill, cripple or blind you."

She thought that Mike might be alcoholic, and in that case it would be better to wean him off whiskey gradually, and she preferred he drink the good stuff. A few of her patients had been poisoned from the bootleggers cutting whiskey with toxic industrial alcohol. Josephine took out her Rx pad again, and flipping through it, noticed that several more numbers skipped. *I'll have to report this.*

Alcoholism had to be treated as a matter of public health— she had heard the doctors speak about addiction at the conference. They suggested a short three day course of liquor, in order that patients don't risk their lives drinking the poisoned hootch from the bootleggers. Some addicted patients even purchased cough syrup full of morphine from unscrupulous tonic salesmen—anything to get "zozzled."

Josephine, like many physicians during Prohibition, was learning how to treat alcohol addiction as a part of her practice. But she'd seen how addicts turn into criminals at the Tombs prison, and was worried about Mike. She decided to check on him in three days. His behavior had been getting rather punchy. She'd look to the medical journals tonight to do some research.

The day continued at its hectic pace with a house call in Bensonhurst for a birth, an adorable baby boy. She made some file notes: Mother had prolonged labour. Placenta regular. Little extra bleeding. Healthy cry." Josephine continued annotating the day's many cases, wiping her brow.

Office hours closed at 6 p.m. and she was exhausted. She asked Dominick to close the front gate, cleaned the examination room and set her medical instruments in a pot of boiling water on the stove to sterilize them. She also brewed a cup of chamomile and linden flower tea, but that did little to relax her. Her mind was in turmoil. As she sipped the tea, she had a moment to think of the day's revelations.

Janus had fought with Goldblum, so that explained the hematoma on Goldblum's head. But that didn't explain who killed him with Aconite. There must be something else I'm not seeing yet, she thought, but the day had been busy with no time to do any more detective work. She realized that she might never find the killer on her own.

She heated up a can of chicken noodle soup, adding some carrots and brussel sprouts. She ate dejectedly, then decided to lie down and close her eyes to rest and fell into a slumber.

Next thing she knew, she was woken by a loud knocking on the front door.

Chapter 13 - A Flapper

Saturday night...

D oc Joe!" familiar voices called out. "It's us! We must see you!"

Josephine opened the door. Sophie and Maria entered in a swirl of perfume and glitz. Josephine was startled and barely recognized them. Andy, Antonio and Mike stayed on the balcony smoking. Josephine noticed that her patients were all in evening attire, the ladies wearing fashionable dresses and the men in evening jackets. The ladies had painted their faces with outlandish eye makeup and bright red lipstick. The men wore pin-striped snazzy suits in bright colors with matching bow ties, high rise cuffs over their baggy wide-leg pants, and sported shiny two-toned shoes. They topped it off with snappy fedoras. The ladies' low cut sequined evening dresses were made of light as fluff gossamer silk, with ostrich feather boas thrown over their shoulders. They must have spent a fortune on these clothes, thought Josephine. The group was sparkling like a Saturday night marquee. Josephine felt like the plain duckling, in her dowdy house dress and lab coat. She pulled her collar up tighter.

"Where are Gianni and Teresa, your babies?" Josephine asked Maria.

"Gianni's all better now. Your *Chamomila* worked, grazie, thank you. Gabe's watchin' 'em wit' my niece, Natalia. Tey are letting me have a girl's night out."

"I think Gabe and Natalia wanted to spend some time alone, too," laughed Sophie.

"We was worried about you, so Antonio, Andy and I tagged along," Mike added.

"Because we 'eard that awful evening radio broadcast," Antonio said. "The police said Goldblum was poisoned wit' Aconite."

"Well, that's a relief, at least I won't be arrested." Josephine replied. O'Malley must have finally believed her.

"No, don't you see?" said Sophie, "that puts you in more danger! You are one of the few people who know what Aconite is. The police now know that."

"And if te murderer can pin te crime on you, maybe by killin' you.... oh, I don't a wanna t'ink about it." Maria began to cry.

Sophie continued explaining. "We were out at Sam's having a good time, but we couldn't enjoy ourselves knowing you are here alone, in danger."

"Sam's? You mean the deli at the corner? Why is it open at night?"

"It's a speakeasy, didn't you know?"

Josephine shook her head. "But Dominick is here, at least I think he is. He wouldn't let anyone harm me. And why would the police want me anyway?

"They're looking for a Homeopath," said Sophie.

"You're a 'omeopath, we saw you wit' tat box," Maria said.

"But my remedies are diluted many times over. There's not enough poison to kill anyone," Josephine protested. "Only a pharmacist would have enough Aconite plants!" She suddenly realized that she now had a stalk of Aconite. Whoever sent it wanted to implicate her. Fortunately, Dominick was there when she found the flowers on her doorstep.

"Maybe he's te murderer?" Maria asked. "Tat professor, Janus Heath?"

"Not Janus. He told me what happened at the cemetery," Josephine explained. "Goldblum wanted to put him out of business. So they fought at Green-Lawn. Goldblum fell down on a tombstone and got a nasty bump on the head, but he was still alive when he left the cemetery. Janus denied killing him. But now I don't know whether to believe him or not."

"He 'ssa got a strong motive," Antonio pointed out.

"True, but if he was in the pharmacy working that night—I have to question him again. Darn, why didn't I think about that before. Well, I'll see him tomorrow anyway. I still don't think he did it. Besides, he wouldn't have had time to get down to The Narrows."

"If he didn't kill Goldblum, then who?" asked Sophie.

"Another Homeopath, maybe one I met, I think," said Josephine, unsure. This detective work was proving more difficult than she thought.

"Let's think about it. Goldblum was killed at The Narrows," Mike had entered and was listening. "Surely, there must be a connection. Tell us what you saw where they found the body."

Josephine began describing the crime scene. "Goldblum wasn't dragged there—his shoes weren't dirty and there were no scuff marks. He must have been meeting someone," she remembered.

"But why would he go to that deserted Brooklyn shoreline? How or why did he take Aconite?" Sophie asked.

"Maybe he was held down and forced." Josephine ventured.

"But you said t'ere was no sign of a struggle, 'cept for 'riggling 'round on te ground from poison, " Maria added. "And his head bump was earlier, from Janus."

"Yes, he took the Aconite from Janus. Goldblum must have believed it was a safe dose." Josephine's pulse quickened.

"At The Narrows, after taking Aconite, maybe he realized something was wrong and cried out. Or maybe his killer cruelly told him the dose was lethal?" said Sophie excitedly.

Josephine felt another spark. "He must have known his killer and trusted him."

But then dismay. *Oh, dear!* she realized, *it still must be another doctor.*

"That Goldblum was in high society, sounds like he liked money," said Sophie.

"Janus claims that Goldblum wanted to sell more drugs," added Josephine.

"Yep, they're our most likely suspects - Homeopathic doctors, pharmacists or those that are in the business. Could be the mob, too. They got their fingers in everything." said Mike.

"How do we spy on any of these people?" asked Josephine.

Sophie spoke her thoughts out loud. "This killer has brains and guts—I read a lot of detective novels. You're right, Doc Joe, to suspect other Homeopaths. The victim is usually killed by someone he knows."

"He thinks he's framed you, but maybe he's unsure if his plan will work. He probably wants to live it up just in case the police come for him," added Mike. "That's what I'd do."

"Or maybe to fool everyone that he has no worries and isn't guilty, he'd go to a flashy place to be seen, with music, liquor, you know, putting on the Ritz," said Sophie. "There's one place that anybody with money goes to be seen out and about on a Saturday night—a Night Club."

"And you, Doc, you, too, might as well enjoy a last night of freedom!" added Mike. Maria and Sophie made a face at him.

"But first," said Sophie, stroking her chin. "You'll need to be someone else."

"What do you mean?" asked Josephine.

"You can't go out, your picture's in te papers," agreed Maria. "You need a disguise."

Sophie whispered to Maria. "Let's find some makeup and an evening dress."

"It's gonna take some work," Maria whispered back. "I mean look atta Doc. She's no flapper!"

"Well, we have to try something." Sophie turned back to the men. "You boys get Dominick and the car ready. Maria and I will go to work." The girls pushed the boys back out on the balcony, and led Josephine to her dressing area.

"If we take off your glasses, why, you've got beautiful baby blues!" Sophie said happily. She and Maria started singing the hit song, "Five foot two, eyes of blue! Could she, could she, could she, coo, has anybody seen my gal? Turned up nose, turned down hose, Flapper yessir, one of those, has anybody seen my girl?" as they began rustling through Josephine's dressing table. "Five foot two, eyes of blue, But oh! what those five foot could do. Has anybody seen my gal?"

They removed Josephine's stethoscope from around her neck, her shapeless white lab coat, as well as the plain housedress underneath,

"There, now you're no longer a Lady Doctor," Sophie laughed and Maria nodded. "Much better."

Then they applied face powder in a puff of dust to Josephine's face, then smokey silver eyeshadow combined with a heavy streak of eye liner and bright rouge to her cheeks. Then they slicked her hair back with glossy oil. Rummaging through her armoire, they found a slinky, low cut evening dress buried in the back, the most elegant one a patient had ever made for her. It was sheer sparkling lilac silk with a crystal beaded overlay and a small velvet bow rested on each shoulder.

"Isn't this rather risqué?" complained Josephine.

"Shhh! Doncha worry," replied Maria. "It's darlin'!"

The skimpy dress had just enough opaque sequined panels, Josephine thought, to reveal and hide vital body parts.

Sophie contributed her own swirling shimmy beads. "See, this is perfect for dancing. And we must find you a slip—when your partner spins you, your dress will lift to reveal these little frills underneath." Josephine's jaw dropped—she felt like she was wearing a beaded curtain over a ballet tulle.

Next they pulled on light matching gloves to her upper arms, and threw on Maria's rope of white pearly beads.

"What'll we do for 'er 'ead?" Maria asked.

Sophie fashioned a headband with turquoise ribbon and a pin, adding one of her outrageously fluffy purple ostrich feathers. Finally, they took two thick silver faux fox collars off Josephine's coats and sewed them together for a boa.

Josephine stood awkwardly in front of the mirror. She adjusted the dress to make sure a few silver sequins covered some of her embarrassment. She felt she could barely move or the dress might fall off or float away.

"Wowee! Doc Joe, you're now an "It" girl, a gorgeous sexy flapper!" Sophie said, posing alongside in her own sheer dress. "You've got to have some T-strap shoes here somewhere, we could paint them with my sparkles, and then you are ready for a night on the town!"

"You're a SHEEBA!" hailed Maria, ever the romantic, thinking of Rudy Valentino's movie. "Let's go find you a SHEIK!"

Chapter 14 - Carpe Noctem

The Packard's big V-8 engine soared, even under the weight of its seven passengers. Dominick had no trouble maneuvering it around ruts in the Brooklyn streets, dodging potholes gallantly until he reached the paved streets in downtown Brooklyn near the courthouse. He took a left on Joralemon Street, passing the large gothic brownstone Brooklyn Female Academy, now renamed Packer Collegiate Institute, with its heavy arched oak doors and the bell tower of its attached chapel. Josephine had been happy with her public high school in Gramercy Park, but she'd longed to go to a private female academy. Was Dominick driving round the block to show her what she missed? He kept checking the rear view mirror, and was driving around in circles. He did like to show off the fancy car, but it was already 11:00 p.m. and they wanted to get to a club before the 12:20 a.m. show.

How she wanted to see singers and dancers perform! She'd heard all about the famous Colored performers and what spectacular performances they gave. Never having been to an evening club, she wondered what the experience would be like. It seemed that everyone went out on the town to establishments serving alcohol, and that a raid was a rarity. It was 1929, and everyone was fed up with Prohibition. Besides, the police arrested the owners and bartenders, but they seldom bothered arresting patrons anymore, when they couldn't get convictions. Even the judges were seen out at evening clubs. More people were flouting Prohibition and now there were hundreds of speakeasies with liquor flowing nightly. Josephine was getting used to the feel of the silky dress on her skin, and the excitement of her patients was starting to rub off on her.

Dominick made several more turns around the courthouse, then opened the manifold. He had recently tuned the engine, and relished the 108 horsepower. He headed for the ramp to the Brooklyn Bridge and gunned it.

The passengers in the rear paid no mind to the forces of physics wrenching them about, for they had discovered Josephine medical liquor bar. It was more extensive than previously thought, with extra bottles of vodka and whiskey in the side compartments.

Andy teased Mike, saying, "Too bad, it's only rubbing alcohol and iodine!"

"Naw, ya kiddin' me," Mike said, grabbing the bottles and sniffing. "Hey, stop pulling my leg, and pass a glass!"

The patients grew even more excited as they crossed over the lighted bridge into Manhattan. It was like entering an island of temptation, and they were now feeling warm and flush from the whiskey. Dominick was having a grand time driving up Broadway, then over to Park Avenue. Josephine marveled at all the skyscrapers and tall apartment buildings with windows lit up brightly like fireflies.

"I wish I lived 'ere," sighed Maria.

"No ya don't," said Antonio, "we'd never fit all your clothes into one of those shoebox apartments!"

"Or your wine barrels!"

The group was as bright-eyed as the lights of the city. What an amazing feat, Josephine thought, that every building was electrified in just a few years and seemed to be lit with hundreds of light bulbs. Even the street lamps were no longer gas and newly electrified.

"Should we go to the Cotton Club?" asked Andy.

"Oh, I don't know," Josephine shook her head. "I heard some clubs are segregated. I don't agree with that and it's my one night out!"

"Even if they've got Duke Ellington? He's playing 'Creole Love Call'?" asked Sophie. Josephine hadn't the slightest idea what song she meant, although it sounded like it must be a hit.

"It's so sad that Florence Mills died a few years ago, she was amazing! What a dancer!" Sophie added.

"Did she die from TB? That's sad. Well, what about Adelaide Hall?" Mike suggested. "Maybe she's performing somewhere tonight."

"I read in Variety that she's in Paris. The best Colored singers perform in Europe - they face less prejudice there. Josephine Baker is now playing at the Folies Bergères!"

"I'd like to see her dancing naked with that skirt made of bananas!"

"Oh, don't be ridiculous, Mike," said Josephine. She was shocked imagining this. She was a little envious that these entertainers were taking those sleek steamers back and forth across the Atlantic. She wished she could go to Europe, too, to see where her mother had come from. Plus, she'd read about medical discoveries in bacteriology in Paris and London.

"How about The Plantation Club?" Sophie interrupted her thoughts of Europe.

"No, Doc Joe won't like the Southern theme," Dominick said.

"The Lafayette?"

"That one closed or was raided, I think."

"How about Texas Mae's Roadhouse —uh, that's in Midtown, naw, forget about it."

"How about The Oasis? It just opened this month and it's got the biggest stage and dance floor, they say. 50 cent cover, though."

"But only the gents pay."

"Wait a minute! I've heard of that one," Josephine interrupted. "Those Yorkvillains, those doctors from my medical school, they were raving about it."

"Good, if they go there, we'll find 'em—it's Saturday night," said Mike.

"Ok, let's head uptown to Harlem. It's the cat's pah-jamas!" Dominick swerved the car. "Hey, Doc, the speakeasies there are integrated—Black and Tan. You've gotta see that at least once in your lifetime."

Josephine thought of Janus' quote: *Tempora mutantur, nos et mutamur in illis,* Times are changing, and we are changed within it. She could only hope!

As they turned onto Lenox Avenue, Josephine rolled down the window. She saw Colored couples walking arm in arm, alongside White couples, and even more surprisingly, several mixed-race couples snuggling. This might be the only area of the city where Jim Crow laws were openly flaunted, and she smiled in relief.

The speakeasies were easy to spot, one right after the other. They passed a few clubs that had been raided with heavy padlocks on the doors, but many more were wide open with jazz music escaping from inside.

"The police can't raid all the clubs," Andy said. "There's literally hundreds. This week, it looks like Connie's and New Amsterdam Roof got raided."

"Yeah, "Prohibition Portia" has been at it," said Mike.

Mabel Willebrandt, US Assistant Attorney General, was still leading the Temperance charge. Nonetheless, there were many other speakeasies to choose from, as they passed Tillie's, Edith's Clam house and the Log Cabin. Party goers filled the streets, holding hands, and shouting in loud drunken voices. More jazz could be heard blaring whenever a door sprung open.

Dominick found The Oasis easily, for it was the biggest and brightest, lit up with strings of lights with a long awning. Couples in furs and silk top hats were seen entering, and some staggering out. Several large police town cars were parked out front. The club's billboard promised "an exotic and over the top" show offering "the famous Maude Russell and her Ebony Steppers" performing songs from their hit show The Blackbirds of 1928. It also teased "a special guest performer for a musical number."

Dominick parked just across the street, and two guys in pinstriped suits stubbed out their cigarettes and walked over. Dominick got out and spoke to them, then handed them some dollar bills.

He motioned for Josephine and the group to follow him as he walked down a few steps to the doorway. He knocked, a slot opened, and with a word he pushed $2 through it.

"You know de password?" asked Antonio.

"Yep, those sharks told me. This is the busiest gin joint tonight. All the big wigs are here. Even Mayor Jimmy Walker's inside, so it's not gonna get raided," Dominick said.

The bolt slid open, and Josephine, Dominick and the group of patients sashayed inside.

"Welcome to The Oasis! Foist drinks are on de house for Cleopatras. Marc Anthonies youz fellas may choose from our fine cigars, after you pay de admission price, 'course." A dark-haired, broad-chested man greeted the group raucously. with a decidedly Boweryese dialect. He wore a traditional flowing *gallebaya* from Egypt with a silly red *tarboosh* with a tassel on his head. Offering the ladies a "Pyramid", which was a triangular chip for a free drink, and the men a camel-stamped box of matches, he encouraged them to "Drink up, get plastered, and enjoy de show!"

Ever since the 1922 discovery of King Tutankhamen's tomb, New Yorkers had been in the throes of Egyptomania. The tomb was excavated bit by bit, revealing more of its multitude of treasures. New photographs of mummies and funereal ornaments streamed over the newswires from the Valley of the Kings. Josephine had seen a photograph of the boy king's magnificent death mask in solid gold—no one could help being mesmerized by that face with its captivating kohl-lined eyes and elaborate headdress inlaid with turquoise, cornelian and lapis lazuli. Nothing like this had ever been seen before from an ancient, previously thought primitive culture. The treasures confirmed that far-flung Near Eastern civilizations were once as glorious and wealthy as Roaring 20's New York. Important artifacts, such as glazed faience beads and small funerary objects, were making their way, with dubious provenance, into New Yorkers' private collections.

"Have you seen the Brooklyn Museum's Egyptian exhibition? I liked the early artifacts from the 1906 de Morgan excavations in Ma'mariya, dating back to 3500 B.C.," Josephine asked Maria, who looked incomprehensibly back. "That bird-like woman fertility goddess figurine was outstanding."

"I'm so glad you went outta your office to a museum —ittsa good place for you to meet a man. Maybe he'll like a science, too."

Their attention was drawn back to the club's over-the-top grandeur as the orchestra began playing. The Oasis was massive, much larger than it looked from the outside. Its numerous tables were packed with people smoking and drinking surrounding the immense dance floor, with the twelve-piece orchestra playing at the far end. The best tables were the ones tightly packed along the dance floor, and at one of these Josephine could see a group of men dressed in pin-stripes with several bleached blonde molls seated between them. Champagne on ice stood in buckets, replenished often by scurrying wait staff.

"You don't have to hide the liquor under the table in this joint?" Mike asked.

"Shush! This is a fancy club!" Sophie admonished him.

The extravagant stage of The Oasis was decorated with giant plaster of Paris pyramids and date palms. Despite the grandeur, Josephine was disappointed by the vestiges of racism: the performers were mostly Coloreds, and the patrons gawking at them were mostly Whites. Next time, she thought, they would try one of the speakeasies on the side streets where she had seen the happy kissing couples.

Notwithstanding, the bright spectacle was unlike anything she'd ever seen before. The smokey air swirled like silken ribbons, and what appeared to be *felucca* sails billowed in the dusky lights. The syncopated jazz music propelled the crowd of swaying couples. Even Josephine bounced a little more in her step. She held her head high, as if she were one of the Nubian goddesses whose likenesses were painted on the club's walls.

Soon the show began. The performers had sexy, sullen expressions just like an Egyptian painting. Bare-chested muscular African men led draped stuffed camels on wheels across the stage. The dancers flashed by in sheer silk tunics that barely hid their lean, smooth-skinned bodies. They wore bejeweled bracelets, neck collars and belts. As they danced, they pulled Pharoah gold masks on and off their beautiful coffee-colored faces, revealing their exaggerated eyes exotically outlined in heavy black kohl. The dancers moved seductively in a syncopated rhythm, keeping their arms and legs outstretched and rigid, like Egyptian hieroglyphs. The beat-heavy tempo of the Arabic drum combined with a flirtatious and lilting *ney* flute were spell-binding.

Soon the dance ended and the famous Fletcher Henderson orchestra made a guest appearance. Couples filled the dance floor, hanging tightly to one another. Josephine thought they danced a little too closely.

"They'z cutting a rug, must be shocking!" Maria said, laughing at her own joke.

Maria's English had definitely improved, thought Josephine. She looked around the evening club with a happiness she hadn't felt in a long time. Her patients were smiling and seemed to like her new alter-ego. Her life had been constrained by her profession— it wasn't respectable to be seen out dancing and drinking. But now she was a flapper, an "It" girl, just like Clara Bow.

The bar was almost a city block long, with twenty barmen rapidly mixing colorful cocktails. They sent them sliding along the counter to wait staff who picked up the glasses and set empty ones down in rapid succession.

A lively man came onstage to thunderous applause, and began singing, "*Toot toot tootsie, goodbye!*"

"Isn't that Al Jolson? I can't believe it!" Josephine said. "Maybe it's a really good look-alike."

"No, it's him!" said Sophie. "Thank goodness he's not in black-face—you'd be mad! They say he helped integrate clubs by getting white people used to the idea of black performers. That's sad, huh? What a world we live in."

Al Jolson was dancing up a storm and swinging his hips to the music. Couples on the dance floor began singing the catchy refrain, "*Toot toot tootsie don't cry!*" Josephine stared wide-eyed. How did he dance so fast?

Dominick seemed to have an "in" with the hosts, the other men in pinstripes seated at the best table, who subtly raised their drinks in his direction. Josephine and her group were shown to one of the larger tables in a prime location with a clear view of the stage.

A pretty waitress soon enough locked on to Dominick. "Hey there, you're a brawny Bruno!" she called. "So handsome and built like a battleship! " She was squeezing his biceps.

"Two Black Cats, doll," Dominick ordered, and she put two packs of cigarettes on the table in front of him.

"Brandy Punch for the ladies and Scotch for the gents?" she asked, then leaned over to whisper in his ear. He laughed. Any closer and she'd fall right into his lap!

Dominick nodded, giving her the Pyramid free drink cards. "And make it the Real McCoy." He patted her rear as she left. Josephine had never considered Dominick a catch, despite his dashing looks, but now she stared at him aghast, wondering what went on in his garage apartment.

"What's a Brandy Punch?" she asked Maria.

"Brandy wit' berries and fruit, shaken wit' ice. They give you a tall straw."

"Or you could try a Cobbler. Dat's sherry wit' slices of orange," Antonio added.

The party at the neighboring table was well under way. A group of well-dressed gents in white tuxedo jackets and black ties were smoking Cuban cigars and ordering buckets of champagne. A gaggle of girls accompanied them. A flapper wearing a thin-strapped dress that looked more like an under slip was pressing against an ebullient man who seemed to be a natural comedian. He had wavy hair parted in the middle, kept long and falling over his eyes to his prominent nose. He sported a bushy mustache on his upper lip and wore unfashionably square glasses.

"Oh, Arnie," the girl laughed, rustling his hair. "You're a hoot!" They were necking.

"You see," Arnie deadpanned, "Some doctors sing to their patients to get them to relax. But I clown around. I wanted to be in Vaudeville, but my mother wouldn't let me."

Josephine leaned in a little closer, trying to get a good look at the joker. She felt a moment of panic; it was Arnie, a Yorkvillain, and alongside him was Vic. He'd written all those awful jokes about her in the yearbook. Boy, would she like to give him a piece of her mind.

"Who feels my beating pulse in sheer delight?" Arnie began a burlesque-style verse, raising his eyebrows up and down and bobbing his fat cigar for a bawdy double-entendre.

"My wife? Oh! how I wish she might!"

"Who then?" the others asked. Arnie paused for effect, then answered loudly, *"My Doctor!"*

The others erupted in laughter. The punchline seemed to be *"My Doctor."*

Vic took a turn with a verse, adding his own overtly carnal spin on the intimacy of a doctor-patient relationship.

"Who thumps my rump and thumps my chest,
pokes and pinches me with zest,
then says go home and get some rest?"

"My Doctor!" the table answered in unison, laughing cheekily.

Sophie turned to look, a bit surprised. "How risqué! And they're flashing a lot of lettuce!" She liked to use grocery slang for money. "All those drinks and champagne."

"Those are the Yorkvillains, from my medical school," Josephine croaked nervously. "They were the worst!"

"That's great. Let's spy on them."

"What if they recognize me?"

"Don't worry, no one could possibly recognize you."

The next doctor added a verse:

"Who, when I groan, this pain is more,

but I can't pay, I'm too poor.

Turns and runs out the door!'"

"My Doctor!" the others answered, laughing more.

It was Arnie's turn again, and they listened to the end of his verse:

"Who asks if I've filled up my tank,

then sends me off with a Booze Blank!"

"My Doctor!" the table shouted, raising their glasses and guzzling more champagne.

"They're funny, I'll give 'em that!" Sophie said. "That one with the mustache is a regular Groucho Marx!"

Josephine continued eavesdropping. Those dastardly Yorkvillains! Could they be murderers? But the Yorkvillains weren't talking about anything of importance to her investigation or Goldblum's murder. They seemed to be interested only in getting dates with the lovely 'birds' around them. How was she supposed to sleuth if they weren't saying anything incriminating? Maybe Detective O'Malley's job was more difficult than it looked.

"Dr. Goldblum and those Yorkvillains went to the same medical school. It's a common link," said Josephine. "I think there's a good chance that one of these doctors is the culprit."

"So you think they're killers? And framing you? They don't seem nearly that cunning, just silly," Sophie responded with disbelief.

"They know about Aconite and how deadly it is. Something's up with them—all that cash. I'm going to the powder room and back around the other side of their table to get a closer look." Josephine took her purse and got up. The men at the table also rose gallantly, then sat back down. She headed towards the Ladies Room.

One tall man watched her. He had been standing by the bar staring at these new arrivals, eyeing Josephine in particular. He was well-dressed in an expensively tailored white tuxedo jacket that set off his fit physique, probably from weekly games of squash, and he was taking long puffs from a cigarillo. His dashing face was framed by dark center-parted hair, with a straight nose and even jaw, and he was not clean-shaven but sported a pencil-thin mustache. The gleam in his eye held just a hint of rogue.

Josephine emerged from the powder room, passing in front of him.

"You never made it to China," he interrupted her with a clear voice that rose above the nightclub's din.

She stopped, unsure. "I don't know what you're talking about, sir."

"Wasn't that your plan after graduation? A nun, I believe?" he smirked, and his mouth turned up at the corners.

She studied his face in earnest. It was Saltzman, the Columbian, a bit more mature now and definitely more handsome. But another Yorkvillain! They were crawling out of the woodwork!

"Josephine Reva!" he exclaimed, "I knew it from the moment I laid eyes on you. You're in there, somewhere under all that makeup. And that outfit! Are you trying to vamp like Theda Bara's Cleopatra?"

Josephine couldn't help laughing at the thought. "Oh, hello, Saltzie," she tried to act nonchalant. "I'm as fashionable as Theda, uh, Theda whatever. And I come here all the time."

He laughed uproariously, and Josephine noticed how his eyes crinkled.

"I've never seen you here before, Joe— but I did see you in the morning papers! Front page, no less! You killed Goldblum? Is that what the police think? Those dimwits. I've never heard anything more ridiculous in my life! Although you were pretty fast with that scalpel."

Josephine took a long look at Saltzie. For one thing, her cover was blown, and so quickly, too. If he revealed her identity to his friends, she would lose the opportunity to find out if any of the Yorkvillains were involved in Goldblum's death. She remembered that back in school, he hadn't been the worst of the lot. While naughty like the others, he alone had a soft spot for her. Perhaps she could enlist Saltzie's aid?

She decided to appeal to his sense of gallantry. He was a man, after all.

"The police suspect me—it's gads awful!" She batted her eyelashes at him. "I've had to go undercover—no one can know

I'm here. Somehow, I must find the real killer or I'll be sent to prison."

Saltzie seemed to be enticed—whether it was her sexy dress or her plight, she wasn't sure.

They were jostled by a fur-trimmed lady with a long cigarette holder who sashayed to the bank of telephones. The woman blew a long stream of smoke, causing Josephine to cough and her eyes to water.

"Hold on there—I hate to see a beautiful doll cry." Saltzie seemed moved by her tears and Josephine did nothing to correct his misassumption. "You'll ruin those baby blues. Please, let me help you." He seemed mesmerized as he stared into her eyes while taking out his pocket handkerchief.

She noticed it was embroidered with his initials CS. Wasn't his first name Charles? She looked at his fine cut clothing. He'd obviously done well for himself. She remembered with a tang of bitterness that her mother used to embroider rich gents' handkerchiefs for the extra money. She looked at his face and he seemed sincerely concerned—she had a moment's hesitation. Had she misjudged him? But Mike and Andy has said to suspect all the Yorkvillains.

She desperately needed to find some evidence before she was sent off to prison by that Detective O'Malley.

With the syncopated jazz music playing, Saltzie seemed to be swaying like a saxophone player. She realized that he was more than a little drunk, more so than she.

When Saltzie moved closer to dab her eyes, they were jostled by another sashaying woman, and Josephine found her hand slipping into his breast pocket, like a natural reflex, quickly removing his wallet. Just like when she was an orphan on the streets of Little Italy, pickpocketing for some cash to feed herself and her siblings. A skill never forgotten, like riding a bicycle.

While he fiddled with the handkerchief, she managed to slip the wallet into her purse. He dabbed at her eyes tenderly, then suddenly grabbed her upper arms, turned her so her back was against the wall. Was he accusing her? No, he was shielding her from the jostling crowd with his body. "Let me help you prove your innocence," he said with vigor.

She hesitated, but looking into his almond brown eyes, felt a warmth course through her body. She nodded.

"Good, that's settled." Still holding her arms, his eyes scanned her body clothed in its transparent sequin dress.

"That's some disguise! I think you should stay incognito like this, um, so we can move freely, without alerting the police." Drunk patrons were pushing them even closer together, and Josephine brushed against his chest and caught a whiff of his cologne.

He smiled broadly, showing his perfect teeth and his eyes crinkled deeper in an appealing way. "Your new look, Joe, it's hotsie-totsie!" They laughed at the expression. Suddenly, they were as they'd been back in school, and he quoted, "*He could see not that which was...*"

And they finished the poem together, "*but what which should have been.*"

Their gaze locked, she felt his warm hands sliding down her upper arms, and it seemed as if they were the only people in the entire speakeasy.

"Lord Byron," she smiled. "I remember how you used to read me poetry at socials."

"Well, you were the only girl there. I had no one else to practice on. Tiny Joe, always falling for our tricks! You were a Pollyanna, despite how naughty we were!"

He hadn't yet released her nor moved back to a respectable distance. "Who are your friends?" he asked, now holding her hands, his breath tickling her ears.

"Oh, they're not friends, they're my patients."

"You know, you shouldn't be out with patients, it's a conflict of interest. I'm on the ethics committee. I could report you."

She frowned.

"But not if you come sit at my table."

"I couldn't! Our old classmates, they'll recognize me."

He raised his eyebrows and looked her up and down again. "That's hardly likely! Come, we'll have a laugh. *Dulce est desipere in loco.*"

Was he speaking Latin? She felt a thrilling tingle.

"It is sweet sometimes to play the fool," he said, tugging her hand and leading her back to his table.

Arnie flicked his cigar. "I see Saltzie, you made quick work of your trip to the bar."

"May I present uh... uh, Sallie." They sat.

"Sallie and Saltzie, that's cute!" a girl giggled. "Like two little lovebirds."

Saltzie hadn't let go of her hand, and he held it tenderly under the table on his knee. Josephine smiled back at him through the thick smokey haze. Having drunk half of a brandy punch, she was starting to feel the effects. The evening club was starting to revolve around her like a merry-go-round. She shook her head to stop the motion, and Saltzie put his arm around her shoulder.

Wasn't she supposed to be sleuthing, not falling for this guy? She tried to get back on course. Saltzie surely had been a Homeopath, but had he switched to Allopathy? In any case, he, like her, would know full well the effects of deadly Aconite. So would all of the Yorkvillains at this table. She wasn't sure of Saltzie anymore, but he said he would help her, and she needed all the help she could get.

Saltzie signaled for the waitress and ordered a round of drinks for everyone. "Wait 'till you see a Blue Blazer," he said to Josephine. He took his arm off from around her shoulder and began patting his tuxedo jacket and pants. "Sorry, I seem to have lost my wallet."

"You're a generous Sheik!" Arnold said sarcastically. "Let's have another round—on me this time." He gave the waitress several twenties, and Josephine zeroed in on his stuffed wallet left carelessly on the table.

Two Vaudeville stars came on stage to more thunderous applause and began the back and forth "Absolutely, Mr. Gallagher, Positively, Mr. Shean" comedy revue as the drummers played a steady beat. The comedians were making silly jokes, pretending to be Englishmen lost in the Tombs of Luxor.

Josephine barely listened, intent on watching the group of doctors. She found her opportunity while Arnie was distracted, and quickly pinched his wallet and added it to her purse. She couldn't wait to examine the contents, and the evening suddenly seemed a success. Of course she would find a way to return the wallets, convincing herself that she was merely borrowing them to find the evidence she needed to save herself.

The barmen were still busy making all sorts of cocktails. Saltzie told Josephine to watch for the Blue Blazers. Suddenly, the lights at the bar dimmed dramatically, and a barman filled silver tankards with Scotch, lemon zest and some hot water. He then set the alcohol ablaze and poured the flaming liquid back and forth, creating an iridescent blue arc. A spectacular sight, if not an outright fire hazard, it added to the carnival atmosphere. When the servers brought the cocktails to the table, the silver cups were still smoldering with a blue-orange flame.

"That's the bee's knees!" Josephine let the drink extinguish, then hazarded a small sip. She didn't have a taste for alcohol and gagged. Tentatively, she took another tiny sip. It tasted sweeter than the first sip and she felt hotter. Saltzie watched her, greatly amused. He put his arm around the back of her chair.

The King Tut dance show and the Vaudeville revue ended, and there was a break while the orchestra members changed places. Then the lights dimmed low once more, and a spotlight appeared on a gorgeous woman in a black slinky sequined low-cut evening dress, her dark wavy hair shining. The low notes of the saxophone called attention and the orchestra violins began playing a steady ascending melody.

The woman began singing in a lustful low voice a love ballad that had made its way across the ocean to the Italian-American community. 'E Pentite," a song of repentance and longing.

Josephine glanced around the speakeasy, searching for her patients and Dominick. They had moved to the owner's table. The singer walked over to that table and the spotlight flashed on

Maria, Antonio, Dominick, Mike and Sophie seated alongside a man in a striped suit, the only man still wearing a black fedora. He smiled at the singer covetously, and she seemed to be singing only to him:

I'm inside this prison called "Regret." Where are you?
And who are you with? I'd like to know.
Do you sleep at night? But I never sleep
and in front of my eyes I see only you.

Io stó dint'e il prigione "Pentite." E tu addó staje?
E cu chi staje? Chésto vurría sapé.
Tu duórme 'a nòtte? Ma io nun dòrmo maje
e 'nnant'a st'uócchie véco sulo a te.

Her melodic voice was suddenly joined by the sonorous soprano of Maria for a chorus. Memories came flooding back to Josephine. How they used to sing! Her mother had a beautiful operatic voice. The orchestra was melodic and the violins were practically crying the notes. Antonio, soon overcome, joined in with his tenor's voice The pin-striped suited men at the owner's table were also tenors and teary-eyed, and others from distant corners of the speakeasy began wailing.

Josephine couldn't resist joining in with her lilting voice as all the singers reached a crescendo:

Repent for what? I regret
To have loved you too much!
Infamy, no one has ever

Been more sorry than me.

Pentita 'e che? Pentita
ca t'aggio amato assaje!
'Nfame, nisciuna, maje,
fuje cchiù pentita 'e me.

"You're astounding, Joe!" Salzie whispered in her ear, sending shivers of pleasure down her spine. "You have a lovely voice, after all." She was enjoying his flattery, even if it seemed excessive.

He winked at her. "You'll have to tell me what the words mean and sing it for me later, privately."

"It's a sad story about a woman driven mad by her lover. She killed him, so she's in a prison called Regret where she can't sleep—she's haunted by his face forever more."

"Gads, that's dreadful. Is that a warning?"

"Not as long as you're a gentleman!"

"That'll be hard with you!" He moved closer and squeezed her waist and she felt a desire to kiss him or slap him.

The mood was brought back as the orchestra picked up the tempo. The club filled with jazz, then the music spiked for a fast foxtrot.

"Let's dance," he stood up suddenly and extended his hand.

"No, no, I don't know how, uh, I mean I'm not much of a dancer. Not in front of all these people!"

"Don't worry, it's easy, you just follow my lead." But she shook her head.

"May I have the pleasure," he asked again more formally, bowing deeply. He looked at her expectantly, his deep brown eyes sparking with their tinges of hazelnut, his charm reassuring her. She laughed. Surely such a fun- loving man had nothing to do with Goldblum's death. But she didn't dare tell him that she suspected his friends.

"Okay, I guess." They stepped out onto the dance floor with swirling spotlights. The other couples were spinning and Josephine felt as though she'd stepped onto slippery ice. But Saltzie was holding her in a firm embrace.

"That's it, you've got it!" He pulled her in tightly against him. They moved side to side until he said, "Fun, isn't it? Now same thing, only faster!"

"Oh, no!" she fumbled in her step. "You forgot to tell me that you walk forward, but I have to walk backward!"

"That's the way it is, Josephine. Men lead, ladies follow. You never got that memo, as I recall!" He laughed and then said, "But we can do it your way. You lead, I'll follow. I'm nimble on my feet."

Josephine clung to him for the faster tempo. She twirled a little too fast, and they laughed. They continued finding their own rhythm. The next spin was more even-paced, and the next was even better.

"See, Josephine, I told you, easy peasy. Trust me!" He spun her, she spun him and they moved around the dance floor at a faster clip.

She laughed and rested her head lightly on his shoulder, letting the music and dizzying motion carry her away. She felt light as a bird in her gossamer dress and ostrich feather, as if Saltzie was simply carrying her around in his arms.

The music tempo changed to a lively Charleston, and they danced on. Balloons were suddenly released from up in the catwalks, and in the excitement, he kissed her on the cheek, just brushing her lips.

When they returned to the table, glowing from dancing, another college classmate showed up. *Oh! That's Jamie again*, Josephine grimaced. But she was incognito tonight, and her mission was to find Goldblum's killer. Her revenge would be sweet if Jamie proved to be the murderer.

Jamie addressed the table with a joke, of course.

"Sorry I'm late.The cabbie looked at the meter and asked me for $4.00. I only had $3.50 so I told him to back up a mile!"

"Jamie, you're a hoot," one of the girls laughed.

"Another round, barman! For the night is young!" He flashed a big wad of cash.

"Woo! He's flush!" Josephine whispered to Saltzie. "Can he loan you cab fare to get home?"

"Don't worry, Joe. We've all got plenty of cash. Haven't you?"

"Getting there," she replied. "Which hospital are you working at?

"Working? That's for the common man! I've my own practice on Lexington and 59th. I specialized. G.I."

"Oh, gastroenterology!" she said, feeling as if she'd missed a boat. "I went straight to being a G.P."

"Well done, that suits a lady more. I remember you did enjoy delivering babies at clinic. Babies give me the heebie jeebies!" he shivered. "Well, we're both working the lower end of the *corpus humanus*," he joked, slurring the last words a bit. She laughed, too, intoxicated from his attentions and the strong blue cocktail.

"But tell me what happened, Joe. I read the flatties brought you to the murder scene. Must have been ghastly. What'd you see?"

"Goldblum was already dead, lying there on the ground. It was awful. You know, he'd been killed by *Aconitum napellus*! Who would do such a thing?"

"So that explains why the coppers are looking for a Homeopath. And they suspect you?"

"I told that obnoxious Chief Detective that I'm not a Homeopath."

"The lady doth protest too much, me thinks. You loved pharmacology and working in that remedy lab." He thought for a moment, then announced, "By Jove, I think we've found our motive! Dr. Goldblum was working on a report to finish the Homeopaths off for good."

"How do you know that?"

"Our gentleman's club at the fraternity. That's the scuttlebutt, anyway. They're making our college fully Allopathic. Our dean saw which way the wind was blowing."

"I went to meet Professor Janus Heath. Remember him? The Homeopathic compounding pharmacist."

Saltzie nodded. Josephine continued, "He's moved out to Brooklyn, near my office. He admitted he had a fight with Goldblum on the very day he was killed. And he told me Goldblum wanted to control the new drug discoveries, to patent them."

"So Janus Heath killed Goldblum. Money is the root of all evil." Saltzie paused to light his cigarillo and took a long inhale. "You're a clever sleuth! So what's your next move, Sherlock?"

"I'm fairly sure Janus Heath didn't kill Goldblum. But he knows more than he told me. He rang me back saying he wanted to show me something." Josephine couldn't help telling him her plans— was it his trustworthy eyes and the way he breathed in rhythm with her? "And I want to take a look around—Janus' lab is the only place I can think of where there'd be *Aconitum napellus.*"

"I didn't know there were any Homeopathic pharmacies left, certainly none on the Upper East Side. They've mostly gone out of business. But you should be careful, Janus could still be the killer, despite what you think. I'd better go with you, Joe."

"I'd feel safer with you there." She allowed herself to rest against his shoulder. "He asked me to stop by tomorrow at one thirty."

"Fine. I'll pick you up at one o'clock sharp tomorrow afternoon. Brooklyn it is! Write your address on this napkin. And please continue to be fetchingly dressed!" he tugged at the little bow on her shoulder strap. "We'll have a picnic afterwards by the shore, and I'll bring Lord Byron."

"That'd be the cat's meow!" she laughed. Was he really flirting with her? Was this what having a man's attention was like? She felt on Cloud Nine. But she reminded herself to come back down to earth—Detective O'Malley was still waiting for her in the shadows. She needed to find out information on Saltzie's friends. Well, if flirting is what it takes, she thought pleasantly.

This might be the best way to get close to him, she reasoned, to find out more about his pals.

She caught the eye of her patients and they were motioning to her from the door.

"It's time I headed home," she said, as he began nuzzling her neck. "You're zozzled enough!" She playfully pushed his face away from her.

"Uh-oh, the bank's closed—no more withdrawals! Forgive me. I don't want to wind up in some Neapolitan Regret Prison!" They laughed and he asked, "How are you getting home, my lady?"

"I've got my motor car."

"You drive? I can't believe it, you could barely handle a horse and cart."

"No, of course not. My chauffeur drives."

"Just as well, there are too many women drivers anyway." He put her boa around her shoulders and they said goodbye to the table of doctors and company, who were too tipsy to notice anyway.

They stood on the street outside The Oasis. Josephine turned and looked for Dominick, then found him easily. His muscular form was standing alongside her flashy motor car, watching her from across the street. "There's Dominick," she waved.

"Well I see you've brought your fire extinguisher! He looks burly—I wouldn't want to mess with him. Until one o'clock tomorrow!" His lips lingered on her cheek and she inhaled his musky scent. "Taxi" he gave a whistle. A Checker cab pulled over and he blew Josephine another kiss, got in the cab and was off.

Josephine's patients were excited as they climbed back into her motorcar. "We 'ad a talk with de speakeasy owners," said Antonio. "Theyz from Napoli, too."

"I couldn't have guessed!" laughed Josephine. "That song, you were all amazing, better than some of the acts!" Maria and Antonio smiled.

"But listen here, Lucky Lou, he's the one in the fedora, knew our guy Goldblum was murdered down at The Narrows," said Mike. "We found out that's the mob's signal point for Rum Row."

"The mob?"

"Nah, don't worry about it. Nothing happens, we're customers—they want us to spend money on booze. They only kill each other."

Josephine was shocked, but she remembered the street gang fights she'd seen at Five Points on the Lower East Side. It was better to stay clear, but she needed to pursue all avenues of investigation. "Tell me about this Rum Row."

"Speedboats bring the booze from big freighters to the smaller inlets off the south shore of Brooklyn and Long Island along Ambrose Channel, out by Coney Island. They make a drop before The Narrows. Then they run the booze on faster speedboats up the East River to Harlem."

"Wow, that's some production! Could there be a connection to Goldblum's death? Maybe it's the bootleggers and not anyone from my medical college who killed Goldblum?"

"Doc Joe, ya know you should be careful," said Antonio, motioning towards the receding taxi. "You still have to suspect your college buddies. Goldblum was one of 'em, too."

"You think Dr. Goldblum or these doctors are rumrunners?"

"There's something not right about that crowd, they've got an awful lot of greenbacks for doctors," Mike added. "And they were splifficated."

"Well, Saltzie's alright. He always was one of the better ones, to me at least."

"You could stay close to 'em Doc," said Mike, "and see what you can find out."

"I think she's already doing that," said Sophie.

Maria added, "He's so 'andsome, *molto bello!*"

"Don't be silly! I'm just going to question him some more."

"Sure ya are!" they said in unison.

Josephine remembered the wallets in her purse. She couldn't tell her patients that she used to pick pockets to survive on the streets of Little Italy. Besides, she wanted to examine Salzie's wallet at home, privately. But for Arnie's wallet, she'd best come up with a story.

"I found this wallet on the floor. It's Arnie's, you know the guy with the Groucho Marx mustache."

Dominick looked up, turning his head and his dark eyes caught hers in his rear view mirror. She felt ashamed but kept on with the charade. "He must have dropped it."

"Let's see!" said the group excitedly.

They took the wallet and started spilling out the contents, using the motor car's reading lamp. "There's no operator's license. Nobody drives in Manhattan anyway with that new spanking subway line," said Sophie. "Wish we had something better than the El."

"That's a lot of cash—must be three hundred dollars!" Andy added. "Wow!"

"How did he get so much dough? That's suspicious," Mike said.

"And there's some girls' telephone numbers on a napkin. The way they were hanging all over him! Oh, here's a little black book with lots of phone numbers. That's not surprising!" Sophie said.

"What's this? It's a membership card to the American Institute of Homeopathy," Andy said.

"That confirms he's a Homeopath," said Josephine. "He's rich and he keeps girls' phone numbers. But that's hardly incriminating. We need some proof."

"So what have we got?" Mike asked.

"Nuttin' much, 'cept that little black book," Antonio said.

"How do we know what these names and numbers mean?" Sophie asked.

"They're mostly women's names, so let's start with the ones that aren't dames," Andy noted.

"Here's one, "Lou." Is that a gal or a guy?" Sophie said. "Do you think it's that mobster?"

"Here's another, "Luigi"—that's a guy." Mike added. "And "Atalanta", "Constantine", then there's "Nancy," "Nerissa," and one that says "#215." Wow! Arnie must have an entire harem!"

"Tomorrow we'll call the guys' numbers first," Andy said, "and see what they have to say."

The group leaned back against the seats for the ride across the bridge back to Brooklyn as the dawn broke over the East River.

Chapter 15 - The Law of Infinitesimals

Meanwhile Saturday...

Detective O'Malley sat at his desk, flipping through the pages of the Goldblum case file. He realized that there was still no Dr. Goldblum's report, and he needed that report. "Get me former Health Commissioner Royal Copeland," O'Malley said. The rookie whispered back, "Do you mean our Senator?"

"Yes, that's exactly who."

The rookie then spoke to the operator in a loud authoritarian voice, mimicking O'Malley's words, and handed him the telephone stand.

After introductions, O'Malley got to the point. "Sir, we know Dr. Goldblum was working on some kind of report. I'm sorry to disturb you, but I really need to know what important, perhaps confidential, things were in it."

"Why don't we meet, Detective. My home on Central Park West. Please come and we'll take some air in the park."

O'Malley didn't have time for a chat in the park, but he needed the information. Well, on second thought, he hadn't been over to Central Park for a stroll in ages, not since he and Evelyn had picnicked there. A breath of fresh air might do him some good. Besides, a jaunt over the beautiful Brooklyn Bridge was always inspiring, in a taxi paid for by the police no less.

Detective O'Malley alighted from the Checker cab and stood in front of an elegant row of townhouses, one of the few remaining. He lamented that he'd never been able to find a detective job here, where the prestige was, and instead had to settle for a position in Brooklyn, Kings County. He looked about—the town homes were being torn down and replaced with new blocky construction, gargantuan buildings reaching taller than any tree. He craned his neck—the top floors looked unsafe. How did they get permission to build that high? He'd heard the scuttlebutt that Brooklyn was even more corrupt—inspectors were supposedly demanding thousands per apartment and police were skimming off of that. "If you want prestige, go to Manhattan," they said, "but if you want riches, go to Kings."

O'Malley didn't need to demand bribes. He had inherited enough money from his hard-working Irish immigrant parents. Besides, he didn't need much more than he had for himself, now that his wife was gone, and they had never been blessed with children. He'd always earned what he needed to buy Evelyn fancy dresses and bring her flowers as tokens of his love. He'd never be able to take her out on the town again, he thought sadly, now that she was dead.

He glanced at the park, remembering Evelyn's soft laugh, and crossed Central Park West to find Senator Copeland's home. O'Malley had grown up in a row house like this one, although not nearly as stately, on the West Side. His parents had bought it after they immigrated, entering Ellis Island with some funds sewn in their waist shirts from selling their farmland and sheep. Once he became a widower, he had no use for so much space, so he sold that row house at a huge profit and bought another in Park Slope, closer to his work. It was already divided into apartments and O'Malley rented out the upper floor units while keeping the parlor and garden floors for himself. One entered into the lower level a few steps down from the street; there was a comfy lounge next to a big kitchen with a huge cast iron coal-burning cooking stove, which O'Malley preferred over gas. The back door led out to a tiny rear plot vegetable garden that Evelyn had tended, now overgrown. The row house had originally belonged to an upper class family, and the servants had lived on the top floor, but in Brooklyn, not many families had servants any longer and most row houses were packed full of as many families as possible. O'Malley was fortunate that he had two floors all to himself. The big kitchen in the basement was where the servants once prepared the family meals—it was his favorite area of the house, dark and quiet, his retreat from city crime.

O'Malley walked up the curving stone steps of Senator Copeland's brownstone and lifted the brass knocker, letting it fall on the iron-hinged oak door. As a child, he'd walked by this very door many times with his parents on their way to the swings in the park. He'd noticed this particular door before with its pointed arch—even as a kid he noticed details, like an obsession. *Three steps to the tree. Passed a newsboy this morning with a mole on his chin. Mum, did you see that?*

The door opened and O'Malley was shown inside by a suitably reserved butler. He sat down on the Victorian curved sofa in the parlor. O'Malley watched as the butler closed the pocket doors to the inner parlor, catching a glimpse of stuffed bookcases, a desk overflowing with papers, several microscopes atop a large table and various chemistry apparatuses. As O'Malley suspected, he was entering the world of science and medicine and fortunately, he had taken time to read up on it.

The venerable former Commissioner and current Senator entered with a respectably stern countenance. He was the kind of man you'd like to see with the surgical scalpel when you're about to be sedated and operated upon. He had a steady no-nonsense gaze, a square face and large jowls and bushy eyebrows, and he managed to look both ornery and wise at the same time.

Senator Copeland's even tone of voice spoke of his Midwestern roots. He was born in Michigan and then headed east to suit his ambitions in politics and public health. The former Dean of Josephine's medical school, he left when he was appointed the New York City Commissioner of Health. O'Malley remembered that his handling of the 1917-1918 Influenza Pandemic won him acclaim, and he had recently been re-elected Senator of New York.

Copeland gazed at O'Malley with sincere eyes. He had thick side parted hair over a large, wide face, and his mouth turned downward in what looked like a perpetual scowl. He wore a plaid light wool suit with belted back, which did little to hide his large frame. O'Malley couldn't help thinking that newer boxy style, which he himself preferred, might have been a better cut for the man. French cuffs and a stiff collar poked out from under the Senator's jacket, and his lapel held a red carnation. The suit spoke of the best tailoring, although old-fashioned—as O'-Malley called it "classic". The cloth was fine, and not from any of the discount shops where O'Malley bought his own suits, like Barney's Men's Store on 17th Street (they offered free tailoring). O'Malley could see the gold thick watch chain across the Senator's middle waist trailing into his vest pocket and envied the large expensive timepiece resting inside.

The Senator asked his butler to bring coffees, and the two men sipped as they spoke about trivialities.

"What about Dr. Goldblum's report, Senator?" O'Malley began, before Copeland cut him off, raising his hand.

"If you've finished your coffee, Detective, let's go for that walk. Fresh air is a requirement for healthy lung function, don't you agree?"

"Yes, Senator, I do." O'Malley could tell that he was going to have to tone down his questioning to a leisurely pace.

Once outside, O'Malley thought that if he could finish with the Senator by early evening, he would have some free time to enjoy Manhattan. But he sensed that the Senator was not the type to be hurried along; nonetheless, he decided he needed to steer the conversation towards the missing report, sooner rather than later. The sun was already beginning to set. He began with a general question, one that he already knew the answer to.

"Was Dr. Goldblum working on a pandemic preparedness program?"

"No, not that I'm aware of," said Copeland. "His area of concern was Preventative not Infectious Diseases."

"And how was he going to stop those?"

"He was aiming to prevent alcoholism, addiction, and other man-made illnesses with public safety awareness campaigns. He believed that the public needed to know more about medicine and the science behind it."

The detective's next question was to the point. He knew that Senator Copeland was a trained Homeopathic physician. "Speaking of medicine and science, was Dr. Goldblum determined to put an end to Homeopathy?"

"It's not a simple matter to put an end to a type of medicine that's been effective for over a century." The Senator hadn't paused in his brisk stride. "When I was City Health Commissioner, I helped coordinate the response to the Influenza pandemic we just spoke about. We developed an exciting new vaccine, with Dr. Park our Chief Bacteriologist. It would later save many lives."

O'Malley was about to say something to bring the conversation to the present day, but the Senator continued. "My point being that vaccines are of Homeopathic derivation. Without Homeopathy, we might not have discovered the very concept.

"To prepare the vaccine, the influenza bacilli were killed by exposure to heat, then dissolved in salt solution. I won't bore you with the many details, but the idea is a simple one—to inject extremely small quantities of the toxin to stimulate a person's ability to form protective bodies against the invasion of the germ. In such diluted doses, it cannot cause any recurrence of the disease in question, but is capable of inducing symptoms similar thereto, which in turn, stimulates a person's vital force— their immunity.

This is the essential philosophy of Homeopathy: *"similia similibus curentur"*, or "like cures like". This axiom expresses the Law of Similars—a toxic substance which produces detrimental symptoms in healthy individuals will, once diluted and potentized, relieve similar symptoms occurring as an expression of disease. Interestingly, the vaccine dose recommended by Sir Wright of London is 1/10000 of a milligram, equivalent to approximately the sixth decimal dilution on the Homeopathic scale. And Prof. Denys of Belgium, speaking of his antitubercular dose, recommended one millionth of a milligram, which is approximately the eight decimal."

"Uh, these dilutions are extreme," said O'Malley with a confused look, after doing the math in his head. "Was Dr. Goldblum against vaccination because he didn't believe in such extreme dilutions?"

"Oh, my good man! As I was saying, the vaccine was new, but it was the application of an old idea—a Homeopathic one. In October of 1918, for the influenza pandemic, we were testing the vaccine on laboratory volunteers so convinced of its efficacy that they willingly subjected themselves to its doses."

O'Malley consulted his notebook, then spoke carefully, "So what you're saying is that Homeopathy—because it uses very diluted doses, like vaccines, but more so—is highly effective? But how can that be when the dilution is so extreme that there's nothing left of the original molecule?"

"Now that is what's called The Law of Infinitesimals. Have you read my book, *The Scientific Reasonableness of Homœopathy*? Physical chemistry has scientifically proven the value of the infinitesimal dose."

"No, I haven't read that one, Senator." The detective preferred dealing with mobsters who cracked under questioning and gave information when he demanded it.

"I wrote," the Senator continued, "if I may attempt to paraphrase: a chemical, which is basically an electrolyte molecule, once dissolved is dissociated into particles known as ions. The more one dilutes the solution the greater the dissociate and thus, the atoms decrease and ions increase, and when infinitely dilute, the dissociation is absolute and the chemical is present in a state of ionization. Importantly, the therapeutic value of the drug is not lost."

"Ions, uh, I read that this holds for conductivity, lowering of freezing point, refraction equivalents." O'Malley had picked up a few books on medicine and poured over them in his basement study.

"Exactly so! I'm impressed by your knowledge," said Senator Copeland. "So you'll understand why Goldblum's report was troubling. He was trying to disprove a finding by an eminent Parisian physician that the 5th dilution of gold metal produced positive therapeutic results, such as an increase in the coefficient of nitrogenous utilization, a positive flush of urinary indoxyl, a decrease in quantity of total oxygen consumed, a raising of arterial tension, oxygenation of the blood globules, etcetera. The ions, once liberated —"

"Uh, Senator, sorry to interrupt again, but I haven't a degree in medicine. So if you don't mind speaking plain English. Would you kindly tell me briefly the conclusion of Goldblum's report?"

"Please excuse me for digressing to the particulars. I've never seen the report itself. Odd thing is that no one has. Dr. Goldblum didn't make any copies for distribution. But he did speak about it—enough to raise an alarm." Senator Copeland stopped and turned to Detective O'Malley. "I maintained to him that certain inert elements and ions in extreme subdivision, such as Homeopathic remedies, are capable of remarkable physiological action. Small doses before considered ineffectual are indubitably found to make a profound impression upon life's processes." His gaze was most assured.

O'Malley scratched his head. "Uh, nobody's seen any of Dr. Goldblum's experiments or results, nor the report. But Homeopaths were worried that Goldblum was trying to discredit the Homeopathic provings?"

"That's it, you've got it."

The two men continued walking across Central Park. O'-Malley was shaking his head again—why was Goldblum threatening to publish results that didn't exist? "Was there anyone else besides Homeopaths who might have been upset by what Goldblum was planning to do?"

"Dr. Goldblum's report," Copeland continued, "targeted several matters of public health and prevention, but in a way that hurt business. My own thought, as a conservative, is to first bring businesses on board and have them comply willingly. It's no wonder that Goldblum became unpopular when he began instituting smoke and noise nuisances and a staggered traffic plan. There were also the matter of polluted water at city bathing beaches—businesses were opposed to cleaning up their own acts."

"Goldblum also instigated prosecutions and convictions concerning corrupt food inspectors, and exposed a ring of people profiteering from the sale of impure milk to babies."

"Yes, but someone had to do something to safeguard the public. Goldblum was forced out of Preventative Diseases and into research."

"And how did he take that demotion?"

"I suppose he was quite bitter about it."

The Senator picked up the pace, and O'Malley's long legs were easily able to keep up.

"You know, the Tammanies still have a hold on the city and on the Democratic Party. My running mate last year was FDR, our governor and I was re-elected as your Senator. Some say I'm too conservative to be a member of the Party..."

"Uh, yes, sir, politics is never ending, and I can see Goldblum made some enemies with businesses. But his murder seems more personal than political. Who else might he have offended?"

"Dr. Goldblum was about to offend many, not just Homeopaths. As I said, he was in charge of preventable diseases, like alcoholism. He was "dry," meaning, as you know, that he was in favor of Prohibition, and he was set on squashing bootlegging. And, come to think of it, he supported other controversial but necessary ideas, especially about curbing habit-forming drugs. There were reports that druggists had increased their sales of morphine, cocaine and heroin substantially—addiction is fast becoming a public health crises. The Harrison Narcotics Taxation Act effectively ended the use of addictive drugs in unregulated tonic medicines, and that was a good first step. But habit-forming drugs are still available by prescription. Unfortunately, unscrupulous doctors are still selling fake prescriptions, thereby resulting in ever more addiction."

Detective O'Malley had been busily writing in his notepad. He looked up at Senator Copeland and nodded for him to continue. But Copeland was raising his hand irately and pointing to a large building in the distance aglow with twinkling lights.

"Here we find ourselves walking towards Mayor Jimmy Walker's Casino, a place of wanton excess—Porterhouse steaks there cost $1.00, and as if that isn't bad enough, you have to pay 25 cents extra for the mushrooms!"

O'Malley had read the muckraking stories about the Casino. The Mayor's associates leased the Central Park building from the city for very low rent, then turned it into their own private evening club by invitation only. After charging admission, selling food and even illegal alcohol at high prices, they were reaping a huge profit off of a city-owned building. Tammany Hall politicians were worried that this blatant corruption might cost them the next election. Already the reformers, led by the Governor Franklin D. Roosevelt, were gaining favor.

"Look there, Detective. It's an outrage that such a den of corruption exists within a public park —it's a rebuke to the good people of this city."

O'Malley looked at the glimmering lights and practically salivated. An anti-corruption investigation into the big fish would be just the ticket to a commendation and promotion. He thought he'd check out this Casino. But first, he needed to find out more about Dr. Goldblum's report."

"You do understand, Detective? It's the embodiment of the principle of the infinitesimally small dose. Excess—it disturbs the equilibrium."

"So you're saying that this Casino, this corruption, is too much? Like large doses... do you mean that Allopathy doesn't work at all?" asked O'Malley.

"No, the Allopathic dose enters the cellular structure, but it wreaks havoc. The damage can be extensive—imagine a fight in this uproarious Club Casino with thrashing about and breaking glass. But Homeopathy, in contrast, with its dilution to mere ions, is the gentlest way to permeate the cell structure. Goldblum would not uphold this philosophy."

Dr. Goldblum was an Allopath? O'Malley thought. He stopped and consulted his notes. "But he was killed with a Homeopathic." O'Malley turned to Copeland. "*Aconitum napellus.*"

"Poor chap, Goldblum! Aconite is known as the Queen of Poisons. A terrible way to go, although I can think of worse, more lingering deaths like influenza, or succumbing to the infections of surgery - bacterial infections are also a ghastly ending." He shook his head sadly. "But Goldblum was killed by the plant, not the remedy. Let us consider, Detective, the action of toxins. It was Professor Clark who discovered the need for the antidotal to neutralize the toxin in the blood stream. Without the antidotal, well, for Dr. Goldblum, it would have been hopeless."

"Did Dr. Goldblum antagonize the Homeopaths, who would wish him dead?" Detective O'Malley asked.

"Well, Goldblum changed his tune, and no one knows why. He was a Homeopath who became an Allopath. We doctors fundamentally disagree. In Homeopathy, there is one law, the Law of Similars to treat patients. But under Allopathy, there is not just one law—instead, there are differing opinions. Dr. A. may prescribe one way, but Dr. B. may prescribe differently.

"In Homeopathy, we have the provings of the remedies. We know what each drug can do. But Allopathy relies upon clinical tests—giving hundreds or thousands of persons the same dose of a drug and monitoring for relief of symptoms, while the other half are given a placebo. But this only measures palliatively the outcome of the patient, each with their own and very different constitutions and immunology. It does not prove the components of the drug itself."

"So how was Goldblum going to show that one was better than the other—I assume he wanted to show that Allopathic drugs were better and safer for the public?"

"For that, it is helpful to consider the relationship of the chemical properties of drugs to their dynamic effects. Mendeleef's periodic law tabulates the elements in order of their atomic weights, and they naturally fall into groups and relationships, by column and by the number of elements between any one and the next similar. If you know the atomic weight of an element you may therefore know its properties. These groupings allow us to find the Homeopathic "Similars" quite easily. Indeed, the proving show the similarity between certain remedies. Of course, Mendeleev found gaps —."

"Excuse me, I'm not sure I'm following...uh....," O'Malley interrupted. "I'm getting one of my migraines."

"Has this come on suddenly, with any pain behind the eye?"

"Yes, it was sudden with a gradually increasing pounding in my temples."

"Ah! Belladonna. Let us consider the dosage." After asking the detective several more questions about his condition, he took out a small case and found a vial. "Here, I believe this dilution is best for you. One tablet, under the tongue."

O'Malley hesitated.

"No need to worry, Detective, you won't meet the same fate as Dr. Goldblum. Remember the Law of Infinitesimals —the remedy is diluted to the point where merely the ions remain and hold therapeutic value. You're perfectly safe."

O'Malley accepted the tablet and upon Dr. Copeland's instructions, placed it under his tongue.

"Now don't speak, Detective, let the remedy dissolve slowly. I remember it was our college's pharmacologist Janus Heath who prepared this vial—here's his insignia on the label. Finest remedies! I recall he had a few fellows, pharmacology students working with him to help with the succussions, most expertly. The pharmacist determines the dilution—in all measures—if you'll pardon the pun." Senator Copeland laughed.

O'Malley waited for the tiny tablet to fully dissolve, then gulped. "What happened to them?"

"It was several years ago, but they were all let go. Janus Heath included. The medical college needed to cut the pharmacology department in its entirety. Abraham Flexner's 1910 report, you know, and its outcomes. Pharmacology should be kept separate."

"Janus Heath—I assume he was opposed to Goldblum's report?" O"Malley was taking notes. "And the students he taught might have been opposed, too, although they certainly had no career at that point."

"No, some students wouldn't have been opposed. They felt no loyalty towards Homeopathy. I recall several were even in favor of making the Allopathic higher toxicity drugs—these sell at higher prices. But Janus Heath was a devout Homeopathic pharmacist, and he was most definitely in disagreement with Dr. Goldblum, from what he told me at the conference last Thursday."

Janus Heath, Dr. Goldblum and Josephine Reva were at the same conference, just before the murder. And Janus Heath was none too happy about Goldblum's report. O'Malley was starting to feel better.

"Is there anything else you can recall, Senator, about Dr. Goldblum's report?" asked O'Malley.

"Yes, Dr. Goldblum was lambasting the production of those unregulated patent medicines. You know, those corner hawkers touting useless tonics, a great many containing poisonous substances. Homeopaths don't get on with them. We believe that the herb must be diluted properly in order to be effective. Herbalists, you see, don't dilute the toxins that far, they merely extract —"

"Quacks?"

"Yes, quacks. Dr. Goldblum concerned himself with preventable diseases, like alcoholism and addiction, and charlatans are known for adding addictive drugs and alcohol to their tonics. This infuriates most doctors. You see, that's how these quacks get their customers hooked, like addicts, always coming back to buy more!"

"And that was going into the report?"

"Yes, we discussed this and I agreed. We both saw the pressing need to curb the spread of "addiction by quackery." Sometimes, doctors, too, are guilty. They prescribe too much morphine, heroin, opium, cocaine to addicts, instead of weaning them off of these drugs. Sometimes, it's a money-making scheme, with prescriptions costing $2, and then the unlucky addict needs to purchase the drug at the druggist for an additional $2! I remember one unfortunate who hadn't any shoes, and they took every last cent he had. Most irresponsible and a disgrace to our profession."

O'Malley realized that Dr. Goldblum probably thought himself a crusader for public health.

This is more complicated than I thought, he winced, trying not to envision the flowers wilting in his upstate garden as his commendation ribbon faded away in his dreams. Then he remembered his sergeant telling him about many phone calls from Dr. Reva about a certain quack, a Dr. Quinn.

"Dr. Reva reported a quack selling on her street corner," he spoke out loud.

"You mean Josephine Reva? A most knowledgeable graduate of one of our Homeopathic medical colleges. We invited her to speak at our recent conference on the future of medicine."

"You did? Why?"

"Because that young lady is the future of medicine. We need more women Homeopaths. Frankly, we need more women to enter medicine—there's not enough Allopaths or Homeopaths. Our ranks are mighty thin."

"I must head off, Senator. It was a pleasure, sir, and you've been most helpful." O'Malley needed to call his sergeant.

"Don't you want to hear about my plans for a new Senate bill including the Homeopathic Pharmacopeia?"

"Sorry, that'll have to wait until another time. I've got a murder to solve. Thank you, Senator, um, *infinitesimally!*" O'-Malley couldn't resist making his own pun.

"Ha, ha," the Senator laughed heartily. "I understand. Duty calls."

"Is there a public pay phone nearby?"

"There'll be a pay phone inside that indomitable Mayor Walker's club. A nickel call, but I'm sure they'll charge 15 cents and keep the change! Godspeed, and I am sure you'll catch Dr. Goldblum's killer."

Detective O'Malley said his goodbye and jogged the path across the park at 70th Street toward the Casino. So soon after its grand opening, the club would be packed.

Chapter 16 - Central Park Casino

The trees of the park in front of the Central Park Casino's entrance sparkled with twinkling fairy-like bulbs, like fireflies in a forest. Customers were arriving for Saturday night dressed to the nines, and the parking lot was filled with sleek phaetons and roadsters. O'Malley stopped to admire one motor car in particular: Mayor Walker's stunning silver and black Duesenberg La Grande Phaeton. It was an outrageously expensive machine, costing over ten smackers. Massive chrome pipes jutted from its powerful engine; he'd heard it could reach speeds of 110 miles per hour. The bold chrome grillwork and headlamps, undulating fenders, wide running boards and sumptuous interior were ostentatious. But O'Malley knew that the ill-gotten gains that purchased this Duesey were the result of corruption, and he, like many others, would like to be the one to end Walker's reign over the city.

O'Malley entered the Casino, checking his pockets for a nickel. Not finding any coins, he headed for the maitre d' station. The club was abuzz with waiters running back and forth like busy bees, unfurling tablecloths, and depositing place settings of bone white china, silverware, and crystal water and champagne glasses. O'Malley entered the enormous ballroom.

From the ceiling hung large chandeliers dripping with crystal, and the ceiling itself was black glass. *So this is where the "high hats" play.*

He saw a bartender polishing crystal goblets behind the bar.

"Where's your house phone?" O'Malley said starchily.

The barman in white tie and dinner jacket was busy prepping for the crowds starting to enter. He looked at O'Malley up and down, and sniffed. The Casino had just opened and tonight like every night was sure to be a smash—only the most upper crust patrons attended by invitation only. Satin-trimmed ladies and gents were being seated.

The barman seemed miffed and didn't budge. "I smell a police officer," he said with a petulant look, not even bothering to look up from his task.

The place reeks of attitude. He was used to people jumping to attention on his command. This twerp was going to need some stronger tactics.

"And I smell gunpowder." O'Malley opened his coat to reveal the high caliber pistol in its holster. "I'm asking politely, where's your house phone, now!"

"Oh, all right, here," the barman pulled a phone from below the counter. "You don't have to take out your heat."

O'Malley called the station house, and spoke to his sergeant. "It's me, O'Malley. Yeah, I know this is the Casino Club's number... Uh huh, the operator told you... No, I'm not out for the evening. Listen up, I want to know more about Janus Heath, he's a pharmacist. Then tomorrow, bring in that quack Quinn... The one who's always on the corner by Dr. Reva's. Keep him entertained until I get there... Don't worry, he'll have something illegal on him—just check his bottles."

The barman looked up at the detective and hurriedly threw several bottles down chutes that were hidden under the counter. They clinked loudly and O'Malley imagined the bottles broke in the sewer below. "Don't worry, Mayor Walker's gin joint is safe —for now," he said.

At that moment, Gentleman Jimmy, as the mayor was called, strolled in with his black top hat and satin evening attire. He was carrying a pearl-handled walking stick and quickstepped, showing off his tall slim frame to his entourage. With high cheekbones that made his rosy cheeks look like apples, his eyes were light and twinkly, but when he saw the detective, his face changed from a smile to a frown. O'Malley thought that he was probably displeased that someone not in evening dress was seated at the bar, or maybe the mayor had noticed he was a flattie, just like the barman had. Mayor Walker left the ballroom abruptly, calling over one of his employees, who shrugged his shoulders.

What a dandy, thought O'Malley, but he was hardly concerned. The Casino was city park property, and supposed to be open to the public. Of course the "public" wouldn't come here, sensing the chilly, unwelcoming atmosphere and the steep prices. Besides, it was invitation only.

He looked around at the fancy furnishings, the shiny mirrors and waxed floors and decided that, nonetheless, it was a very fine evening club indeed. He would have liked to have taken Evelyn dancing here, if not for the wealthy patrons who made the place unbearably stuffy. He hunched his shoulders and sat down on a bar stool.

The barman watched him for a moment. "What can I get you, Detective?"

"Nothing."

"We've got whiskey, port, gin—pick your poison."

"Oh, I prefer sherry!" O'Malley's haughty accent and puckered face sent the barman into a fit of laughter.

"I'm glad you flatties have a sense of humor. But please do us all a favor and next time come in with a tailored suit."

"Can't," O'Malley patted his revolver in its holster. "Hazards of the job." The barman laughed.

"What'll it be? It's on the house."

"Whiskey, straight up." The barman found a bottle of oak barrel aged Scotch, and O'Malley nodded.

"I see you're opposed to Prohibition?" The barman smiled wryly.

"Getting rid of it would sure make my job a lot easier."

"That long arm of the law reaches too far, into restaurants, clubs, our kitchen cupboards and even into our bedrooms."

"My job is strictly to enforce that long arm of the law, no matter where it goes."

"Hmm, I see. The man in blue is always true to his job. But even you, Detective, have to admit that you'd like to take your wife out for dinner and drinks to a snazzy place like this."

"I'm a widower, so no. And she'd never have come here, although she'd have been the most beautiful woman in this joint. There's no joy in hobnobbing with these rich folk when they're often guilty of more crimes than I can list for you. Besides, I've got better things to do with my time than putting on the Ritz."

"A slick oil or rubber baron? A titan of industry? It'd be nice to have that cash."

"No, it wouldn't. Thieves, clever thieves —. I've seen what they do to their workers. I don't know how they can sleep at night."

"Well, drink up, Detective. It may all come crashing down upon their heads. What goes around comes around."

"Yeah." O'Malley motioned to the glittering couples seated at tables around the dance floor. "This club should be open for everybody to come dancing. This is a city park."

"You wanna tell me about it?"

"What? I can't talk about my investigations."

"I meant your wife. You said you were a widower."

"Oh," O'Malley looked down, fingering his whiskey glass.

"It must be lonely, losing your wife so young,"

"How did you know she was young?" O'Malley looked up startled.

"Some people have the look, like they've been sad a long, long time. You have that look."

"I should add you to the detective squad."

The barman continued polishing glasses with a cloth. O'-Malley knew he'd never come back to this club, nor was it likely to be raided with such a powerful benefactor, so he unburdened himself.

"She was a beautiful woman, fair hair, blue eyes, a smile to light up a room brighter than anything here," he waved at the glass chandeliers. "But.... the life I had... it was hard for her to be a police officer's wife. She worried too much. She was scared that I would die first, in some gunfight. You know, I've been in so many. But in the end, it was her...."

"How did it happen?"

"Crossing the street. She was crossing the damn street."

"So many accidents—you do take your life in your hands when out for a stroll. I'm truly sorry. It must be a terrible loss."

"Nothing to be done, nothing." O'Malley voice was very quiet.

"Have another whiskey, and maybe you want something to eat? The chef makes a great Porterhouse steak."

"No, and uh, thanks," said O'Malley, putting down his glass and standing up. He regretted his momentary lapse in judgement confiding to an unknown bartender. Taking a box of matches monogrammed with two C's, he lit a cigarette. He reached deeper into his pockets and put a nickel on the counter.

"I'll be back one day, and it won't be for pleasure."

He took one last look at the dapper Mayor Jimmy Walker, smiling and toasting his flimflamming friends. He wasn't called "Gentleman Jimmy" for nothing.

Chapter 17 - The Laboratory

Sunday...

Hello Joe!" Saltzie bounded up the sidewalk like an overgrown pup to meet Josephine halfway, "Wowee! You are looking gorgeous!" He lifted her up in his arms and spun her around, as she put her arms around his neck.

Josephine had chosen a floral afternoon tea party dress that was a touch revealing. It was short and kept riding up even shorter to just below her knees. She pulled at it now, trying to stretch it back down. All her stockings that weren't ripped were white medical ones, so she had run to Sophie's to find silk stockings, also borrowing a brimmed straw hat with a ribbon and daisy flower. She'd tried her best to apply face powder, and had taken some care to draw a bit of eyeliner at the corners of her eyes. Finally, she'd puckered her lips and dabbed on the bright red lipstick that her patients had left on the dresser.

She looked pretty enough for a "date"—but she stopped to remind herself that her true intention was to sleuth. *How difficult can it be?* she'd asked herself in the mirror. She'd already discovered that Janus Heath wasn't a killer.

Detective work must be easy if that Detective O'Malley could do it. He'd even let her do most of the talking.

She was ambivalent about the job she'd pulled last night—but didn't detectives pinch wallets and break into people's homes? Admittedly, she hadn't been the best spy, carried away by the atmosphere of the speakeasy and her first taste of mixed cocktails.

She'd already looked in Saltzie's wallet. It hadn't revealed much of anything, except a lot of cash. There was no little black book, thank goodness, and there was no Homeopath membership card. Secretly, she was relieved that there weren't any girls' telephone numbers on napkins from last night.

She dropped Saltzie's wallet into her medical bag; the bag would be just right for hiding any other evidence she could collect—if an item found its way into her hands, well then, she wouldn't turn it away, which technically wasn't stealing.

"Oh, dear!" A moral conundrum— her "collecting" evidence now meant she'd have to somehow find a way to return it. How was she going to get close to Saltzie and slip the wallet back into his pocket? It was going to be a long day.

Saltzie led her to his cherry red Roadster convertible with the top down, as it was fine summer weather.

"What a peachy motor car!' Josephine said, as she hefted her medical bag into the back seat, next to Saltzie's. "I see you've brought your medical bag, too."

"Yes, of course, I never leave home without it. Our bags are nicely nestled together, the same as we shall soon be. People are going to think we're going away for a nookie."

She had no idea what he meant, but it sounded delightful.

He held the door open for her. "Your chariot awaits, Miss Reva!"

Behind the wheel, he opened the throttle, pulled out the choke, set the motor car in gear and they bounced down the bumpy street. He began to whistle and then sing in a jaunty voice, *"Ain't Misbehavin', I'm savin' my love for you."* After a few bars, he said, "Great to enjoy the weekend off with a beautiful gal by my side!"

"I've never taken a day off—until today."

"What? Don't you ever close your office?"

"Nope, never."

"You can't do it all, Joe. Find another doctor to be on call for you. Take a break and have a little fun. With me!"

"With you? I'd like that."

"You know, one day, when we're married, you won't have to work at all."

"But I'll always work. I'm a doctor."

"Not when you're part of Dr. and Mrs. Saltzman."

Was that a proposal? No wonder everyone's married. Her last beau had been slow-footed, taking years to ask her and sealed the deal with a handshake. But Saltzie seemed to be fast off the mark.

"You mean Dr. and Dr. Saltzman." Josephine wasn't ready to stop working.

"Okay. Women's rights. I like the sound of that, too!" He turned to look at her and began crooning.

"A lovely day in June
A couple's over the moon
The bride's a snapper

The groom's a napper
They'll be wedded soon!"

Saltzie reached over to squeeze her hand. Josephine was delighted that he was already singing about marriage. On their first date, no less.

Then he continued with the next verse:

"Brides can't wait for their day in June
Grooms can't wait
for the honeymoon
Is there a reason, only the season
to wait for whoopee!"

He kissed her hand. "Bing's got nothing on me!"

Josephine couldn't help laughing. He sung off-tune, but he certainly knew how to make her chuckle.

"You're a hoot!" The day was going to go well indeed.

"Hey," Saltzie said, "let's backtrack to that deli we passed for a quick coffee before beginning our detective work. My head is still banged. I'm afraid I was way out of line last night."

"You weren't. I had a spliffin' good time." Josephine attempted a flapper expression.

He stopped in front of Sam's Delicatessen, and turned to look at Josephine. "You know, I had a spliffin' time last night, too. Joe, I always felt something, well, that there was a special bond, like a chemical bond between us. But I want to apologize for those days back in med school. I was young and reckless."

"There's no need. We all got through it."

"Remember that time we locked you in the morgue. That was dastardly."

"I didn't mind as much as you thought. I could study there —it was quiet." She gritted her teeth, but then laughed. "When the night janitor came in, boy, he had a start - he thought I was a ghost!"

Saltzie laughed. "You're so forgiving. Is that something the nuns taught you?" He touched her cheek. "We did tease you mercilessly. What else could we do? You were so determined and smarter than any of us."

"I suppose you teased me because you felt threatened."

"Yes, I suppose. I didn't deserve to be there. It's as if I just had to show up and collect my diploma."

"Was that before or after you borrowed my notes?"

He chuckled in response. "Touché!"

Saltzie stepped out of the motor car. "Don't go away!" he winked.

Josephine looked up and saw a seagull soaring. "Please forgive me, again." She said a quick prayer to Mother Cabrini, crossed herself, then rifled through Saltzie's glove box. There was a publication of Lord Byron's poetry. *How sweet!* she thought. But there was also a little black book just like Arnie's. She took a peek: girls' names, too, and numbers.

Angrily, she threw the little black book in the glove box and slammed it shut. Sam came running over.

"Hey Doc, you're finally out of your office. It's a fine day! Youz going for a picnic? That *mensch* of yours is buying sandwiches, fruits, and a bottle of my best cellar booze."

Saltzie emerged from the deli, stopping to light a cigarette, so Sam lowered his voice.

"Doc, those numbers in Arnie's little black book aren't girls' phone numbers. Dominick thinks they're some kinda code. Some of the numbers repeat. He's working on it."

Josephine felt relief that Saltzie didn't have his own harem. She quickly took the little black book out of the glove box and handed it to Sam.

"Here, give this to Dominick and the gals."

Saltzie approached, so Sam raised his voice back to normal and said cheerily, "Have a good time, you kids!" he winked at them, rubbing his palms together.

"Gee, it's like a little village out here in Brooklyn. Everyone is so friendly," Saltzie said.

"It's not Fifth Avenue, that's for sure," she said, putting her nose up in the air.

"Ha ha! I'm always put out on the street anywhere I go, it would seem."

"I'll bet!" She smiled at him, but was wondering what messages were in his and Arnie's little black books.

Saltzie was excited and talkative. "You studied, Joe, and never got in any trouble. We stayed out all night, fell asleep in class, didn't do our homework. The professors were always mad at us."

"I didn't have it so easy."

"Not like us men," he added.

"What do you mean?"

"We're not all good like you, sorry to say."

They drove along and he reached over to touch her knee again.

"Joe, I didn't defend you enough. All those pranks. I hope you can forgive me—*ambo te ignosce me.*"

"*Numquam!* Certainly not!" She was kidding, but he still looked downcast with his soulful puppy eyes, and it was her turn to touch his cheek and make him smile.

He began quoting poetry.

"How beautiful she look'd! her conscious heart
Glow'd in her cheek, and yet she felt no wrong.
O Love! how perfect is thy mystic art,
Strengthening the weak, and trampling on the strong..."

"Byron," they said in unison. "Don Juan."

"I remember you standing on top of that apple crate in Autopsy Class. You were six foot tall! I laughed so hard, I almost split apart like our poor cadaver."

"That crate got me through Anatomy, too."

"I was secretly rooting for you," Saltzie added. "I have a little sister, and she's feisty, always demanding her rights, just like you."

They drove up to the front of Janus' large brick compounding laboratory and found a parking spot around the back. They walked to the factory door. Josephine knocked, but no one answered.

"Janus!" she called, "It's Josephine. I've brought a friend from college. Saltzie—remember him?"

The door was slightly ajar. She pushed it open and they walked inside. The pharmacy was cavernous and silent. Sunlight filtered in through streaked skylights, bathing the laboratory in eerie light. Josephine could see several enormous round distillers made out of steel. Dust covered tables with scattered broken paraphernalia —the entire laboratory looked abandoned and forlorn.

"How the mighty have fallen," Saltzie whistled.

Shelves were filled with glass bottles and jars of all different shapes and sizes. Everything was in disarray, but some bottles were still grouped in alphabetical order.

Josephine pushed some cobwebs aside, and beginning with the "A's" read: *Aesculus hippocastanum, Antimonium tartaricum, Argentum nitricum, Arnica montana,* and *Arsenicum album.* Witch Hazel, Silver Nitrate, Arnica, Arsenic. She took a second look for *Aconitum napellus,* but found it missing.

They passed into a glass-ceilinged atrium, filled with flowering plants baking in the hot house. Josephine's love of botany allowed her to easily recognize the blossoms, and all were poisonous, like Foxglove and Belladonna. She searched for the distinctive dark purple flowers of the Aconite plant, but it wasn't in this area either. There were tables lined with shells, hammers, anvils, and lots of other tools for beating, grinding and succussing. Josephine and Salzie roamed the laboratory, naming more compounds: *Calcarea phosphorica, Calcaria carbonica, Helleborus niger, Gelsemium, Mercurium solubilis...*

"I remember all this stuff," Saltzie said. "Janus used to be so busy, with his pharmacology students making all these remedies and employing dozens of people. It looks like the Allopaths have put him out of business."

"Yes, it appears so." Josephine called out again, "Janus, I'm here, it's Josephine. Where are you?"

"Someone's back there. I heard something," Saltzie motioned to a door.

They entered the rear storeroom.

There was broken glass everywhere and signs of a struggle. Shelves were toppled. Janus was lying in the middle of the floor moaning. He was holding his throat, making slight gurgling noises.

"He's in distress! Oh, no! Do something, find a phone and call the ambulance!" Josephine said frantically.

"We're doctors. We know what to do!" said Saltzie.

They looked at each other, then bent down at the same time in a rush and collided, banging their heads together. Saltzie rubbed his temple and said, "We can do this. You listen for breathing and I'll check for a pulse."

"He's still alive," Josephine said.

"What's he saying?" Saltzie asked.

"Oh, no! He said 'Aconite!'"

"Who did this?" Saltzie asked, leaning over Janus closely, listening for any response. "That sounded like 'X.'"

"His ex?"

"Maybe he said 'Rex'?"

Janus stopped breathing. "We've got to start his heart!" Josephine shouted.

"What do you mean?

"You know, pound on his chest."

"What are you talking about? I work the rectum."

"I read about this new technique in a medical journal." Josephine pounded hard several times on Janus' upper chest over his heart. "Any breathing now?"

"No. You know, if it's Aconite, he hasn't got a chance."

"Keep pounding! We have to try—I'll find something." She spotted a leather bellows by several Bunsen burners, ran over and grabbed it. She then put the tip up Janus' nose. Squeezing the bellows, she pushed and pulled, forcing air into Janus' lungs as his chest moved up and down. Saltzie pounded on Janus' heart repeatedly. They kept at it, pounding and blowing, for fifteen minutes.

"It's no use," Josephine said in exhaustion. "He's not breathing on his own."

"No pulse. He's gone."

They leaned back, exhausted and panting. Josephine shuddered and Saltzie put his arm around her, pulling her close. "You were amazing, Joe. Pounding like a bear cat—I never saw that before! And that bellows, golly, that was quick thinking."

"Thanks, you weren't so bad yourself," she exhaled, breathing hard. "But Janus, poor Janus. Aconite is the perfect poison. Why would he take it?"

"No. I heard someone rummaging about," Saltzie said. "The killer must have left just as we got here. Maybe we should look around before we call the police. We might find an Aconite plant here somewhere."

They got up from the floor and began searching the laboratory.

"Oh dear, I wish we'd gotten here sooner," Josephine said sadly. "We might have saved Janus."

"Yes, poor devil...."

Josephine took a last look at Janus. What a terrible waste, she thought. He knew so much about Homeopathy and now his knowledge would be lost. She looked at his desk in the hopes of saving something of his and saw a square envelope marked with *"Mouse"* scrawled across the front in black ink.

"Look, Saltzie. It's for me. "Mouse" was the pet name Janus gave me. He used to joke that I was so tiny and quiet and snuck up on him like a little mouse. He said that if I wasn't careful, he would use me as a laboratory rat!"

"Janus always had a morbid sense of humor. Remember when he crushed that skeleton's metacarpals. When the Anatomy professor shook hands with it, the fingers came right off the bone."

"That was funny."

Suddenly, they could hear the front door squeak on its hinges. "Open up! Police!" They heard rushed voices and footsteps.

"It's that Detective O'Malley!" Josephine recognized his iron voice. "They must have found out about this Homeopathy lab." She grabbed the envelope and stashed it in her purse.

"They're going to think we killed him. Let's get out of here, Joe. Quick, out the back!"

Saltzie yanked open the back door just as the tall shadow of Detective O'Malley stepped into the frame. The two men scuffled and O'Malley landed a blow to Saltzie's jaw. Saltzie staggered backward into Josephine, who was rushing forward in her attempt to escape. Saltzie was sent reeling head first back into O'Malley's solar plexus. The lanky detective crumpled to the ground, gasping.

Saltzie grabbed Josephine's hand and pulled her towards the street, stepping over the fallen detective. But O'Malley's hand shot up from the ground, taking a firm hold of Josephine's ankle. With Saltzie trying to pull her by her arm out the door and the detective holding her by the leg, she was caught. She stared wide-eyed as Saltzie suddenly let go of her hand, also slipping her purse off her wrist. Now free, he looked stunned for a moment as if he couldn't decide what to do next. Then he mouthed the words *"trust me"*, and turned to run off down the street.

"Nice boyfriend you have, Dr. Reva," said Detective O'Malley, getting up and dusting himself off. He was still holding Josephine's arm in a vise-lock grip. "A purse snatcher as well as an escape artist."

The sergeant rushed over and said that Janus Heath was dead.

"Janus was alive when we got here—I can explain this. We were trying to save him. He was dying—it's the Aconite killer again. Saltzie will tell you."

"It looks like your alibi just took off and left you," Detective O'Malley said. "Josephine Reva, I'm arresting you for the murder of Janus Heath, and on suspicion of murder for the death of Anthony Goldblum. Sergeant, take her away."

Chapter 18 - The Pit

Sunday afternoon...

D r. Josephine Reva lowered her head to her hands, exasperated, as she sat on the hard bench.

"*Miseria! Sono innocente!* Darn! I'm innocent!" she shouted to the emptiness. Josephine reverted to Italian when she was in distress.

This was no place for a medical doctor, locked away in an interrogation room deep in the bowels of Brooklyn Precinct 962.

"I haven't made it this far from a Little Italy orphanage to medical school to be tossed in prison like a common criminal." Josephine looked around and sighed.

A bolted door. Stone walls. A barred window high above. A room with no means of escape.

"Detective O'Malley thinks poison is a woman's weapon of choice." Josephine stood up, then paced back and forth, clenching her fists. *"I'll teach him a thing or two about women!"*

That detective was toying with her like a cat who'd cornered a mouse. He wouldn't look for the real killer, now that he'd caught her in his claws.

"Aconite is a poison. But I'm a trained Homeopath —I've sworn on the oath of Hippocrates to never do harm.

"I cure people with Aconite, I don't kill them."

It was a paradox that Aconite was toxic in its natural form as a flowering plant, but when diluted, it became a Homeopathic remedy. Hadn't she explained this to the detective?

"O'Malley's not so smart. When I figure this out, *he'll wish he'd never messed with me!*"

Josephine was expected to be ladylike in society, but it was another matter in a jail cell. She pulled her amplifying stethoscope from around her neck and aimed to fling it at the door. But she relented. It had taken an entire year to save up $4.25 to buy it.

Josephine sat back down dejectedly. How could she prove her innocence when she was found at the scene of a second death by Aconite? She knew both victims, and she knew all about the poison "weapon." Nor did she have an alibi for either crime. Josephine realized the killer was manipulating her like a Pinocchio puppet on a string, right into Detective O'Malley's trap.

Who wanted to frame her?

She didn't meet many people, apart from her patients.

But she'd recently attended an unusual event—the prestigious Manhattan medical conference. It was a surprise to be invited, and Josephine was the only female doctor on the panel. Had she offended somebody by speaking her mind? Whom?

While she sat locked away, the Aconite killer roamed freely, ready to strike again. Josephine was livid. *This killer must be stopped,* she thought. *There has to be a way out of this prison.*

She banged on the steel door. Then she tried to jump up to the window, but it was too high. Searching nearly every inch of the walls, she found they were rock solid. The rookie officer hadn't called it "The Pit" for nothing. Exhausted, she gave up.

"If I can name the murderer, I'll be set free."

It seemed hopeless, and Josephine sighed. How could she solve these poison murders? *"I'm a doctor, not a sleuth!"*

Her patients had convinced her to go undercover as her alter-ego, a sexy flapper, to spy on suspicious doctors, quacks and bootleggers. What had they found? She recited a list: *little black books, an abandoned laboratory, a missing envelope, an Aconite plant, and doctors with too much cash, drinking champagne and putting on the Ritz.* Nothing pointed a finger at the murderer.

Her patients! What must they be thinking to see their doctor in prison? She'd only just gained their trust. Most female doctors failed their first year, but she had survived and built up her practice. The sooner this killer was found, the sooner she could get back to work and help others.

She hunched her shoulders and thought hard, back to the conference and the people she'd met. Where were those telltale signs? Someone must have been so full of sin to commit murder.

"If I'd only known then who was about to die."

* * *

On the other side of the door, Chief Detective O'Malley was using his own stethoscope—a surveillance one—to listen in through the keyhole. His grin was as wide as a Cheshire Cat's. Satisfied with what he'd heard, he padded off.

Once in his office, he leaned back in his chair and put his feet up on his desk. The sergeant poked his head around the doorway.

"How much longer are we going to hold Dr. Reva? We can't keep her locked up with these new Wickersham rules."

"No one here inflicts any pain, physical or mental, to extract any confession, whatsoever," O'Malley deadpanned. "That Lady Doctor's one of those suffragette types, always banging doors until they open.

Now she's in The Pit, and desperate. Mark my words, she'll crack."

What he really meant was that Dr. Reva would crack this case. She wasn't the type to buckle under pressure and confess to a crime she didn't commit. A street orphan raised by nuns, newly graduated from medical school. No, she wasn't guilty. But he was sure she'd use her brains to solve these crimes, just in time for him to earn his Detective Second Grade commendation.

"Let's begin questioning her," he called to his rookie and sergeant to accompany him to Josephine's cell. "Watch me and learn."

The bolt of the steel door slid open and Detective O'Malley and his men walked into The Pit. Josephine was sitting on the bench. She looked up warily at the trio.

"Miss Reva," O'Malley began, taking a chair opposite her, "it seems we meet again under less fortunate circumstances. Less fortunate for you, that is. Let's begin with you telling me why you poisoned Janus Heath with Aconite?"

"I didn't kill him and I'm not confessing to anything," Josephine said flatly. "If you would simply listen to what I have to say, then maybe it's not too late to catch the real killer."

"I'm all ears. Go right ahead and tell me why you were in Janus' lab at the same time he was dying from Aconite poison."

"He telephoned and asked me to come."

"And why would he do that?"

"I have no idea, but he clearly wanted to tell me something important. By the time Saltzie and I arrived, Janus was in distress. We tried to revive him, but..." Josephine stopped, for Janus' death had hit her hard. It wasn't often that she lost a patient. Besides, Janus was going to tell her, in all likelihood, who the murderer of Goldblum was. Now she realized that this suspicion pointed to her. With Saltzie gone, it would be nearly impossible to extricate herself from this mess. She sank in the interrogation chair.

"Are you sure it was Janus Heath who called you?"

"Well, no. I mean Sophie took the call. The caller identified himself as Janus." Now Josephine was wondering if she'd been set up. That meant that it wasn't Saltzie, she thought with a small measure of relief. She hadn't yet met him at the speakeasy. Could she trust him after all?

A loud commotion of tires squealing and breaking glass could be heard in the street outside. Detective O'Malley, the sergeant and rookie quickly left the room, bolting the door tight.

Josephine wondered what was going on, when suddenly, Saltzie's face appeared through the bars of the window above. He was using a scalpel to break the window seal.

"Joe, stack the bench and chair on top of the table. I'm crushing you out of here!" he yelled. She could just make out what he was saying through the glass. A chain was pulling the bars away from the window.

"I can't leave. I'll become an outlaw." But she stacked the bench and chair on the table, and grabbed her medical bag.

"Don't worry! Your patients and Dominick made a fracas in the street for a diversion. We've figured out something big. Hurry up! I'll explain in the car."

Her patients were helping her break out of the police station? The bars tore off from the window, and Saltzie pulled the glass out. Josephine tossed her medical kit up to Saltzie, then climbed on top of the wobbly pyramid. Saltzie grabbed her wrists and pulled her up. Her tiny figure squeezed through the window into Saltzie's arms.

Together they ran, passing Sophie and Andy's delivery jalopy, which had spilled vegetables into the street. Dominick was outside the Packard, yelling and waving his arms, pretending to be in an accident with the grocers. Mike, Sam, Gabe, Maria and Antonio formed a wall of pedestrian onlookers, and were motioning for her to hurry along behind them. Josephine and Saltzie ducked in a side street, then jumped in Saltzie's roadster and sped off.

"I've some experience in quick getaways" Saltzie said, a little too gleefully.

"Yeah, I found that out once before," Josephine replied.

"Joe, I had to leave you so I could come back and save you."

"That doesn't make any sense. I don't know how you pulled this off, and I'm grateful. But now I'm in worse of a pickle."

"Don't worry, we'll find the killer somehow. Here's your purse. I couldn't help taking it at Janus' lab when O'Malley grabbed your arm. The contents must have spilled during my getaway. Why don't you see if you can find a comb and powder to fix your face? I'll drive as fast as I can."

"That O'Malley is going to come after us."

"We'd better get out of town until things cool down. I know just the place."

He turned his roadster to the south and sped towards the ocean at Coney Island.

Chapter 19 - Sea Gate

How self-deceitful is the sagest part
Of mortals whom thy lure hath led along—
The precipice she stood on was immense,
So was her creed in her own innocence.
—Don Juan by Lord Byron

T he sunset was shooting colors across the sky—bright orange, vivid purple and glowing pink. Venus, the bright evening star, had risen and sparkled on the eastern horizon.

Saltzie turned on the radio.

"Latest update on Director Goldblum's murder: toxicologist determined that poison was the cause of death. Breaking news: Police found pharmacist Professor Janus Heath dead in his apothecary in Borough Park. Preliminary findings show he was poisoned. Both poisoning victims knew each other. Police stated that the public should not be alarmed. In other news, Mayor Jimmy Walker calls for a relaxation of Prohibition rules and for the District Attorney to end prosecutions of liquor..."

"Enough news," Saltzie said, turning off the radio. He extended his arm around Josephine, drawing her near. "Don't worry, it'll be okay. Let's enjoy this beautiful sunset together. I'm hoping it won't be our last."

"I won't be opening my office tomorrow for the first time."

"You and me both, but we're wanted dead or alive. I don't know about you, but I'd prefer alive."

They drove on in silence over the causeway leading to the barrier island. The salty sea air was rushing in through the open windows, and the early summer was casting its spell. If it was their last night of freedom, at least it was beautiful.

"*Puer puellam pulchram amatum,*" Saltzie uttered after some time, relieved. He'd clearly been puzzling out the grammar of this sentence in Latin.

"What?"

"My feeble attempt to be romantic. I was trying to say "the boy loves the beautiful girl."

"That's sweet, but "*amatum*" is past tense, or "loved." As in, it's over. It should be '*pulchram puellam puer amat.*'"

"If you're going to get grammatically high and mighty, then I'll add that *amatum*, past tense, fits!" Saltzie looked offended.

"*Formosus puer puellam amat,*" she said to soothe him. He had helped her escape from O'Malley's clutches, after all. "The girl loves the handsome boy. It is a dead language, anyway. I only had the nuns teach me, and they didn't teach such things!"

"Those nuns in the convent, hmmm. Are they the ones who taught you to dress as a flapper?"

Josephine wondered if he was joking or serious. "No, those were my patients."

"Your patients are much more helpful than mine." He paused and took his eyes off the road to look at Josephine. "You should listen to your patients and wear that flapper disguise more often!"

He reached over and squeezed her thigh. She was surprised by the intensity of his touch. But she didn't brush his hand aside, either.

They drove on, stopping to marvel at the height of the Cyclone roller coaster. "Where are we headed?" she asked.

"To my father's house."

Shops on Stilwell Avenue were open for summer beach goers. They stopped off for some water and other provisions. Saltzie left Josephine in the car and came back with a bag of oysters and lemons.

Instead of heading left at the boardwalk towards the area with the big hotels at Brighton and Manhattan Beaches, Saltzie turned the motor car to the right on Surf Avenue. He drove to the furthest point west on the barrier island. They entered a small community of beach cottages—a sign read "Sea Gate." Saltzie drove to the end of the road.

"Look up, Joe—it's the Coney Island Lighthouse," he said.

A beacon towered above them. It was a tubular black and white striped column planted firmly in the rocks at the point. The pulsing light flashed every few seconds. The lighthouse keeper's brick Victorian cottage stood alongside and a sign marked the area as Coast Guard property. There was no one around, and all was quiet.

The sky was darkening to violet and pink, illuminated by the rhythmic flash of the beacon, like lightning across the sky.

"We used to climb to the top when I was little, and Mr. Grady would yell at us. Now hardly anyone comes out here anymore. The really rich head over to the North Shore of Long Island to their mansions."

Josephine looked around. The houses didn't look shabby at all—she saw beautiful beach homes with lots of glass windows. If this was "rich" then she could only imagine what it meant to be "really rich." She'd read in magazines about the "Robber Barons" and seen pictures of their million dollar estates on Long Island. This area was less ostentatious, but Josephine was still awed.

Saltzie parked the car alongside the lighthouse facing the ocean and turned off the motor. They watched the magnificent sunset in silence as the beacon continued to flash over the water.

"Look, there's Gravesend Bay and beyond that, The Narrows. This seaway is part of The Bight—where Long Island meets New Jersey and Staten Island, as if a shark took a bite out of the shoreline. We're only about ten miles from Manhattan, there's a ferry to the Battery, but here's another world! My old motor car did a fine job getting us here so quickly."

"This is incredible. We're on an island." But she looked nervously at the black water in the distance, remembering the gruesome corpse of Dr. Goldblum.

"Yes, it's one of my favorite places. I'm glad you like it, Joe. It's special. I loved fishing here off the rocks with my father, uncle and cousins. A nice escape from the crowds in Yorkville."

"I can see why. The view is incredible and the ocean is, uh, dark."

"Here, I'll show you the beach area." He drove around the bend, and pulled the motor car to the side. "This point is rocky, but there's a few sandy spots we locals know about." The setting sun was still glowing orange and the sky had turned a darker purple.

"Take off your shoes and stockings!" he ordered. "Don't be shy, we're at the beach!"

Then he was like a boy again, clamoring over the rocks. "I wish I had a fishing pole—I'd catch us dinner. Come this way. Don't worry, the rocks are smooth and there's a patch of sand over here." He returned and held out his hand to help Josephine over the rocks to a spit of soft sand.

Saltzie found some reeds and placed them down for Josephine to rest upon.

They sat down together, hips touching.

"Did you know, back in the 1600's, this island and Gravesend, all of it, was first settled by a woman? I don't mind women being in charge—I rather like it." He looked expectantly at Josephine.

"So you wouldn't mind a wife bossing you around?"

"Not at all! And you're the only bossy woman I know, besides my sisters."

She wondered if she should be the one to kiss him. Then Saltzie asked if she was cold, and took off his jacket to put around her shoulders. They moved closer until their arms touched and watched the sun turn a blazing orange as it began its rapid descent towards the horizon.

"You've been through a lot today," he said hesitantly. "It's getting cooler—maybe we should head up to the house."

"Oh wait. I want to watch the sun completely disappear," she replied, "I can't wait for this day to be over." With Janus' death and her jail break, she realized that now she and probably

Saltzie were on the lam, and she wanted to push that thought away. Saltzie put his arm around her shoulders, drawing her into his chest.

Then he reached over and kissed her. It was a strong kiss and his mouth opened greedily. She felt his tongue touch hers and was momentarily surprised and jerked away. Her fiancé had never done that. Saltzie felt her resist, so he pulled her tighter. She pushed back reflexively, not being used to amorous advances, sending the two of them reeling backwards on the sand and landing Josephine on top of Saltzie.

"That's right, Josephine," he said, aroused. She hadn't meant to take the initiative. But he was excited and pulled her more firmly down against his body. The sun was fast slipping below the waterline.

When they stopped petting to take a breath, Josephine took stock of the situation and realized that she couldn't fully trust Saltzie. Besides, it was getting dark. She asked, rather urgently, "Do you have a flashlight?"

He laughed no, the moon was quarter full, so they'd have enough light.

But the spell was broken and he got up, saying they'd better walk back before they were forced to spend the night on the little beach. "We'll be more comfortable at the house," he said.

They dusted the sand off their clothes, and made their way gingerly back over the rocks. Josephine noticed the stars just beginning to emerge in the night sky.

Saltzie parked the roadster in front of a wooden cottage built on stilts with a deck and dock perched over the rocks at sea level. It was a simple place, two stories, but all the rooms were aligned for the best views along the water. An outdoor deck above and a terrace below extended towards the sea.

"I'll make up your room. It's not much. This is just a shack, a weekender now."

"It's very nice," she said. The neighboring houses were packed in like sardines, for the waterfront lots were narrow, and the other homes were shuttered. She wondered how the rich managed to take care of all their extra properties. They seemed to like leaving them vacant, strewn about like discarded packages. If she had the extra money, she'd prefer to stay in a fancy hotel with room service and valet parking and travel to a different one all the time. But Saltzie seemed to have a deep affection for this house on the cove.

"My father built it, so it's very sturdy, even if it doesn't look like much. It's withstood a few storms, well, most of it has. A fisherman's battered home."

"Wow, he was a fisherman? I'd have never guessed."

"Yeah, not many people would. He had good woodworking skills, even built several wooden boats and an oyster trawler. He was a carpenter in Manhattan, doing custom work in wealthy people's houses. They paid him a lot of money for his carpentry. He was very talented. I guess I'm good with my hands, too, for surgery!" he laughed. "Soon, he had enough money to take on an apartment building in Yorkville. Back then, it wasn't a ritzy area, more like a muddy hilltop. Then he bought some lots, built some more. He put everything he had into it, and did most of the work himself. He met my mother and the rest is history."

"That's quite a story."

"So this cottage, they used to bring me here when I was a child, to rest and recover. I had gotten ill, you see. Tuberculosis...." Saltzie's voice broke. "I loved it here, the sea air—the doctor thought it would do me good, and it did. The lesions on my lungs were mild. Soon I was running all over the place. I think this house saved me. I'd do anything to keep it." He suddenly brightened. "Here, I'll show you around outside while there's still a bit of twilight."

He led her outside to the terrace and down to the rough hewn dock. The ocean crashed onto the rocks below. They walked out as if standing upon the ocean, and Josephine could feel the unsteadiness as the force of the waves pushed the timbers. The deck heaved and groaned under the pressure.

"Sorry, it's just barely standing. I apologize. My father's too old, and well, I never got around to repairing it after the last storm knocked out most of the side section there. Another storm might wash it completely away. Maybe the house, too."

"That would be terrible to lose those memories." Josephine realized that there weren't many memories from her childhood that she'd like to keep.

"Yes." But then he turned to her. "Sometimes I wish it would wash out to sea."

"Why ever?

"Oh, I don't know." He went silent.

"This view, and this dock, it's like we're out in the middle of the ocean." Josephine said. The lighthouse was still radiating light beams across the sky. "The only time I've been this close to the water was on the Staten Island Ferry!"

He laughed. "We have a small boat, too, but it's a little rough tonight. Maybe I'll take you out sometime." She nodded, but was frightened because she couldn't swim. The surf looked turbulent crashing on the rocks, and the water dark and deep. She saw the silhouette outlines of two points of land. "Isn't that The Narrows way up ahead?"

"Yes, it is, and that's Staten Island across the way."

"The Narrows is where Goldblum was killed, and now, Janus is dead, too. I don't know what's going on!"

"Oh dearest, don't be upset," he put his arms around her and began kissing her. They were being jostled on the unsteady deck by the crashing ocean, and she stumbled.

"Let's go back inside, eat some dinner, then get some rest, so we can think clearly in the morning. It's been a distressing day." He took her hand and led her back along the dock to the dark cottage and turned on some lights.

"We've got these old sandwiches from our picnic that never happened. But how about some Long Island oysters, clams and spaghetti—you Italians love that—and a glass of champagne?" He opened the bag he'd bought on the avenue, and reached into the icebox. He popped the champagne cork, and poured out two fizzy glasses.

"Cheers!" he said, "To my *pulcerimma Josephinna!*" They laughed and sipped the champagne.

"We shouldn't be celebrating after we left the coppers red-faced and empty-handed," Saltzie said. "But I'm going to get you out of this mess."

"We're a couple of outlaws!" she said. She wished she had something more romantic to say. She should have paid more attention to flapper speech at The Oasis. She'd never been alone with a man for the evening, so, feeling awkward, she set about boiling a pot of water, which was about all she could manage. Saltzie, however, was a fine cook, and sautéed the clams with some olive oil, garlic and then drizzled some lemon juice on top. Next he shucked the oysters, and fed one to Josephine, who gagged at first as the mollusk slithered down her throat.

"Wow!' she exclaimed, "that's raw? It tastes pretty good!"

"Yes, it's one of my favorite things to eat at the beach. They've still got some oyster beds out past Jamaica Bay and the Rockaways in Long Island, where the water is cleaner," replied Saltzie.

After dinner, he opened the door to the terrace and announced it wasn't too chilly, and it would be pleasant to sit outside. He lit a campfire with some driftwood stacked on the side.

"The fire and moonlight is beautiful, romantic," she ventured, but Saltzie was silent. Josephine assumed it was because they were alone, and neither knew what to say. They sat on Adirondack chairs by the fire. A foghorn from a ship in the distance blew, and he looked up quickly. She could see some twinkling ship lights on the water, far out from the dock.

"Josephine, do you realize that we've been together the entire evening, and you haven't mentioned your work or your patients hardly at all?"

"I guess I've been too busy, breaking out of jail and fleeing the law. I can't believe it myself."

"If that's what it takes to make you quit worrying about your patients and have some fun!"

Then he reached over to kiss her.

Josephine suddenly felt adrift. In fact, she had never strayed so far from her office, ready to attend to her patients at a moment's notice. Her patients were always telling her to take some time off, and urging her to date. The gossip mill must already be churning, spreading the news that she wouldn't be opening her office tomorrow morning because she had escaped from jail. But she was alone in a strange place by the shore with a man she hadn't seen since college. If this is what dating was, it didn't feel right. She went rigid, and he sat up.

"I can see you're not that flapper after all. I'd better be a gentleman and set up a cot in the living room."

He put out the fire and they went back inside. Josephine settled in the bedroom. Saltzie came in angrily and pulled one of the blankets off the bed for himself, then turned to look at her once more.

"Don't go!" but she didn't know what else to say. Her eyes met his bashfully, giving a little flutter.

"Oh, Josephine!" he moaned with desire and strode over towards her, throwing the blanket down. "You're driving me crazy!"

He pulled off his shirt, exposing his taut abdominals, then reached for Josephine's dress bow, pulling on the ribbons. He slipped her dress over her head, and she tugged on his belt, unzipping his pants.

"Undress me, " he said. And she complied, staring at his hardness. It was a medical marvel, far better than the textbook drawings.

"You just wait," he breathed. "It's your turn for an anatomy lesson."

He pulled off her slip and girdle, tossing them aside, and began stroking her breasts, eliciting sighs and trembles. His hands went all over her body, something she'd never experienced before, then moved lower, below her pelvis. An area of the body she associated with birth now became erotic. She moaned in rhythm to his fingers playing a slow song.

As they were lying on the bed necking and petting, touching skin to skin, a fog horn blared twice offshore.

Saltzie sat up abruptly. "I'll be right back, Josephine. Please don't fall asleep." He grabbed his pants and left.

But she fell asleep, lulled by the sounds of the ocean and the caressing of Saltzie's hands over her body.

A short time later, a rumbling noise awoke her. It was pitch black and the middle of the night, but she heard male voices. Was she dreaming?

She sat up and listened.

"What a beauty!"

"Got a V-12, liquid cooled..." That didn't sound the least bit romantic, nor like medical terminology. She listened more.

"Tie her off!"

Josephine grabbed her clothes, got dressed, then peeked out the bedroom window overlooking the ocean. She could make out the shadow of a very large armored speedboat that had just pulled up to the dock. A rope flicked across the air, and the silhouette of a bare-chested man, yes it was Saltzie, caught it. Then he wrapped the rope around a cleat. The huge double engines purred loudly. There were two men aboard, one running about the deck. The bearded man at the helm had an Italian accent, and the other sounded English. The captain laughed as Saltzie apologized for being late. "You caught me at a bad time."

The boat had a large enclosed cabin, and Josephine could see that its metal hull was welded with heavy rivets. It had strange antennae, and Josephine could hear a radio channel with a voice repeating numbers.

Josephine was stunned. She'd never seen anything like this mini naval destroyer, with large guns attached to the stern and foredeck.

The men jumped off the boat. Should she hide? Run? But where? Behind the lighthouse? This rocky point offered few hiding places. She heard voices, some curse words. She decided it was safer to keep still and not let them know she was watching.

"She's fast, made it here in under 20 minutes." The captain was talking to Saltzie.

"Any patrols?"the other man asked.

"Not tonight. No one at the station." That was Salzie's voice.

So that's why he took me to the lighthouse, Josephine thought.

The men worked hard, pulling crates out from behind the bushes. Liquor, Josephine saw, a lot of it. Then they loaded the crates into the boat's hold.

"*Madonna mia!* Cast off!" The captain was crossing himself for luck.

Well, at least he's religious and might one day have remorse for his life of crime, thought Josephine. The men untied the ropes and jumped back in the cockpit.

"Here's yours," one of the rumrunners said, tossing a duffel bag to Saltzie, "And we left some bottles of whiskey and French champagne for your doll— she'll love it."

The loud engine revved up. Josephine watched as the speedboat raced off, heading for The Narrows. Machine gunfire echoed in the distance.

She was just about to run outside and confront Saltzie when a loud pounding hit the back door at the terrace.

Chapter 20 - Bootlegging

A very zozzled Arnie, his long dark waves of hair falling across his face, his square-framed glasses fogging in the sea air, was yelling. "Let me in! I know you've got some giggle water here. I'm no cellar smeller!" He slurred his words and fell as Saltzie dragged him inside.

"Oh, great, Arnie. What did you do, swim here in a whiskey sea?"

"Fishermen took me most of the way. Hey, the drop was tonight, I saw that boat! Gimme some booze!" He walked over to the kitchen, took a glass and leaned against the counter, breathing heavily. He collapsed in a heap on the floor.

Josephine ran forward, her medical instincts overtaking any need to keep herself hidden. Saltzie looked surprised to see her awake, but he, too, rushed towards Arnie, rolling him onto his back, and they both began administering first aid. Josephine grabbed her medical bag, opening it, then leaned over Arnie with her stethoscope.

"I think I got some poisonous hootch..." Arnie spat out and suddenly sat up and grabbed Saltzie by the collar. "Be a good lad and pump me."

He turned towards Josephine, who was trying to check his heart rate. "What a pretty little nurse!" he began, but then looked startled. "Wait, I remember you.... the smart one! You're that girl who used to carry around her own pedestal!"

He suddenly swooned and fell back. "He's semi-conscious," Josephine said, "but his heartbeat is strong." Saltzie slapped Arnie hard across the face. Arnie came to and gasped as Saltzie forced him to drink Syrup of Ipecac.

"He'll vomit everywhere. Do you have an emesis basin?"

Saltzie found a bowl on the counter, just as the emetic began working.

Arnie burped up some foul whiskey and turned to Saltzie. "You've got hootch! The gang were here - you've got the Real McCoy!" He coughed up more alcohol, then had the presence of mind to recite Byron:

"Sweet is the vintage, when the showering grapes
In Bacchanal profusion reel to earth,
Purple and gushing: sweet are our escapes
From civic revelry to rural mirth"

Josephine, having treated alcoholics, replaced her stethoscope in her bag tiredly. She turned to glare at Saltzie. "*In vino veritas*—wine speaks truth," she said. "Arnie says you're working with the mob—bootlegging!"

"No, it's not like that, Joe," pleaded Saltzie. "Let me explain."

Arnie lurched and grabbed at them, then flailed about, knocking over Josephine's medical bag. Out rolled the wallets, spilling cash.

"Hey, that's my wallet," Saltzie said in shock. "Josephine, can you explain this?"

"I accidentally found, well, I took them at The Oasis. I thought maybe you had something to do with Goldblum's murder."

"You're a thief!" Saltzie said angrily.

"You're a bootlegger!"

"Oh, and you're not? Here's your Booze Blank!" Saltzie reached in his pocket and threw down a metal forger's plate. It was engraved with Josephine's Rx. "This was in your purse."

"That's not mine."

Josephine and Saltzie glowered at each other.

Arnie interrupted, waving his hand. "You both look like mad cats in heat. Please, would someone get me a drink!"

Josephine gathered her purse, the metal Rx plate and her medical bag, and stormed out the front door.

Saltzie ran after her. "Is that why you danced with me, and why you came here.... and why we...?"

Josephine yelled back, "No, I didn't know then. But now I do!"

"Josephine, where are you going?" Saltzie stood in the road. "Come back inside!"

Arnie groaned loudly from inside the shack, then yelled, "Saltzie, help me! I need that gastric lavage." He called out louder, "*My doctor!*"

"Wait, Joe," Saltzie ran forward and grabbed Josephine's arms. "I'll explain, please trust me. I was only trying to protect you." He paused, searching for the right words. "*Condemnant quo non intellegunt.*" He begged her not to condemn him without knowing the full story.

"Trust you? Are you crazy!" She shook free of his grasp and stalked off. Latin came easily to her when she was angry. "*Acta deos numquam mortalia fallunt*—mortal acts can not fool the gods."

She turned to look at him one last time. If this was love, then why was there deceit?

They both heard the blare of sirens rapidly approaching. Saltzie hung his head.

Josephine quickly reached the road, looking for a place to hide, when she saw the shape of a large motor car parked to the side. Its headlamps suddenly illuminated, blinding her. Was it the bootleggers? The car headed towards her at a fast speed. It screeched to a halt next to her, and the muscular figure of Dominick got out. Josephine exhaled in relief. He opened one of the suicide doors for her.

"At your service, Doc!"

"How did you.... Oh, never mind!"

"Let's get you outta here."

On their drive back from the shore, police cars with sirens wailing were heading in the opposite direction toward Sea Gate.

"That'll be the end of that rumrunning gang!" Josephine said.

"I was just about to pull you out of there, when you came barreling out. I should have figured."

"I can take care of myself," Josephine said. "But how did you know I was way out here on Coney Island?"

"Quite a trip, I'll say! The police have been following you. When we drove to the speakeasy, I could see them in my rear view mirror. I took evasive action, of course."

"Now I know why you keep the Packard running so well." Josephine sank back against the red cushions with a mixture of relief and regret. "That O'Malley is welcome to the lot of them! I hope I never see Saltzie again."

Dominick looked up and their eyes met in the rear view mirror. Dominick then spoke with some hesitancy.

"After your jailbreak, Detective O'Malley made me follow you instead of using his own men. When Saltzie took you to Coney Island, I knew something wasn't right. I waited to see if you needed my help. You seemed fine—I didn't want to interfere. It looked like you were having a good time, making a nice campfire... all cozy."

Josephine blushed. Surely Dominick hadn't seen anything in the bedroom through the curtains.

"But it was suspicious, so I kept watch from the road. Sure enough, I heard that speed boat come in. I mean, the engines were louder than an airplane taking off!" he laughed. "Those rumrunners don't seem to care if the whole world hears 'em."

"Yes, if they want to bootleg, they should be quieter," Josephine agreed. "The noise woke me up, too."

"My guess is that they pay off everyone—cops, Coast Guard, and probably your boyfriend. I think they saw the fire as a signal that the coast was clear. Saltzie probably figured you'd be pleased, maybe take a share of the profits!"

Josephine frowned. Saltzie was in cahoots with bootleggers. And he thought she was selling forged Booze Blanks.

Was that what these murders were about? Rum and whiskey! She told Dominick to continue.

"I crept over by the bushes out back. I heard that Italian and that Irish guy—sounds like Dwyer's old gang. They control the liquor running off Coney Island from Rum Row through The Narrows.

"I put two and two together. Those mobsters are killers. I didn't want you to get hurt. I waited and saw the whole thing at the dock. You were safe inside. Right after the bootleggers left, I drove to a pay phone to call O'Malley—the police are probably arresting the whole gang right now. The bad news is that O'Malley wants you. I'm to bring you back to the Precinct house for questioning."

Josephine thought Dominick sounded rather official.

"Do I have time to freshen up?"

"Yeah, take as much time as you need, but we'd better get there soon."

Dawn was breaking over the city as they headed back towards Bensonhurst.

Chapter 21 - Hospital

So, we'll go no more a roving,
  So late into the night,
Though the heart be still as loving,
  And the moon be still as bright.
—*Lord Byron (George Gordon)*

Monday morning...

Josephine walked up her steps slowly, and opened the door to her office. She walked through the scrubbed but empty waiting room silently, and then entered her bedroom. Peeling off her flapper clothing, she put on a bathrobe. In front of her vanity mirror, she vigorously scrubbed off every trace of make-up. That's better, she thought, looking at her good ole plain self in the vanity mirror. *No more of that silly flapper nonsense!* She'd only found disappointment, and she was no closer to proving her innocence. Dejectedly, she brushed her hair. She noticed the Aconite flowers, still fresh in their vase. Who had sent her the bouquet? It seemed like she had more questions than answers.

Things had certainly gone from bad to worse. First, she was a suspect in a murder, then another murder, then arrested, then escaped, only to end up in a bootlegger's lair! How had she gotten into such a mess?

She put on her slippers and scuffled to the kitchen to make herself a cup of tea.

Iacta alea est, she said to herself as she sipped the herbal brew, just as Julius Caesar was quoted by Suetonius before he crossed the Rubicon. The die is cast. She'd have to plead her innocence and hope that Detective O'Malley believed her. Or she'd better think of something else quickly.

A knock pounded at the front door. She ran to open it, desperate for anything or anyone that might help her. Maria, Antonio, Sophie, Andy, Mike, Sam and Gabe entered, looking sad and worried.

"We heard they're taking you back to the Precinct house," said Andy. "We wanted to see if we could help."

"We all know dat you're innocent!" cried Maria, blowing her nose into a handkerchief. "This is *pazzesco*, crazy!"

"The detective surely will let you go," said Sophie. "He can't be that blind."

"And dumb," said Antonio.

"'fraid so," said Sam, "he's not kiddin' around."

"What can we do?" asked Gabe.

"Well, let's get you changed and ready," Sophie and Maria said together, ushering Josephine into her bedroom and shooing the men outside. Sophie went to the large armoire and sorted through it, picking out an elegant flowing dress of beautiful white and grey silk. It had an extra-long matching scarf at the neckline, to trail elegantly along behind her, like the flowing wings of a butterfly. Josephine protested, but the ladies shushed her.

"White makes you look innocent," said Sophie. "You wouldn't want to wear black, or worse red."

"And dis scarf, it shows you're free as a bird, just like dat dancer Isadora Duncan."

"Didn't she strangle herself when her long scarf got caught in the spokes of her motor car's wheels?" asked Josephine.

"Doncha worry none!" Maria said as she set about putting lots of makeup on Josephine. "You wanna look beautiful for the cameras."

"Yes, you must face O'Malley and the press looking like the new Josephine—undercover sleuth and successful modern woman doctor. This dress suits you." said Sophie, as the three women looked in the mirror at Josephine's new attire, telling her to stand up straighter.

"You'll never attract a man if you look like a frump."

"I'm not frumpy," Josephine protested. "I'm just a doctor, a professional."

"That doesn't mean you can't look fabulous!" said Sophie. "And you do now."

"Besides, you'll be set free and outta dis mess," said Maria determinedly. "You're gonna crack dis case."

Josephine hugged the two women. Her patients were supporting her, just as she had always helped them. Perhaps working in Brooklyn, not Manhattan, was truly her mission, as the nuns had foretold. She sighed with a feeling of hope she hadn't felt in days.

The women went outside to join the men. Josephine looked at each of her patients to say goodbye.

But Sophie's face was turning a ghastly shade of white.

Andy cried, "Sophie, Sophie, darling, what's wrong?"

"I don't know, I feel weak."

"She's pale like a ghost. Maybe she drank too much alcohol at The Oasis?" Maria asked.

Josephine reached over to touch Sophie's forehead and check her pulse. "Dominick, quickly, get my medical bag out of the car." Dominick retrieved the kit and came rushing back. He gave it to Josephine and she pulled out her stethoscope.

"She's unwell. Her heartbeat is slow, her eyes and mouth dry, her pupils dilated. She's dehydrated. We've got to get her to the hospital now. Sophie, did you eat or drink anything unusual?"

"No, uh, yes, I took something to help me get pregnant."

"What did you take, Sophie?"

"It was Mother's Special Cordial, from Dr. Quinn. I thought it would help me..." She leaned against Andy and was too weak to speak.

Josephine tried to control her anger. If that Quinn had made Sophie sick or if she died...

They hurriedly climbed into the back of the Packard.

"Doc Joe, please stay in Brooklyn. I know you love Manhattan, but we need you here." Sophie fainted.

Dominick drove as quickly as he could to the hospital. Once they arrived, Sophie was transferred to a gurney by the orderlies and wheeled inside. Josephine made to follow.

"Not this time, Doc," said Dominick, pulling her arm gently. "Let the other doctors take care of her. She's in good hands. I need to get you to Detective O'Malley."

Josephine understood that her future was in jeopardy. She saw that Sophie was conscious again, and that the doctors and nurses were giving her fluids.

She went to Sophie's side. Sophie smiled and said, "Don't worry about me, Doc Joe. You go get yourself out of trouble." Josephine held Sophie's hand until she was wheeled away.

"We'll all stay right here until our Sophie is back, fit as a fiddle," Mike said. "But you go and solve the crimes, and give that O'Malley a helluva lesson in sleuthing."

Josephine turned to look at her patients.

Maria and her husband Antonio - they sang beautifully that Neapolitan song of regret. Hadn't Janus been repentant? Why did he feel so guilty if he didn't kill Goldblum?

Sophie - laughed at the 'My Doctor' jokes and noticed that those Yorkvillains had a lot of "lettuce" at the speakeasy. She drank Quinn's tonic and fell ill.

Mike - jolly Mike, put out of business by Prohibition when he had to close his bar. Janus was about to be put out of business, too, with new regulations.

Andy - sweet Andy, pretending to have a cold from his storage cellar, when I know he was really making whiskey down there. But he and Mike both wanted the Real McCoy.

Dominick - handsome, strong, protective. He'd told that story of the Three Generals—why was that sticking in her mind?

Then there was Speakeasy Sam - he delivered her bagels every day. Bagels with a hole, not bialys. That hole! What's missing in this case?

Her patients seemed to want Booze Blanks. Could there be a connection? Someone had stolen her Prohibition prescriptions.

And those little black books filled with names and numbers. A code. What did it all mean?

Dominick rapped on the hospital door. "I think it's time we headed over to the police station and face the music."

Chapter 22 - Sweet is Revenge

Sweet to the miser are his glittering heaps,
Sweet to the father is his first-born's birth,
Sweet is revenge–especially to women,
Pillage to soldiers, prize-money to seamen
  —Don Juan by Lord Byron (George Gordon)

Dominick pulled up in front of Brooklyn's Nine Six Two Precinct. A mob of reporters were waiting, and flashbulbs started exploding like popping firecrackers. Josephine got out of the Packard, shielding her eyes with the curved brim of her felt hat and feather. Her scarf flowed behind her and her skirt skimmed above her knees as she ran up the steps, but she didn't care. Escaping the pack of journalists was her main goal, and she could feel every part of her being illuminated by the flashes.

The reporters were shouting questions at her, asking if she was a temptress caught in a lover's triangle. "Did you poison Professor Heath and Dr. Goldblum for love or money?"

Like a mouse caught in a maze, Josephine didn't want to show any fear. In her purse she had placed a vial of Aconite, the last of the ones she and Janus had made together. Pulling open the door, she stopped just inside, and took out one little pill, placing it under her tongue.

"Best get this over with," she said, seeing O'Malley, who had been watching her every move.

He looked her up and down sardonically, and asked who she was.

"I'm Dr. Josephine Reva, remember me?"

"My! I didn't recognize you with that... get-up. Where's your usual plain dress and lab coat?"

"I've been working undercover. I think it rather suits me."

"I see." His eyebrows went up half an inch.

He accompanied her down the stairs to the dark basement interrogation room. This was the room Josephine remembered. The Pit. The one place she didn't want to ever see again. The window was now nailed shut with plywood.

Soon enough, she could hear the echoing voices of Saltzie and Arnie complaining, then the muffled curses of the two bootleggers from Saltzie's dock, and Quinn's obnoxious loud voice. They were shepherded into other rooms. Josephine seethed that Quinn was so close, believing that he had harmed Sophie with his tonic. But she didn't have any proof to accuse him.

O'Malley re-entered the Pit. He wasn't smiling.

"I see you've caught the rumrunning gang. They're the criminals, not me," Josephine said.

O'Malley sat down quietly in front of her and picked up the case file. "Now comes the good part, Miss Dr. Reva." He turned to his sergeant and rookie. "You boys start with those doctors and the medicine man. Make them sing. And those bootleggers— we need to find out who's higher up in their network. Rattle their cage."

The rookie looked at O'Malley and asked, "Don't we need to abide by Wickersham."

O'Malley grimaced. "Blasted Wickersham."

"There's no law against it—yet," the sergeant said, grinning like a dentist who can't wait to do some extractions. "Wickersham is only a *recommendation*."

"Good, you understand perfectly. Get to work. I'll begin with Miss Lady Doctor," O'Malley said, opening the case file.

"Doctor Reva," he began, twisting his fingers together, "seems like I'm playing catch up to you after every crime. Do you want to tell me what you were doing at Janus Heath's laboratory at the time he was murdered? The truth, this time."

"Well, it's really quite simple. I thought Janus might have some Aconite flowers," she began hesitantly.

"And why would you concern yourself instead of telling me that you suspected him of Goldblum's death?"

"I guess I couldn't believe he was involved, so I wanted to ask him myself."

"What happened?"

"First time I met him, I called him to ask him some questions about his argument with Dr. Goldblum at the conference. But he wanted to meet me at Green-Wood Cemetery. So I had Dominick drive me there."

O'Malley motioned to an officer to get Dominick.

"What happened at the cemetery?

"Janus admitted to fighting with Goldblum, knocking him down. Goldblum's head hit a tombstone by the Altar of Liberty.

There's some blood still there, if you look. Goldblum was going to shut down Janus' business - he wanted Homeopathic medicines to be sold without any prescription. They fought about it."

"Obviously, the knock on the head didn't kill Goldblum because he made it to The Narrows. Did Janus give Goldblum any Aconite?"

"Well, yes, he gave the Homeopathic remedy *Aconitum napellus,* but not the deadly flower. Janus confessed, thinking Goldblum later died from the remedy, but it couldn't have been..."

"And you didn't tell us? You're in trouble, young lady. Withholding evidence from the police is a serious crime."

"Janus didn't kill Goldblum. He only knocked him down. Goldblum left on his own two feet."

"Uh huh. So someone else killed Goldblum. I do agree. Are you ready to make your statement?" He brought out a piece of paper already typed out and put it on the table before her with a jar of ink and a fountain pen.

"Please listen. Janus didn't kill Goldblum. *Aconitum napellus*—the remedy—is dilute and non-toxic. Janus' remedies couldn't kill anyone. But Goldblum died with purple flowers in his mouth—I saw that."

"Yes, I know. I spoke with Senator Copeland. Homeopathic drugs are potentized, diluted over and over, to the *infinitesimal.*" O'Malley rubbed his temples. "There's only ions left, no poison molecules."

"Yes, that's right." She realized the Senator must have given O'Malley an involved lecture on the delicate process.

Dominick entered and sat down.

"So you see, Janus couldn't be the murderer," she continued.

She looked warily at Dominick. "That afternoon, Janus rang back and said he had something he wanted to show me in his laboratory. Saltzie drove me to his lab the next day, but when we got there it was too late."

"So you went with that fellow, Saltzie, the one we found at the dock with all the booze? The bootlegger."

"Well, yes, he's an old college classmate. When we got there, Janus was already dying. We tried to resuscitate him, but we couldn't save him."

"Uh huh," he said with disbelief. "How did you meet this Saltzie fellow?"

"I met him at The Oasis, it's an evening club. The patients took me out for the night, and I met doctors from my medical school. I was spying on them because there seemed to be a common link. Goldblum, the doctors and I graduated from the same school, and Janus taught pharmacology there. But that's not got much to do with it, after all. You see, Arnie and Saltzie had these little black books with numbers in them."

Dominick leaned forward to explain, "It's not phone numbers, it's a code."

"Where are these little black books now?"

Dominick took both little black books out of his pocket and put them on the table. "That's all of 'em."

"Anything else you two took? You'd better show me now."

Josephine reluctantly opened her purse and pulled out the "Mouse" envelope. "I took it when we were leaving Janus' laboratory because, well, he used to call me 'Mouse.'"

O'Malley reached over and snatched the envelope. He opened it and pulled out a thin metal plate with engravings on it. "Well, well," he said. "It's got your name on it, backwards! Do you know what this is?"

"It's an engraving plate of my Prohibition Prescription blank. I have no idea how or why —"

"So you know nothing of this counterfeit Rx plate? It's not only against the Prohibition Act, but against the US Treasury. We could charge you with a whole host of crimes and you'd never see the light of day again! We found alcohol in the distillers at Janus' lab. He was making whiskey and selling it from his dispensary, apparently with your prescriptions."

Janus had stolen her Booze Blanks? No, she thought, that's not like him. But he was saying "Rex" with his dying breath when he was lying on the floor. Maybe he'd been trying to repent, as he lay dying.

"Janus didn't tell me any of this at the cemetery, I swear! Maybe when he called me back, he wanted to confess that he was using my forged prescription blanks. Only he didn't get the chance, someone killed him first. Maybe he was forced to use my Booze Blanks and felt badly? There was somebody else there, we could hear him scuffling about like he was looking for something. He left out the back. Everything was a mess, broken jars, like a fight had taken place. Janus was lying on the floor, already dying from Aconite—the poisonous plant that is, not the remedy."

"Was Janus ever at your office?" The detective was tapping the paper again with the fountain pen.

"No, he couldn't have stolen my Prohibition Prescription blanks. I don't know—it just doesn't make sense."

"Who had access to these Booze Blanks?"

"Just me when I'm with patients. I keep it in my pocket, or my medical bag when I go out on house calls. I suppose anyone could have pickpocketed me, I was so busy, I might not have noticed if someone bumped or sandwiched me and reached in." That would have been easy, she knew herself how easy it was.

But who would do such a thing? Surely none of her patients would steal her Booze Blanks. She remembered that the numbers skipped. "Whoever it was was clever and took off a sheet in the middle, so I wouldn't notice. Then they put it back in my pocket."

"Or you could have given a sheet to Janus yourself," O'Malley said, shooting off accusations in rapid fire. "You wouldn't be the only doctor profiting from Prohibition, working in cahoots with a pharmacist to sell alcohol for a profit. This plate is evidence that you were supplying fake Booze Blanks."

O'Malley looked ready to pounce. "Here's what I think happened," he began menacingly. "You and Janus Heath were working together, distilling and selling alcohol with your fake Booze Blanks. That's how you got the money for all your elegant dresses, your chauffeur and your fancy car." He motioned to her and to Dominick, and Josephine awkwardly wrapped her silk dress with its flowing scarf tighter around her.

"Goldblum was on to you, and he was going to turn you both in. So Janus fought him, hit him on the head, took him to the lab where you both finished him off with deadly Aconite flowers. The poison killed him. You tried to make it look like a suicide by dumping him at The Narrows. But one man wasn't enough—you had them on a leash. Your new boyfriend Saltzie killed Janus —probably because he was jealous or because Janus double-crossed you."

"What? That's crazy!"

Dominick interrupted, "What about the bootleggers and the code books?"

"Why don't you tell me about that?" he glared at Josephine. "In your examination room, we found this." O'Malley slammed down on the table the *Aconitum napellus* vial from Josephine's wooden Homeopathic remedy box. "You're a Homeopath. Aconite is causing a lot of headaches for you, Miss Queen of Poisons."

"I didn't kill either of them, neither did Saltzie!" Had she just defended Saltzie? Somehow, she believed him to be innocent.

O'Malley continued to tap the table and the statement. "You're facing double murder charges, absconding with evidence, Federal counterfeiting charges, obstructing a murder investigation and more. Now's the time to confess and work out a deal. You can testify against your boyfriend. He's probably singing about you right now."

Josephine had never been one to panic in an emergency, but it was time for her to panic. She needed to save herself. Who knew what Saltzie was saying to the cops? She couldn't dare imagine!

A knock at the door, and O'Malley was called outside. Before leaving he tapped the statement again, looking Josephine in the eye, as if telling her to sign it. Josephine didn't need to look at it to know it was a confession. She turned to Dominick. "What am I going to do?"

"Doc, you'd better pray." Dominick got up. "I'll go get some coffee, and you a tea. We need a clear head."

He left and went into the hallway. Josephine cradled her head in her arms on the table. She was tired and hadn't slept much at Saltzie's. All was silent.

The door opened again and a woman officer in uniform came in. She was surprisingly beautiful, like a movie star, with long wavy reddish golden hair that glimmered under the harsh lights and pale green eyes. Josephine wondered if female police officers who glowed even existed. She sat serenely across from Josephine and placed a cardboard box on the table marked "Evidence."

Josephine opened it. Inside were Goldblum's belongings. She recognized that gold ring he wore - it had the seal of her medical college. Josephine took it and fingered it, slipping it on and off. It kept rolling sideways because it was so top-heavy. The woman police officer closed the box and seemed to float out of the room.

Josephine looked closely at the large ring slipping on her finger. The side carving was thick. Was that a little hidden latch? Yes, it was. She opened it, and purple flower petals spilled out. "*O, Dio buono!* Good Lord!" she gasped. She used O'Malley's confession pen to carefully push the deadly Aconite back into the ring without touching any powder and closed the latch tightly.

"Dominick!" She ran out into the hall to find him at the coffee stand. They both re-entered the interrogation room together.

"Don't touch that ring! It's full of poisonous Aconite! Dominick, can you get O'Malley and everyone else in here? I think I know what happened!"

O'Malley strutted back into the room with Dominick. The sergeant and rookie brought in Saltzie, Arnie, the two bootleggers and Quinn. They all sat down and faced Josephine, who was standing at the front of the room.

"Okay, Miss Doctor Reva, we're all ears," said O'Malley. "Ready for whatever game you're playing."

Josephine suddenly felt nervous. What if she was wrong? She'd surely go to prison. *Fortes fortuna adiuvat.* She took the fountain pen, let it soak up some ink, and turned the confession O'Malley wanted her to sign blank side up and pinned it to the wall. She twitched her toes in her shoes to keep herself steady and took a few deep breaths, then began in a small, high-pitched voice.

"It all started with Dr. Goldblum's report. Let's call it a bagel." She made a drawing of two concentric circles around a hole, looking like a bagel.

"Nobody has a copy? Why?" No one said anything.

"We've been looking at everything all wrong," she continued. "To solve this crime, we have to assume one important thing—that report doesn't exist. It's missing, like the hole in the bagel!" She pointed to her drawing. "Goldblum found out a lot of dirt on everyone, but he wasn't going to squeal or publish any of it. Why not?"

She looked around the room, searching for a better way to explain her theory. Her eyes rested on Dominick. "Well, to answer that, it's the story of the Three Generals, from the Battle of Brooklyn."

"Miss Reva," O'Malley let out a loud guffaw. "What do bagels and the Revolutionary War have to do with murder?"

Josephine hesitated, but then continued. "They were three: General William Howe, General George Washington, and Admiral Richard Howe." She drew three stick figures under the bagel. "General Howe was the old-fashioned one who believed in honor," and she wrote 'Honor' under the first figure. "He was outwitted by Washington."

She pointed to the second stick figure. "Then there's the Admiral who blockaded The Narrows." She wrote 'Blockade' under the second stick figure.

Lastly, she put an X under the third stick figure and wrote "Escape" underneath. "Washington was a rebel, an escape artist in the Battle of Brooklyn, ready to do whatever was necessary."

The group looked at Josephine as if she was delusional. Arnie spoke up, "Honor, blockade, escape—how? By boat? Is this somehow going to save us?"

"I don't think so," said Saltzie, "but with Joe, you never know. She always manages to hit it out of the ballpark. Let her continue." He winked at Josephine.

"Okay, then," began Joe, drawing three lines to connect each stick figure with the bagel above. "You see the first one, Honor

—that General is Janus Heath. He wanted to help people with Homeopathic remedies, and wanted to keep making them in his lab—he wanted the status quo, just like General Howe." She wrote Janus' name under the first stick figure.

"Then, the second square, the Admiral—I bet you're thinking that's the head bootlegger?

The others nodded.

"Nope, that's Anthony Goldblum. He was powerful, like Admiral Howe, and he had the power of blockade. You see, he told me at the conference that he wanted to modernize medicine with his report on prevention. His report was going to block many people by ending their livelihood." She put his name under the middle stick figure.

"And then there's the third General—it's not Washington, of course. We'll call him X, the one who always slipped away. That's our murderer."

"Surprisingly," said Detective O'Malley, "I'm starting to see a pattern."

"Arnie, Saltzie, Quinn. You are all connected through the gentleman's club. Am I right, Quinn?"

O'Malley turned to him. "You'd better admit it. I heard all about you pharmacologists."

"Uh, yes, I worked in Janus' lab, and I'm a member of the club. But we all were, well, except women, like Josephine."

"And there's the Dwyer gang," Josephine continued. She drew two squares on the paper. The two bootleggers looked like bull dogs waiting to sink their teeth into her. She took a step back. "I'll get to them later."

"So did they fight for honor, blockade or escape?" the rookie asked.

"Well, we know Goldblum found out about wrongdoings, and he threatened to block the others. He held the power to blow the whistle on them with his report. But he didn't. At least he didn't present his report at the conference."

"Why not?" Saltzie asked.

"He got greedy, that's why." Josephine continued with renewed vigor. "Goldblum was a city official with a small salary. He wanted to turn his knowledge into profit— he knew who his report would harm the most, and he wanted to make them pay him *not* to publish it."

"Blackmail! He uncovered a lot of dirt," said O'Malley.

"Why wouldn't he publish his report and gain fame and recognition?" Saltzie asked. "Maybe even be promoted."

"I think he gave up on that idea. He was a political outsider, and what he really wanted was wealth. At the gentleman's club where you meet, he saw many people getting rich off Prohibition, except him. At the conference, I overheard Quinn tell Goldblum that his tonic business was growing three-fold. I saw the crowds around your booth, Quinn. I don't doubt you were adding whiskey to your tonics. Maybe you were stealing from bootleggers?" Josephine pointed to the two boatmen.

"Saltzie and Arnie, you were aiding and abetting the bootleggers and I bet you flaunted your cash at the club, like you did at The Oasis. Saltzie, I saw the bootleggers throwing you a bag that probably had your cut. Arnie, you were the Manhattan contact in Yorkville, close to the speakeasies in Harlem—maybe you own warehouses or your townhouse has a secret door to a cellar to hide the booze?" She looked at Arnie, and he looked down at the ground, heaving a sigh. "Then there's the bootleggers, too, who didn't want Prohibition to end."

"If Goldblum was threatening everyone, which one murdered him?" O'Malley asked.

Everyone looked up at Josephine again.

"I bet you still think that the General X, the murderer, is the head bootlegger?" She asked the others.

They all nodded, except the bootleggers who seemed ready to bite. The sergeant and rookie held them gruffly by the shirt collars.

O'Malley poked one of the burly bootleggers with his blackjack. "Dwyer got arrested, so start talking."

"Now Costello's running it. It's called The Combine," the bearded man said. "Dwyer switched to gambling. I ain't saying nuttin' else."

"The Combine owns a flotilla of Mother Ships coming in from Canada and the French islands selling liquor and making millions," said O'Malley. "We can't catch 'em— yet." He eyed the bootleggers as if they were two baitfish dangling on the end of his hook.

"At first, I thought that behind these murders was bootlegging, too," said Josephine. "Goldblum was found down at The Narrows, where they drop the liquor. But then I started thinking about my missing Booze Blanks. Whiskey is also *fructus spiritus* medicine, and perfectly legal under Prohibition—if a doctor prescribes it."

"Did your patients take your Booze Blanks to buy whiskey from the bootleggers?" asked Arnie.

"No, of course not." She paced in front of the room, searching for a way to explain. "I remembered Maria and Antonio, at the speakeasy, and how they sang about regret. That's Janus. He regretted printing my fake Booze Blanks. Goldblum found out at the medical conference that Janus and the murderer were using forged Booze Blanks to buy bonded liquor legally at low government prices, and then selling it off with fake prescriptions at higher market prices for a huge profit. But they needed a constant supply of doctor's Booze Blanks to fool the US Treasury. When they ran out of Booze Blanks, they had to start distilling their own *fructus spiritus* recipe. They were running a big operation out of Janus' laboratory."

"Yup, we opened Janus' steel tubs," O'Malley added. "We tasted the liquor inside. Not bad at all." The rookie and sergeant nodded in agreement.

"Janus' Homeopathy business had gone way down with the rise of Allopathy, so he switched to Booze Blanks. He and the murderer were making a fortune."

"Did Goldblum turn on them?" the sergeant asked.

"Yup, but not at first. I saw Goldblum confront Janus, giving him pieces of paper - those must have been more stolen Booze Blanks. I think Janus balked at forging Booze Blanks and distilling whiskey, but Goldblum told him he'd better do it. Goldblum was now a partner in this scheme."

"So who's X, the murderer? It has to be someone who could have stolen your Booze Blanks. It must be Janus." Dominick asked. "He bumped Goldblum off because he wanted to stop the Booze Blank scheme."

"Nope," Josephine said. "Janus only fought with him."

"So it's these bootleggers. Or Saltzie and Arnie—they're doctors. They have Booze Blanks, too." Quinn said.

"Nope. Sophie showed me at the speakeasy that the Yorkvillains were rich, richer than most doctors, so I got suspicious and realized they must be making extra cash on the side. But it wasn't from Booze Blanks."

"The bootleggers paid them a cut to use their properties," said O'Malley, looking sternly at Saltzie and Arnie, who seemed to be sliding under the table.

"Yep ," said Josephine. "I doubt they'd risk their medical licenses by selling Booze Blanks."

"So did they kill Goldblum?" asked Dominick.

"Nope," said Josephine.

"How do you know that?" asked O'Malley, leaning forward.

"Because the murderer made a mistake," Josephine continued. "He tried to make Goldblum's death look like a suicide. An unhappy man goes to a lonely area at The Narrows and takes Aconite poison. The murderer put flowers in the victim's mouth and even in this 'poison pill' ring." She picked up Goldblums gold ring and pulled the latch open, spilling out the Aconite contents.

The group pulled back in shock, knowing the flowers were toxic to the touch.

"The police didn't search the ring because they saw the bump on the head and declared the death a homicide," said Saltzie.

"Yes, and that's when the murderer got worried. He now had to finger a Homeopath who knew about Aconite—Janus or me."

"It could be a mob killing," Quinn pointed at the bootleggers.

"They bump people off with bullets, not with purple flowers," said O'Malley.

"But the murderer didn't know that Goldblum would never kill himself with *Aconitum napellus*—he was an avowed Allopath," continued Josephine. "It was the words he used at the conference: drug fabrication and testing, not dilution, succussion and provings. That's why the poison struck me as odd—Goldblum wouldn't kill himself with a Homeopathic botanical. He would've overdosed on any number of highly toxic Allopathic drugs.

"Then there was the hematoma," Josephine continued. "The murderer couldn't have known about that. If he did, he would've given up on the Aconite suicide plan, knowing the police would see it was a suspicious death. I think he would have resorted to more violent measures, like hitting Goldblum on the head with a rock and pushing him off at The Narrows to drown."

"Shocking to admit, but this is beginning to make sense," O'Malley said. "Please continue."

"So who didn't know about the hematoma?" asked Saltzie. "Who's the murderer General X?"

"Janus Heath knew about the injury, he caused it, so we can eliminate him. And Janus didn't kill himself in his lab, we know this because the lab was smashed up—a fight was going on. When Saltzie and I arrived we heard someone leaving. That must have been the murderer."

"Who's this mysterious General X?" asked Dominick. "I still think it has something to do with The Narrows and these bootleggers. Why was Goldblum even there?"

"The murderer lured Goldblum to The Narrows, probably by agreeing to pay him blackmail money. He knew the spot because that's probably where they stole whiskey when they ran out of Booze Blanks."

"Okay, it's not Janus, but that still leaves us with Arnie, Saltzie, Quinn, and these two bootleggers," O'Malley said, pointing around the room. "One of you is the murderer."

"But remember, Goldblum couldn't blackmail bootleggers with his report. The mob doesn't deal in Homeopathics—there's not enough money."

"And the mob don't need doctors' Booze Blanks—they control the liquor supply," added the sergeant.

"So that leaves us with Arnie, Saltzie and Quinn," said O'-Malley. "All of you knew about deadly Aconite. None of you knew about the blow to the head in the cemetery. And any of you, given Goldblum's weakened condition, could have pushed the flowers in Goldblum's mouth and tried to make it look like suicide."

"But why would the murderer choose Aconite as the murder weapon? Why poison?" Dominick asked.

"Yes!" said Josephine, nodding proudly at her chauffeur. "Precisely the right question to ask." She looked at everyone in turn. "The murderer, this General X, must have been involved with both Janus and Goldblum in their duplicitous dealings."

"Why is that?" asked O'Malley.

"Because of Aconite. General X was very cunning. He had a backup plan, in case the police discovered the report. He would throw suspicion on his partner in crime, Janus Heath, a Homeopath, and also on me, whom he disliked and thought was also a Homeopath—on anyone except himself, by using Aconite."

"So the murderer isn't a Homeopath, after all?" Saltzie asked.

"That's right. A Homeopath believes that the more dilute the remedy, the more powerful it becomes. Less is more."

"The Law of Infinitesimals," said O'Malley. "A most fervent Homeopath, Senator Copeland, explained it to me, infinitesimally."

"But the murderer General X didn't believe in that paradox. So he's not a Homeopath."

"That still leaves Saltzie, Quinn and Arnie," O'Malley said.

"But what about the Aconite plant?" Quinn asked. "You found it at Dr. Reva's."

"The murderer planted it to point the finger at me. Another ruse. He or an accomplice put the Aconite in a bouquet and left it on my doorstep while I was out delivering babies."

"Nice touch," said the sergeant sarcastically.

"I wondered why you got that bouquet of flowers," Dominick muttered.

"Yeah, me, too. I think the murderer got worried. Goldblum no longer could have been considered suicide after the police found the blow to the head. A Homeopath would be the logical suspect, someone like Janus Heath, or me. But then General X must have realized that if Janus were arrested or questioned, he could turn on him and implicate him."

"So at that point, General X knew he had to kill Janus, too," said O'Malley. "One crime led to another. And that's when he needed to frame you, who he thought was a Homeopath." He looked directly at Josephine as if reading her thoughts.

She was relieved he finally understood. "Yes, and the police wouldn't know about the Law of Similars—that Aconite is a poison, but it's also a cure."

O'Malley returned her gaze. "You're innocent. As I knew all along."

Josephine looked surprised. Had she been wrong about Detective O'Malley?

Saltzie interrupted their connection. "But Joe, if General X tried to frame you, he must have had a reason."

"Who better to frame than me, the very person they were stealing Booze Blanks from?"

Josephine then turned to point at each of them in turn. "*Qui totum vult totum perdit*—Who wants it all, loses it all." Her finger rested firmly on Quinn.

Quinn looked outraged, and shook his head. "What about you, Josephine Reva? Goldblum was blackmailing you! Those were your Prohibition Booze Blanks."

"Perhaps he thought about it when he met me at the conference. But he must have figured out that I wasn't interested in money. I was interested in more equality for women doctors. And I clearly didn't profit from my Booze Blanks in any way."

"That's true," admitted O'Malley. "We could find no extra money coming into your bank account and you certainly don't spend lavishly on yourself. It all added up to what you earn."

Then he pointed to her dress. "And what your lady patients must be sewing for you."

"It has to be you, Quinn," Josephine said. "The second murder sealed your fate."

"That's where murderers usually trip up," O'Malley added.

"Why would I kill Janus Heath? He wasn't blackmailing me!" Quinn said.

"No, but he could implicate you. Goldblum also blackmailed you, claiming his report targeted addictive tonics. Before Goldblum died, he probably begged for his life, telling you there was no report. But you didn't believe him. After all, he'd made you pay him money saying there was a report."

"So you went to confront Janus. You probably got mad and tore up his lab looking for that report, which we now know didn't exist. You killed Janus in anger—and to make sure he wouldn't turn on you," Saltzie said.

"It could have been you or Josephine," said Quinn in defense. "You both were there when Janus died. You realized that Janus was selling your Booze Blanks illegally and together you went to kill him."

"At first, I thought Saltzie was involved because he delayed in driving to Janus' lab, leaving the poison time to work. But Janus wasn't dead when we arrived, and we took about an hour to get there. Aconite begins to work quicker than that, and Janus was already on the floor and barely breathing by the time we arrived. The murderer must have just given Janus the poison at the same time Saltzie and I were driving. Therefore, I'm Saltzie's alibi, and he's mine." She looked at Saltzie, and he sighed in relief.

"With Janus' death, there was a struggle. Janus knew the deadly effects of the plant. Poor Janus probably fought very hard. But he was older and not as fit as you, his younger assistant.

"Your other mistake, Quinn, was taking the Aconite plant from Janus' lab after you killed Goldblum. Who else would bother to send it to me in a bouquet?"

"Yes, who would want to implicate Josephine?" asked Saltzie. "Only someone who wanted to get her out of Brooklyn. Quinn, you would have benefitted the most if she were gone. You could then control that territory like before Josephine arrived, with no Lady Doctor to take away your customers."

"What about Arnie?" Quinn asked. "He could have done any of these things."

"Arnie had no reason—he could easily sell his own Booze Blanks, if he wanted," Josephine countered. "And he'd have no reason to take the Aconite plant because he's a Homeopath and could get one himself. Arnie, we found your American Institute of Homeopathy card in your wallet at The Oasis."

Arnie looked like a student who'd been dozing in class when suddenly the teacher asks him a question. But he rose to the occasion. "So Quinn used Janus! To make fake Booze Blanks to get the whiskey to add to his tonics?" Josephine applauded him.

"What about that phone call? A gal called in the murder and pointed a finger at Dr. Reva," asked the rookie.

"Maybe that was the same girl Quinn used to pickpocket me and steal my Booze Blanks." Josephine turned back toward Quinn. "Probably one of the times I was checking the labels at your tonic stand." Josephine chided herself that she hadn't recognized the bump, a jostle while standing in the crowd.

"It'll be easy to find this girl," said O'Malley decidedly. "She'll testify against you, after I show her the inside of a prison cell."

Quinn sank lower in his chair.

O'Malley stood up, towering over Quinn. "It'll go easier on you, Quinn, if you start talking."

"I needed the money. I couldn't add morphine or cocaine any more after the Harrison Act," Quinn said, "so my tonics stopped selling. But with Prohibition, if I added booze, my tonics sold even better than before. Janus was easy to convince—he was flat broke. We used his steel distillers to make the whiskey. But then my customers demanded the good imported stuff - the Real McCoy. It goes down smoother. We began switching it at the docks. But that was too dangerous. So then, I realized that with Janus' lab, we could order the Real McCoy, if we had doctor's Booze Blanks. Josephine's were there for the taking." He looked defiant.

"I didn't do anything but try to help people. When they have pain or troubles, my tonics with whiskey help them feel happy and go to sleep. What's so bad about that? They're safer and better than most drugs."

He turned angrily to Josephine. "I give tonics to people who can't afford doctors like you or prescription drugs to ease their pain. I was doing the right thing. I didn't want Goldblum to regulate my production or I'd go under. But that Goldblum, he wanted a piece of my business. He was so smug after that conference, demanding 50% of my sales."

"And Janus?" Josephine asked.

"He got in the way. He wanted out, but he knew too much and threatened me, just like Goldblum."

"And Sophie, and others like her, who you made sick?"

"I didn't mean to. I didn't know she had a medical condition. She wanted a baby. I thought a little whiskey and a few herbs would help her conceive."

"Sergeant, book him," said O'Malley with disgust. Then he pointed to Saltzie and Arnie and the bootleggers. "And get these criminals outta my sight. But you, Dr. Reva, you stay right here."

The sergeant and rookie led the men to the booking station in the hallway, leaving the door open. Saltzie looked back sheepishly at Josephine, then left.

"Miss 'Lady Doctor' Reva," O'Malley began.

"Yes, Detective," answered Josephine sweetly.

"You do realize without Quinn's confession, the evidence is circumstantial, at best. It's a good thing that you walked him into it. I'll give you that. But you're not out of the woods yet.

"There's a little matter of hiding information from me, and larceny for stealing wallets, and taking Goldblum's belongings out of the evidence room."

"But the female officer brought that box to me. You know, the beautiful woman with the golden-red hair and bright green eyes."

"Female officer?" O'Malley said. "That's ridiculous! We don't have any female officers. And I'd remember if we had a beautiful one with golden-red hair and bright green eyes." He looked at her strangely.

"You must be under a lot of stress—you're seeing things." O'Malley stared at Josephine as if he'd pushed her too hard, to her mind's limit. "Don't worry, it's over now. I'll make the charges stick against Quinn, Saltzie, Arnie and those bootleggers. They won't bother you again after they're sent up the river."

"And, of course, you'll take all the credit for solving both murders," said Dominick.

"Hmmm," said O'Malley, more than likely imagining his Detective Second Grade commendation and his pleasant garden upstate.

"Detective, Arnie didn't really do much wrong. Surely, you can see he's ill, an alcoholic. He needs treatment," said Josephine. "And Saltzie, well, I think he, too, was coerced by the bootleggers—his dock is one of the last before The Narrows and by the Lighthouse. They're both only pawns."

"I"m most certainly not a pawn. I'm a knight," Saltzie protested loudly from the hallway.

"Or a rook. Rooks are noble," Arnie added.

"And rook rhymes with crook," O'Malley yelled back, telling them both to be quiet.

"Arnie and Saltzie's little black books will help you catch the Combine mob. Surely you can be lenient once they agree to cooperate," Josephine interjected.

"Harrumph!" said O'Malley. "That depends on the D.A."

"And Dominick, you and the patients keep working on those codes. We want to alert the Coast Guard if we're going to catch the big fish.

"We'll be ready at The Narrows!"

"We?" asked O'Malley.

Chapter 23 - Josephine's Office

Several months later, in early October...

Reddish golden leaves haloed the trees, and the sky was clear without a rain cloud in sight. A slight chill hovered in the air with the threat of a bleak winter to come.

A long black Town Car driven by the sergeant pulled up in front of Josephine's office. Detective O'Malley got out with his rookie tagging along behind him carrying two over-stuffed duffel bags. They nodded at Dominick, who continued to polish the silver Packard, then hastened up the stairs to the doctor's waiting room. Josephine was in the midst of another hectic day treating patients.

Sophie told the detective to fill out a form and wait.

"I'm not here for a consultation," O'Malley said gruffly. "But I'm glad to see Sophie fully recovered. I came to inform you of the outcome of the case."

"Well," Josephine said, "we're all ears. But let me examine you while you talk—you look a little piqued. Aren't you taking those *vitamines* I recommended?" She pulled her stethoscope from around her neck and placed it on the detective's chest, as he loosened his tie and unbuttoned his shirt. Sophie and Maria helped remove his jacket, oohing and aahing over his shiny new Second Grade Detective badge.

Josephine began her examination. She felt that his muscles were well-developed.

"Quinn's been singing like a bird, giving us lots of information on his and Janus Heath's illegal whiskey and Booze Blanks racket. Not only that, but Quinn was planning the importation of heroin and cocaine with the mob. They were starting that up, for when Prohibition ends. Quinn confessed to both murders, was arraigned and will be going on trial soon. He's in the Big House, so you needn't worry.

"And best of all, Dominick's code breaking skills led us to a huge Mother Ship lode of whiskey. We nailed a ring of rumrunners from Canada, with warehouses all over the city. They were using local oyster boats and speed boats to make runs through The Narrows. We nabbed the whole lot of them and confiscated 20,000 cases of liquor. Dominick is getting a special commendation. But that's top secret."

They looked out the window to the driveway below. Dominick tipped his cap to the detective and Josephine. That's my chauffeur, thought Josephine proudly.

"Quinn also admitted that he tried to finger you with the phone call and the bouquet of Aconite flowers. A gangster's moll called Carla made that citizen's tip, she's a Ziegfeld girl."

"She sounded swee-eet. Is she in any talkies?" the rookie asked. O'Malley rolled his eyes.

Josephine asked the detective to open his mouth and say "ahh!" He complied, then got up, tucking his shirt back under his suspenders and straightening his tie.

"Funny thing is," O'Malley continued, unzipping the larger bag. "We found this load of dough at Janus' pharmacy, with your name on it."

Josephine looked at the bundle of cash and her mouth dropped open. She'd never seen so much money. Indeed, it did have a label reading "Josephine Reva, M.D." Quinn and Janus had made a fortune from her Booze Blanks.

O'Malley said in a wry voice, "It's technically your property recovered at the scene."

Maria and Sophie clapped their hands in joy. Josephine was in disbelief as he handed her the duffel bag.

But there was more. "Janus' building was seized by the police," O'Malley continued, pulling on his jacket. "It's coming up for auction. I don't know anyone who'd want that old factory, a bunch of poisonous flowers and lots of glass bottles with little pills in them. Plus there's all kinds of weird shaking instruments that look like they could harm somebody. And there's the matter of those big steel distillers—they'd have to be used legally, of course, not for any booze."

Josephine laughed, nodding her head. O'Malley reached into the bag and took back half of the cash. "I'll see that your deed is dropped off." He started to walk away, but then shook his head and turned back.

"I've one last surprise for you," he continued. "I've saved the worst for last, but you've worked with prisoners from the Tombs before." He motioned for Josephine to look out the window.

Saltzie got out of the back of the police car and came bounding up the steps into her office. "Joe, isn't this the cat's pajamas!" he yelped like an overgrown puppy. He swooped

Josephine up in his arms and spun her around. "I'm free! Arnie, too! The judge said the bootleggers were trespassing on our property. He ruled that all charges should be dropped."

"Why?"

"Because we acted under 'duress'—those bootleggers held guns to our heads and said they'd kill us."

O'Malley turned to Saltzie and handed him the other duffel bag stuffed with $100 bills.

"This is technically your dough because it was found at your dock. We seized the rum and whiskey, but the owner of this dough can't be traced to the mob."

Saltzie's eyes lit up with glee, like a kid on Christmas morning, until O'Malley took back almost all of the money.

"That's your contribution to the Policeman's Retirement Fund, and for me putting a bug in the judge's ear to let you off the hook for cooperating."

"Oh, fine," Saltzie said, "lesson learned. I had to promise to give free rectal exams to the judge and his wife for life—as if that isn't punishment enough!"

O'Malley and Josephine walked Saltzie down to the street.

Saltzie turned to Josephine. "I hope you can forgive me. Deep down, I didn't really believe you were selling Booze Blanks."

She looked at him disapprovingly. "*Amore et melle et felle es fecundissimu.* Love is both honey and venom. What will you do now?"

"I think it's best to get out of Dodge 'till this blows over. My front page picture isn't as pretty as yours," he laughed. "I'm off to a Gastro conference in London. There's some new techniques

I need to learn, if I'm to keep up with you and your chest pounding and bellows blowing."

Suddenly, he asked, "Why don't you come with me, Joe?" She shook her head no. "I promise to repent!"

His puppy brown eyes looked as if he were waiting for a petting.

"Come sail with me on the *Ile de France*—First Class, like the Jazz singers. I have an extra ticket. My sister isn't going anymore. She's getting married. Imagine that, her before me, making whoopee! It'll be *amore*. Remember, you still have to sing me that Neapolitan prisoner song."

"Saltzie, you're too much! You'll get us mixed up in another fiasco."

Josephine admitted the voyage was tempting. Hadn't Mrs. Porter-Graves sailed on the *Ile de France*? It must be luxurious. She'd always wanted to visit Italy where her parents were born. In London, she could see the laboratories of Dr. Fleming working on Penicillin. Maybe she could window shop for all the new fashions in Paris, after visiting the Pasteur Institute.

But she shook her head firmly. "No."

"*Omnia vincit amor*," Saltzie said with a wink. "Love conquers all."

Dominick let out a guffaw, but Saltzie gave Josephine a peck on the cheek.

A policeman pulled up in Saltzie's cherry red roadster, released from the pound.

"With time, you'll forgive me," he said to Josephine. He took Josephine's hand and kissed it affectionately.

With that he said goodbye and went to retrieve his prized possession. He fastened the top down, hopped inside and drove off with a wave.

Dominick was leaning against the shiny silver Packard, his arms crossed over his chest. "Bon voyage!" he shouted.

O'Malley escorted Josephine back into her office. He was still tucking in the tail of his shirt and smoothing his silvery hair that had been rustled from her examination.

"I'm sure I'll be seeing more of you, Doctor Reva. I've decided not to retire yet."

"I'm very glad to hear that, Detective. Brooklyn needs you." She looked into his steel grey eyes, and their gaze locked. But once again, she turned away first.

Static was blaring from the police car. "Well, then, until next time." Detective O'Malley rushed out, calling for his men to move on to an urgent radio call.

Sophie and Maria held onto Josephine's arms tightly.

"Now there goes a fine looking man. Dress him in an evening jacket, and he'd be a real cake eater," said Sophie, nodding towards the Chief Detective. "You should solve another crime for him!"

"I dunno," said Maria, "Saltzie's de one for ya, Doc Joe. You can 'ave little doctor babies."

"They both almost got me arrested for murder!" Josephine laughed. "Besides, I've got other things to think about now."

"Yes, we're rich!" Maria said, throwing some of the money around.

"Janus' laboratory is perfect. We can turn it into a modern doctor's office," said Sophie, "with four or even five examination rooms. You can get some of that new fancy equipment you've always wanted."

"Such a nice atrium, to let in te summer sun," said Maria happily. "While your patients wait, tey can enjoy all te pretty flowers."

"Oh, no!" Josephine exclaimed. "Those flowers are poisonous."

"Speaking of poison, where's that Aconite bouquet?" Sophie asked. "I want to see what caused all this fuss."

"Here, I'll show you." Josephine led the ladies to her bedroom. "Be careful not to touch! They are beautiful, aren't they?"

The Aconite stood in the vase of water, reflecting over and over again in the mirror. The purple blossoms were as bright and fresh as ever, their wispy leaves still green.

"Such lovely flowers! No one would imagine that they're deadly," Sophie sighed. "Maybe you can make a remedy from them?"

She, Maria and Josephine stared at the cascade of deep royal purple flowers shyly tucking their heads under their hoods as if in prayer or hiding some secret wisdom.

"I suppose I'd better throw them away," Josephine sighed.

"I suppose," sighed Sophie.

"Or you could keep 'em," said Maria. "'Omeopatics work. My babies nevva felt betta. Let's put te Aconite back in te lab to grow. Look, te roots are still alive!"

ORDER THE SERIES:

DR. JOSEPHINE PLANTÆ PARADOXES
www.lmjorden.com,

https://www.amazon.com/author/l.m.jorden/

BASED ON A TRUE STORY

In Roaring 20's New York, **a feisty orphan rises from the slums to become a doctor**. When no one will hire a female, Josephine Reva, M.D. hangs her shingle in Brooklyn as the area's first woman doctor. Her loyalty to the Hippocratic Oath will be tested under Prohibition, but Josephine has graver concerns. She's fighting for women's equality, and she isn't going to stop using her botanical poison cures.

Murder intrudes when a man is found dead from Aconite, a beautiful flower known as the "Queen of Poisons". The Chief Detective suspects Josephine, and the two begin a cat and mouse chase. Josephine must race to prove her innocence. She goes undercover as a flapper to spy, but complications arise when she falls for a debonair suspect.

Can Josephine unmask the murderer? Can she follow her heart and save her career, while keeping her dark secrets hidden?

BELLADONNA Bitter Conduct, a 1935 Mystery Voyage

An Italian opera star spouts strange verses and collapses during the final act of Romeo and Juliet. Dr. Josephine Reva is in the audience and rushes to render aid. She believes the soprano was poisoned by Belladonna, a plant with deadly black berries.

Meanwhile, the Chief Detective uncovers plots to overthrow President Franklin D. Roosevelt. Could these events spark another World War? Josephine enlists her friends to follow the opera stars and spy on the high seas.

Who's the killer aboard the luxurious SS Rex? A shocking surreal artist, an avant-garde fashionista, a cardinal and priest carrying the relics of an American saint, a mysterious Mussolini official, a British lord, a Nazi doctor, or any of the narcissistic opera divas and dons?

Also along is a handsome paramour—is romance on the horizon for Josephine, if she can survive the trip?

Josephine must hurry to solve these Belladonna crimes with deeper roots, before the ship docks in Fascist Italy and it's too late.

CINCHONA Coney Island Bones, a 1941 Mystery

As Pearl Harbor draws America into another World War, a grave from long ago is dug up on Coney Island. The bones are almost demolished in the name of progress, but Josephine and an archaeologist must put aside their differences to find out what happened. Alongside the skeleton are several strange artifacts.

Josephine must use her brilliant powers of deduction and her knowledge of medicinal plants to solve this paradoxical crime. The message from these Coney Island bones will have deeper implications for Josephine's life.

GELSEMIUM, Memoir of a First Woman Doctor

In early 1900's New York, an Italian aristocrat falls on hard times, and struggles to protect her children as the Spanish Flu grips the city. Help arrives from an unexpected source, and her young daughter, Josephine, finds a way to save her family and realize her dream of becoming one of the city's first female doctors.

DIGITALIS Garden of Death

Chief Detective O'Malley lovingly tends his deceased wife's garden in her memory, but one day he finds an invasive and highly poisonous plant among the blooming varietals. He needs help from Dr. Josephine Reva, Homeopath MD, expert in botanical poisons, to find out who added the poison to his garden and why.

HELLEBORUS Death on the Hudson

An untimely horrific death on a river boat cruise leaves Dr. Josephine Reva, Homeopath MD, wondering: which botanical poison is the murder weapon disguised as a remedy, and which of the passengers administered the deadly dose?

ORDER HERE: www.lmjorden.com,

Thank you for reading! Kindly leave a review on your favorite reader sites.

Order more books in the series here:

www.lmjorden.com,

SOLIS MUNDI

Historical Notes

The past is never dead. It's not even past.
   — *William Faulkner, Requiem for a Nun*

This is a work of fiction based in part upon the life of the author's trail-blazing grandmother, Dr. Josephine Rera (1903-1987), the first woman doctor in Bensonhurst and Borough Park, also serving parts of Gravesend and other areas. Dr. Rera received her M.D. degree from New York Homeopathic Medical College, having attended from 1922-1926, after pre-medical studies at New York University. Dr. Rera practiced medicine from 1926 until the day she died, and received a special commendation from the American Medical Association for 50 years of service—she was a physician for over six decades. There were many societal and discriminatory forces hindering women doctors during the first part of the 20th century, but a few brave women like Dr. Rera in the 1920's persevered. They helped reclaim women's traditional role as medical healers and opened the door for more women to follow.

Homeopathic Medicine has seen a revival in the US, although it has been continually practiced in Europe, the United Kingdom, India and other countries. Congress created the Office of Alternative Medicine at the National Institutes of Health in 1992, and undeniably, integrative and complementary medicine deserves further research. But Homeopathy in the US is constantly under attack —we shouldn't throw the baby out with the bathwater.

Please excuse the use of offensive terms for African-Americans in the 1920's style dialogue. The author used respectful terms otherwise. One hundred years later in the 2020's, racism, prejudice and sexism continue. Times have changed, but unfortunately, society hasn't changed much; a hierarchy that undermines women and minorities continues. Literature, too, has lost its genuine Muse. (See The Dancing Goddess, by Heide Gottner Abendroth, Beacon Press, Boston, 1982).

The author researched and fact-checked meticulously to avoid anachronisms with knowledgeable persons at historical societies, and located primary documents, visited actual sites, researched journals and newspapers (internet sites are often unreliable.) A few items warrant further explanation. New York Homeopathic Medical College existed as a highly regarded institution in the Yorkville area of Manhattan, and the author's grandmother, Dr. Josephine Rera, graduated there in 1926 with an M.D.degree, the same year as our heroine, Dr. Josephine. The medical college (affiliated with Flower Hospital during Dr. Rera's studies) was founded by William Cullen Bryant ((1794-1878), a homeopathy devotee, abolitionist and noted Romantic poet and editor of the *New York Evening Post*. Bryant Park, next to the New York Public Library, is named in his honor. NYHMC is now New York Medical College, located in Valhalla, NY. The New York City College of Homeopathic Medicine is entirely fictional. The "Yorkvillains" classmates are entirely fictionalized in the novel. Their behavior would be considered offensive in the #Me,too generation, but similar experiences were reported by my grandmother and other female medical students during the 1920's. Metropolitan Hospital was Homeopathic in the 1920's and located on Welfare Island (today's Roosevelt Island.) As an interesting note, doctors like Dr. Rera took a boat to get there (an elevator from a bridge was also added.) It was one of the largest municipal hospitals and staffed almost entirely by NYHMC, an unbroken affiliation since 1875. All characters, dialogues, settings and instances associated with NYHMC and Metropolitan Hospital are entirely fictional and creations of the author for this novel.

The Brooklyn Daily Eagle was published from 1841-1955, and was once edited by Walt Whitman.There is a new Brooklyn Eagle publishing since 1996, but the use in this novel of the original Brooklyn Daily Eagle and any articles printed are entirely fictionalized. United Israel Zion Hospital no longer exists, having been incorporated into Maimonides Medical Center, and all events and persons mentioned within are entirely fictionalized. Senator Royal S. Copeland was a Homeopathic doctor, former Dean of NYHMC, a New York City Health Commissioner, and esteemed United States Senator from New York from 1923-1938. Israel S. Kleiner, Ph.D. (1885-1966), another former Dean of NYHMC, was the 1959 recipient of the Van Slyke Award in Clinical Chemistry from the American Association of Clinical Chemists. The portrayal of any real-life persons is not meant to laud nor disparage them.

In creating The Oasis speakeasy, the author "borrowed" famous performers and musicians from other clubs to perform there. Mayor Jimmy Walker's Central Park Casino opened in June of 1929. It was later torn down by Robert Moses and replaced with a playground, reportedly to end this symbol of greed, corruption and profit-taking from public land. The author created the story about the fictional Billingsford family. Oyster harvesting in New York City waters was an important food business until 1927, when it ended due to pollution.

U.S. Public Domain law is gratefully acknowledged: "'E Ppentite," a 1925 Neapolitan song with music by Ferdinando Albano (1894-1968)/ Libero Bovio; Gustav Kahn (1886-1941) wrote Toot Toot Tootsie, Goodbye" in 1922; "Five Foot Two, Eyes of Blue," was a hit song from 1925 (Music by Ray Henderson, Lyrics by Joe Young and Sam Lewis). Several songs are still catchy today.

Writing a historical novel is to engage in a reconstruction of the past, what Michel Foucault called "the archaeology of knowledge." See The Archaeology of Knowledge (A.M. Sheridan Smith trans., Pantheon Books 1972). Kindly excuse the author for any discrepancies.

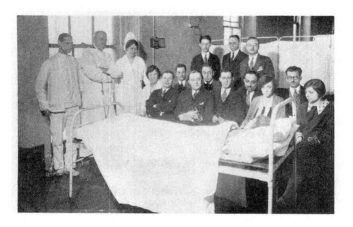

Dr. Josephine Rera, c. 1925-1926, New York Homeopathic Medical College clinic at Metropolitan Hospital, New York City (seated far right).
Photo by Champlain Studios, New York, NY and courtesy of New York Medical College.

Acknowledgements

Many friends and family helped with research and encouragement for this book. Firstly, I'd like to thank my grandmother, Dr. Josephine Rera, who taught me in her lab and patiently answered my many questions. My parents, who insisted that the life of a "Lady Doctor" in the early 20th century was a story worth telling. My cousins, the Carrolls, and my cousin Anthony Bellov for his knowledge of New York City history. Thank you Alexi for being joyful, Tara for making me laugh, and Nicky for succeeding so well in life. You encouraged me to continue writing a historical and biographical mystery.

I'm grateful for the support of Sisters in Crime, the Mystic-Noank writers, Hampshire College, Cornell University and Columbia University alumni writers. The Groton Public Library staff deserves a special thank you for making suggestions and promptly pulling books off the shelves for safe pick-up during the Covid-19 pandemic, and The Mystic-Noank Library for its delightful Victorian cat and toy mouse filled reading rooms. Several other libraries provided books on inter-library loans. We must keep supporting our libraries and return to confidential borrowing.

I'm greatly indebted to both past and present New York Medical School (Dr. Josephine Rera's alma mater) archivists and their medical historian Nicholas Webb for sending many helpful documents, The Brooklyn Public Library, The Museum of the City of New York, the New York Academy of Medicine and the Sisters at Cabrini Medical Center in New York and Mother Cabrini College (now University) in Philadelphia, especially Sister Philippa, for assistance. I am thankful to have researched at the Cabrini Medical Center archives in New York before the hospital closed. My apologies to anyone I've inadvertently left out.

About the Author

L.M. Jorden is an award-winning journalist and former professor who lives between Europe and the US with her family, furry friends and lots of plants. She holds a Master of Science from Columbia University Graduate School of Journalism, and received the New York Press Association Award.

Her company **World 3i** offers multilingual global research and fact-checking for individuals and companies.

The Dr. Josephine Plantæ Paradoxes is her debut mystery series.

www.lmjorden.com
https://www.amazon.com/author/l.m.jorden/
https://www.facebook.com/LMJorden/